RAVE REVIEWS FOR CAROL CARSON'S PREVIOUS NOVEL, *BAD COMPANY*

"Ms. Carson has a writing voice all her own that is refreshingly different, warms the heart, and brings a smile to your face."

—*Rendezvous*

"Carol Carson is a deft voice at telling a rollicking romantic tale. *Bad Company* will tickle your funny bone."

—*Affaire de Coeur*

Carol Carson "breaks into the romance scene with a fresh and amusing plot line [and] gives the reader a new name to add to their keeper shelves."

—*Heartland Critiques*

"Keep an eye on this budding writer. She has talent and imagination coupled with the delightful comic turn."

—*Romance Communications*

"Carol Carson's warm sense of humor will keep you smiling."

—Debra Dier, author of *Saint's Temptation*

THE RIGHT TIME

His eyes fluttered, then opened and captured hers in a heavy-lidded gaze. "I thought I was dreaming," he said. He gifted her with a heart-stopping smile. "Or maybe I'd died and gone to Heaven."

She smiled back. "No," she whispered. "You seem to be very much alive."

"I do at that."

His free hand cupped the back of her head, and tenderly, yet firmly, he brought her face close to his. "I'm laying claim to you, Janie. You can forget about that good lookin' Smith fella," he murmured in a hoarse whisper. "I should have done this before now. I waited until I thought the time was right and that appears to be now."

Other *Leisure* books by Carol Carson:
BAD COMPANY

Family Man

Carol Carson

LEISURE BOOKS  NEW YORK CITY

For my parents, Jean and Eugene Carson. Thanks for your love, your support, and your generosity through the years. Mom and Dad, you are simply the best.

A LEISURE BOOK®

November 1999

Published by

Dorchester Publishing Co., Inc.
276 Fifth Avenue
New York, NY 10001

ISBN 0-8439-4625-3

Printed in the United States of America.

Family
Man

Prologue

Drover, Kansas, 1888

Jane Warner perched on the edge of a slat-back chair, her spine stiff, her throat dry. Perspiration trickled between her breasts and clung to her sweat-soaked chemise. The chair grew harder by the minute as she observed Doctor Hendricks. The expanse of scratched mahogany desk stretched endlessly between them.

The elderly gentleman studied the imposing medical book that lay open in front of him. His brow furrowed as he scanned the pages of tiny print. He scribbled a note, one of many he'd already taken, in a thick, yellowed journal.

John Michael, eighteen months old and unused to sitting still, fussed in Jane's lap and squirmed to be let down. Six-year-old Teddy plucked at her skirt, watching the doctor with round eyes and a gaping mouth.

Not minutes before, Doctor Hendricks had prodded, poked, and probed what seemed like every last inch of her body. He'd asked Jane dreadful, embarrassing questions. Even now she felt humiliating heat work its way up her throat as she recalled the personal nature of his examination. Another drop of perspiration trickled down the nape of her neck.

Now the inquisition was over. She wanted to take her nephews and go back to the peace and quiet of the farm.

"Miss Warner, I'm afraid the news is not good." Doctor Hendricks pulled off his wire spectacles and pinched the bridge of his nose.

Jane tried to swallow. Her throat, parched as last year's corn crop, refused to cooperate.

The doctor continued. "You say you keep losing weight. Correct?"

"Yes, but I feel fine." Her voice came out little more than a whisper.

"And, furthermore, you claim you haven't lain with a man, however—"

Jane stiffened. "I don't *claim* I haven't lain with a man. I have *not.*" Jane's voice rose with each word she spoke, and John Michael began to cry. She gently held his head against her chest, muttered a few soothing words, and rubbed his back. Taking a deep, fortifying breath, she continued. "I have never been with a man, Doctor."

He cocked his head to the side and stroked his chin. "I apologize, Miss Warner, but I've had single ladies such as yourself lie about their circumstances before, in hopes of, oh, I don't know, somehow changing what will eventually happen."

"I don't lie."

"I'm certain that you don't." Doctor Hendricks straightened the corner of his desk blotter and tugged down his black waistcoat. He glanced at his notes. "I just want to get my facts straight. Since you haven't been with a man, and yet your courses have stopped, I can only come to one conclusion based on my medical books and what little knowledge I have of curses."

"Curses?"

"I think—and mind you I'm not certain—but I believe you've had a curse put on your, er, womanly parts."

"A curse?" Jane met the concerned glance from the doctor. She'd never had occasion to visit him before, nor had she heard anything—good or bad—about him, but he appeared deadly serious. He didn't even flinch from her unwavering stare. "Did I hear you right?"

"I've never actually treated a cursed patient before, but according to what I've read, it can attack the body in strange ways, including the internal organs. In your case, the female organs."

"You read about a curse in your medical books?"

He clamped his mouth shut and his lips thinned. "There is nothing *precisely* mentioned in my medical text."

Jane took a deep breath. "What you're saying then is that someone put some sort of evil hex, or maybe a spell on me?"

"Have you been visited by any traveling gypsies or other odd types like that out at your farm?"

"Of course not, and even if I had, why would they put a curse on me?"

"Who can say?"

"I can! No one has put a curse on me! I'm perfectly fine."

"I, well, I can give you something for the pain later when you need it. I'd suggest you get your affairs in order."

Shock yielded quickly to anger. She jumped to her feet. "Are you out of your mind?"

John Michael stopped crying and commenced wailing. Teddy gripped the fabric of her skirt so fiercely she could feel his hand trembling. "I refuse to believe any of this . . . this superstitious blarney." Jane bit back the desire to lash out at the half-wit. "It simply can't be true."

"I'm sorry. I truly am, but, my dear, there's always prayer."

Jane hiked John Michael higher on her hip. She took a jar of apple butter from her reticule and handed it to the startled man. "I have no money, so this will have to do as payment. Thank you, Doctor. Have a good day, but beware of any hobgoblins you might run across on the street." She straightened her shoulders and stalked from the office, slamming the door behind her.

The man was obviously incompetent. *Incompetent.* Ha! He was crazy as a bedbug. Teddy knew more about doctoring than he did.

Jane marched home, clutching John Michael in one arm and holding Teddy's hand. Still, she couldn't help wondering. Why had her courses stopped?

What would happen to the boys if she got sicker? If one day she simply didn't wake up? If she died in her sleep?

What would happen?

She needed a plan. A darned good plan. One that didn't include the hiring of a witch doctor to cure her.

Children are the anchors that hold a mother to life.
—Sophocles

Chapter One

One month later

''I don't like you.''

Rider Magrane jumped. With his hand poised to knock on the weather-beaten door, his heart pounded in anticipation of what awaited him on the other side. Rider glanced down to see a boy, about knee-high to a grasshopper, standing beside him on the sagging porch.

With serious button-brown eyes, the youngster stared up at Rider. ''I don't like you,'' he repeated. Dressed in mud-spattered britches of indeterminate color and a shapeless, threadbare jacket, the ragamuffin looked as pitiful as a hind-teat calf.

Rider wiped a damp palm down his thigh. He removed his dusty Stetson and squatted before the child. ''But you don't even know me.''

The tyke glared, his head cocked at a stubborn angle. "You got a dirty face."

"That so?"

"And your hair needs combin'."

A grin tugged at Rider's mouth. "So does yours."

"You have hair growing on your chin."

Rider rubbed his beard-roughened jaw. The little urchin had him there. He'd been three days riding hard and resting little to get to this sorry run-down farm. He questioned his sanity.

Rider scratched his itchy beard. "I do at that. So will you one of these days."

"Will not."

Rider shrugged. "What's your name?"

"I'm not s'posed to talk to strangers."

"I'm not a stranger. We've been talking two whole minutes. We're almost friends."

The youngster's brow furrowed as he mulled that over. Finally, he said, "Teddy, but Jane sometimes calls me Thorn when she's mad at me."

"Why Thorn?"

"Because I'm a pain in the backside," he stated, as though he'd heard it a few times before.

Rider chuckled. "Are you Teddy Warner?"

The child reached into the pocket of his pants, ignoring Rider's question. "Know what I got here?"

"No. What?"

Grinning from one end of his dirty face to the other, Teddy carefully lifted his hand to show Rider what he now held. "A hoppy toad."

Rider took the squirming creature from the boy's eager, outstretched fingers. "He's a good one, all right."

"I can't bring him in the house, though."

Rider nodded, then handed the toad back. "I reckon he belongs outside."

Teddy gave Rider a grave nod. He patted the critter's knobby head, then tucked him back inside his pocket. "John Michael sure likes hoppy toads."

"John Michael?"

"He's my baby brother. He's sleeping."

"Hmmm." Rider took a long breath and released it through clenched teeth before asking, "So tell me, Teddy, where's your pa?"

He shrugged his thin shoulders.

"All right, where's your ma?"

"She's in heaven."

Rider swallowed hard around the lump that suddenly clogged his throat. Guilt bit at his conscience. Had his misdeeds contributed to her death? God, he hoped not. He slowly rose to his feet, but he had no intention of retreating now. "Who's taking care of you and your brother?"

"Jane."

"Could you take me to her?"

"I reckon."

Teddy surprised Rider by taking him by the hand. The boy's fingers were sticky and dirt-encrusted, but the simple gesture warmed Rider's heart. He smiled. "Do you like me now?"

"Nope." He didn't drop Rider's hand, though.

As they stepped off the porch, Rider noticed the dismal condition of the lonely homestead far from Drover, the nearest town. The right side of the porch drooped and several boards had gone missing. A good gust of Kansas wind would likely blow away the few shingles on the roof before winter arrived. As they circled the clapboard house, he noted the peeling and chipped paint flaking off the sides. He passed two broken windows with nothing but billowing grain-sack curtains to keep out the coming cold.

Guilt gnawed anew at his gut. He shook his head to dispel the feeling. He'd served his time for the crime he'd committed. He had nothing to be sorry about.

If he believed he wasn't to blame, then what the hell was he doing back in Drover?

Rider stepped around a rusted, broken-down plow and over an empty bucket minus its handle. Several scrawny chickens pecked listlessly at the meager corn scattered around the yard. He sidestepped the birds, pulling the youngster alongside.

"There's Jane." Teddy pointed his grubby finger at a woman kneeling on her hands and knees in the garden. At least Rider thought it was a garden. He stopped to take a better look-see. By November most crops were harvested. He wondered what she could possibly be doing.

She did present him with an enticing view of her backside. Each time she dug into the dirt with a hand spade, her buttocks wriggled.

During his five years of incarceration with nothing but men for company, Rider had almost forgotten what a woman looked like. Almost.

She dusted off her hands, then settled back on her heels. A pile of egg-sized potatoes lay on the ground beside her. She shaded her eyes from the sun and turned. "Teddy, who is that with you?"

Rider strode forward and tipped his hat. His back to the sun, he cast a shadow across her face. "Ma'am."

Rider offered his hand to help her up. Either the

woman didn't see the gesture or chose to ignore it. She rose to her feet and wiped her hands on the front of her dress. She stared at him a second, taking in his height and new clothes in one swift glance. Her expression changed to one of surprise when she saw his fingers entwined with the boy's hand. "Find a new playmate, Teddy?" Her lips turned up in a friendly smile a moment before she turned her gaze on Rider.

He found himself looking into compelling toffee-colored eyes. Clear, direct and completely without guile. If he looked hard enough he could see his own reflection staring back at him. Rational thought flew from his head. He stared at the mousy-brown hair braided on top of her head, the chapped hands, and her work-worn calico dress that ill-disguised the womanly, though thin, figure beneath.

His heart thudded in his chest like a lovesick schoolboy. How could such a plain woman cause his blood to course through his veins like a rapid mountain stream?

Suddenly remembering the reason he'd searched for this particular farm in the first place, Rider swallowed his dread and spoke up. "Is your man about?"

She gave him a questioning frown. "You here about the advertisement?"

"Umm, yeah," he lied, stalling for time. As soon as she heard his name, she'd commence to chasing him around the yard with a pitchfork anyway. He could wait awhile.

"Why didn't you say so?"

"Good question," he muttered beneath his breath. If he'd known he'd gain a smile from her, he would've said it sooner.

Teddy trotted over and stood beside the woman. She

tousled his hair, then left her hand on his shoulder.

"This is Jane," the boy volunteered.

She smiled at Teddy. Her expression stilled and grew serious. She slanted profoundly deep brown eyes once again toward Rider.

His heart lurched in his chest.

She inclined her head. "Miss Jane Warner to you."

"Miss?" Rider questioned. "Are you related to David Warner?"

"I'm David's sister, Teddy is one of his boys. And you are?"

"Rider Magrane." He waited for a spark of angry recognition or a rush of furious indignation. Nothing. Not even a blink. She didn't know him from Adam. He released a slow breath, then slapped the side of his leg with his Stetson. "Where *is* Mr. Warner?"

"He's gone."

Shock rendered him momentarily speechless. When he found his voice, he said, "Dead?"

"No. He just rode out one day and never returned."

The man just rode off? And left his family? Damn. He'd wanted to find David Warner and have a straight talk with him—man to man. Apologize and offer his help, but this woman's penetrating gaze and straightforward speech dashed all coherent thought from his head. Just being this close to her rattled him so badly his hands shook. He gripped them behind his back and cleared his throat.

She brushed back a loose strand of hair and strode to the house. "Well, I've got work to do, and I've got to check on John Michael. Come up to the house and we'll discuss the details."

Without a backward glance, she left him standing in the yard.

Teddy capered up alongside him. "You best do what Jane says."

"Oh?"

"Yeah, Jane can't abide lollygagging."

"Teddy," she called over one shoulder, never slowing her stride. "Come along. You, too, Mr. Magrane."

The boy scampered off after her.

The back door shut, leaving Rider alone with a yard filled with rusted tools and a played-out garden. His desire to make amends abruptly changed.

Maybe David Warner wasn't around but Rider could still do what he intended—give the man a hand. Now he would just help his sons and his sister. But what had he walked into? And what was this advertisement he supposedly had read? He wasn't used to conversing with anyone, much less women. He was sure once she found out whom he was, and before he had a chance to explain things, she'd come after him with a double-barreled shotgun.

Determination alone sent him following her up to the neglected farmhouse.

Jane checked John Michael, still sleeping soundly with his thumb tucked in the corner of his mouth. She couldn't help but smile, although a lump formed in her throat. Her gaze skittered to Teddy who found his toys and plopped down on the floor. He began stacking misshapen wooden blocks and then knocking them over with a jarring crash.

"Where did that man disappear to?" Jane looked around, as if he'd followed her and was now hiding in a corner. She then remembered the potatoes she'd left in the garden. "Damn."

Teddy looked up, his eyes round. Jane put a finger to her lips. He grinned, then went back to playing with his blocks.

A knock on the opened back door startled Jane. She swirled around. There stood the lean, dark-haired stranger, with the salvaged potatoes in his cupped hands. She'd noticed his height before, but he looked like he'd missed a few meals of late. A distinct pallor marked his thin face.

"Ma'am," he said, "I brought you your potatoes."

"I see that." She pushed open the screen door and motioned him inside. She took the potatoes from him. "You might as well come in and see what you're letting yourself in for."

He stepped across the threshold and removed his hat, but stood in front of the door, slowly taking in the room and its meager contents. He rolled the brim of his hat several times. Jane saw him catch Teddy's gaze and wink at him. Teddy attempted to wink back but both his eyes closed, then opened, which gave him the expression of a dazed owl. The stranger turned to see John Michael sleeping and his gaze softened.

"Sit down, Mr. Magrane."

He ambled over to the kitchen table and sat down holding his hat in his lap.

Jane pumped water into a cup and handed it to the stranger. "I'm afraid I don't have any coffee. Haven't had any for some time." As she sat down across from him she felt his gaze on her. A spreading warmth in the pit of her stomach took her by surprise. She met his penetrating gaze for a heartbeat. She blinked at the unwavering honesty clear upon his every feature, then turned away, her heart thrumming in her chest.

Jane cleared her throat. "I expect you want to know the chores involved."

"The advertisement, you mean?"

"Of course, what else?"

"Yes, ma'am. That's exactly what I was wondering about."

Understanding dawned on Jane. "You haven't seen it, have you?"

He shook his head. "No, ma'am."

"Can you read?"

His left brow rose. "Yes."

She handed him the newspaper folded neatly on the table. Pointing, she showed him her post.

He bent his head and read. He stopped once, lifted his head, his eyes wide, and his mouth turned down in a frown. Then he glanced down to read it again.

Jane knew the contents by heart. She'd agonized over the wording for well over a week.

WANTED: FAMILY MAN TO HELP RAISE TWO YOUNG BOYS. MUST LOVE CHILDREN. PAYMENT NEGOTIABLE. HOUSE HABITABLE AND CLEAN. SEE JANE WARNER AT THE WARNER FARM FIVE MILES DUE SOUTH OF DROVER FOR ARRANGEMENTS.

Jane watched him as he read. He had a young face but his eyes were old, and dark as a moonless night. His eyes were surrounded by long, sooty lashes. Bushy black brows curved across a furrowed brow. His beard, several days old, and as black as the hair on his head, grew thick and coarse. A tuft of sable hair stuck out above the starched, new chambray shirt he wore.

He curled his right hand around the tin cup of water

and as Jane watched, his thumb began a slow, thoughtful back-and-forth motion across his lip. She stared, fascinated, until she felt his gaze upon her again.

He stared at her a moment, then his gaze dropped. He eyed the cup almost as if he'd forgotten it was there. He took a long swallow and carefully set it down. "I like kids," he stated without ceremony.

"That's good, Mr. Magrane, because what I need is someone to father the boys."

"There's a few things I don't quite understand, though."

Jane nodded to encourage his questions.

"Is the farm for sale?"

"Yes."

"Why?"

Jane's temper caught fire like a dry Kansas wheat field in the middle of August, and she jumped to her feet. She moderated her reply before responding. "You've seen the place. It's falling down around my head, and it doesn't belong to me. You understand?" Her voice rose. "It's not really mine. It belongs to the boys but I can't take care of it myself. I need help."

Rider jumped up, too, his eyes wide, his hands spread out in front of him. "Now, Miss Warner, Jane, I meant no offense. It's just that those boys over there . . . why, this is their inheritance. I wouldn't take anything away from them."

She pointed at him. "You can sit back down. I'm not going to shoot you."

One black brow tilted uncertainly, but he sat down and stared at her with questioning eyes.

"The reason I didn't advertise for a couple was because then their own children would inherit. So the farm would be yours for now but when you died, it would, of course, go to the boys. You've got to understand the most important thing is that you love these boys."

"All right, but *you've got to understand* I have little money."

"If you'll take care of the farm and the boys, it doesn't matter. This farm is only for sale because my brother is a thin-skinned, cowardly fool. When his wife died, he acted like he'd been struck dumb. I understood his grieving but he wouldn't do anything, not care for the boys or the farm or the house or even the darn chickens. He just took off." She slapped the tabletop, then waved her arm around the room. "Just look at this place and it's only been six months. What will things be like in a year?"

He glanced around, nodding his head. "Didn't your brother leave you any money?"

"No."

His eyes rounded. "And you've got no family to help out?"

"My parents are gone. I have two younger sisters but . . ."

"You *are* in a bit of a jam, aren't you?"

Jane couldn't help the sigh that escaped her lips. "More than you know."

"And the farm—"

Jane interrupted, "Have you really looked at it?"

"Yeah, it needs work—"

"Lots of work."

"But all the same, I would have taken it sight unseen."

"You would have?"

"Of course," Rider's voice wavered as he replied in an odd tone. Jane blinked in bafflement.

"It may need some work, but look at all the wide, open space you've got. The freedom to do whatever you want, whenever you want. This is my idea of heaven." He glanced away from Jane as his cheeks flared red. "Excuse me, ma'am. I'd better take care of my horse."

He rushed out the door before Jane could open her mouth. What an oddly poetic man. He acted like this hardscrabble scrap of land really was heaven and he couldn't wait to dirty his hands on every last clump of soil.

It seemed her problem was solved. So why did she have this throat-clogging lump at the thought of seeing him do just that without her? Jane shivered, unwilling to allow her thoughts to drift away in such a sentimental direction. Besides he was a perfect fit for her plan.

No doubt about it, he'd made a fool of himself in front of that woman. Rider shook his head as he walked his horse around the side of the house toward the ramshackle barn. As he came in sight of the tumbledown building, he noticed a faded hex sign painted just beneath the gabled roofline and above the sliding double doors. He couldn't remember if the traditional German geometric design was to ensure good luck or to ward off bad luck. Either way he looked at it, his own luck seemed about to forever change.

He wanted to work this farm so bad, his mouth watered. He had a bit of trouble seeing himself raising those boys, but he wanted the falling-down barn, the run-down house and everything else that came with it. And he wanted to be the one to fix them all up.

He would even take Jane: plain-spoken, plain-dressed, plain-faced. Plain Jane, a mousy woman with eyes like brown sugar and a soft mouth . . . that begged for his kisses.

He'd come determined to redeem himself, but now that wasn't enough. He wanted it all.

Had he just gone and spoiled it?

She wouldn't let him stay. He probably reminded her of her thin-skinned, cowardly fool of a brother. He felt like a coward for running out like that, but he'd opened his heart to her, a virtual stranger. Afraid that she'd laugh at him, or worse, ridicule him, he'd found the most expedient way out: through the door.

Jane didn't know Rider Magrane. She didn't know he'd robbed her brother. She didn't know he'd spent the last five years in prison unable to speak to another soul, unable to move farther than a four-by-eight-foot space, unable to breathe clean, fresh Kansas air.

Unable to do anything but wait.

Just waiting to get released and right things with David Warner, the man whose livelihood he thought he'd stolen.

And if she did know, she'd hate him for what he'd done to her brother. He vowed right then and there to never tell her. He was determined to make the farm a better place for those two youngsters, and he could only accomplish that if he kept his true identity secret. It was only a little lie for a good cause, wasn't it?

As Rider stepped into the shadowy barn, questions plagued him.

Where was David Warner and why did he really run away? The death of his wife? The farm? Lack of money and the wherewithal to take care of his family? He wished he knew.

Rider removed the gear from his horse and led him into a stall. He was here now and, by God, he could help. He had a strong back and a not-so-feeble mind. He could make this farm work. He could learn to love those children.

He took a deep breath, pushed his Stetson to the back of his head and marched up to the house. He knocked on the door.

Jane opened it, surprise on her face. She held the baby in her arms. ''I figured you'd high-tailed it back to wherever you came from by now.''

Rider swallowed the retort that jumped to his lips. ''No, ma'am. I'm here to stay.''

''Good. Take this child.'' She thrust the wiggling boy into Rider's arms. ''He needs changing.''

''Changing? Into what?''

She rolled her eyes. ''His diaper is wet. Can't you tell?''

A moist warmth spread across the front of Rider's shirt. He held the baby away from his body. ''I can now.''

''Good. See you later then.''

Rider stared at the smiling, gurgling bundle in his hands. ''What's his name again?''

''John Michael, and if you don't change him right soon, that cute little grin of his is going to disappear.'' Jane picked up a wooden bowl and clutched it to her midsection.

''And?''

''And he'll start caterwauling loud enough to wake the dead.'' She headed for the door.

"Where are you going?"

"See if I can find more potatoes."

"Hardly worth the effort."

"You haven't been in the larder lately, have you?"

John Michael pulled Rider's nose and laughed. A sweet bubble of a laugh that turned Rider's stomach to mush. Rider noticed two teeth, tiny, and white as pearl buttons, protruding from the top of the babe's gums.

"I'm not sure I can do this."

Jane's voice came softly from the doorway. "That's what you wanted, isn't it, or did you leave something out of our discussion?"

"We didn't exactly finish."

"Well, call this practice. See how you take to fathering. I'll be back shortly and start dinner."

Teddy showed Rider where Jane kept the clean cloths and even explained the basic fundamentals of changing a diaper. After warning Rider about the potential hazards of John Michael's anatomy, Teddy left Rider on his own and went back to playing with his blocks. Rider lay the child on the kitchen table and pulled up the baby's gown. Two flailing arms and two equally flailing legs occupied him as he attempted to figure out the ins and outs of diaper changing. He marveled at the child's good nature through it all.

When Rider finished, he tipped the baby's chin up and looked into his face. "John Michael is an awful mouthful for such a little boy."

The baby grinned, again exposing the two bright front teeth.

"You look like a gopher to me."

Teddy, playing on the floor, hooted with laughter. "He does kind of look like a gopher."

"Well then, Gopher it is." Rider picked up the child and settled him in the crook of one elbow. He smelled warm and moist, reminding Rider of his mother's kitchen on baking day when he was young. "You can call me Rider."

"Wide," John Michael gurgled.

"R-R-Rider."

"Wide."

Rider grinned. "Wide, Rider, I guess it doesn't much matter. Teddy, what do I do now?"

"Do?"

"Yeah, what am I supposed to do with him?"

"You can put him on the floor but since he's learned to walk you have to really watch him. He puts everything in his mouth. Jane says he has curious ideas about what he's s'posed to eat and what he's s'posed to play with."

"Well, I guess I'll find out about all that soon enough when Jane and I marry up."

Rider heard a gasp from the doorway. Jane stood there, her face pale, her expression horrified. The bowl she held in white-knuckled hands tilted. Potatoes spilled out and rolled across the floor. John Michael gurgled happily and, on short, wobbly legs, chased after them.

She glanced at Rider with a look that said he must have lost his mind in an all-night poker game. "When did I ever say anything about getting married?"

Where there is whispering, there is lying.
—English proverb

Chapter Two

"I just assumed . . . that is, well, from what you said . . ." Rider sputtered, feeling like a chucklehead. Heat worked its way up beneath his collar, as he stooped over and began gathering the scattered potatoes. As he leaned over, their heads collided with a sickening, thwacking sound.

Jane moaned, then swayed, her eyes blinking rapidly.

Stars danced before Rider's eyes, but he managed to catch one of her elbows and ease her against the door frame. Appalled by his clumsiness, he stood beside her and tipped up her chin. He stared into a pair of glazed eyes. "Are you all right?"

She clasped a palm to her forehead as a wan smile crossed her features. "What do you mean? The shock you've just given me with your talk of marriage or my now-throbbing head?"

It took him a moment to realize she was joking. He

released her chin and returned her half-smile. "Well . . ."

Her smile deepened into laughter. "You must have thought it was a good idea to crack me over the head before you hauled me off to the preacher."

Rider surprised himself as he burst out laughing. It had been a long time since he'd really had anything to feel good about, except healing his relationship with his brother, Chance. The laughter fell easily from his lips even though he found himself standing beside a virtual stranger. "Next time I'll get down on one knee and propose like a real gentleman."

She stared at him in amazement. "What next time?"

John Michael chose that moment to grab onto her skirt hem. He held one of the larger potatoes in both his chubby hands, trying, without much success, to take a bite out of the dirty thing. She picked him up and held him against her chest. He laid his head down, still trying to nibble on the potato. "So, Mr. Magrane, what do you think of our John Michael?"

Rider settled one shoulder against the opposite door frame and folded his arms across his chest. He eyed the child. "I don't know all that much about children," he admitted.

Jane gave an unladylike snort. "You'll soon learn."

"Kind of a big name for such a little boy."

Jane nodded, ruffling the hair on the toddler's head. "Mary Therese named this one. David wanted something simpler, but she generally got her way."

"The boy's mama?"

"Yes, she was a lovely woman but a mite eager."

"Eager?"

"Eager to get married, eager to have children, eager for David to make something of his life."

"But you're not looking for an eager bridegroom, I take it?"

She eyed him with a calculating expression. "To be perfectly honest, Mr. Magrane, I never once gave marriage a thought when I placed the advertisement. I don't want a husband, just a father for the boys."

"It makes sense."

"To you, perhaps." Jane gently put John Michael on the floor, grabbed the potato and playfully swatted his bottom. He scooted off into the adjoining room. She moved toward the kitchen area.

Rider jerked away from the door frame, then swayed on his feet. This time Jane took his elbow to steady him. He gave her a grateful, though sheepish, look.

She raised her gaze to find him watching her. His eyes glittered with faint amusement. "You see? It makes perfect sense to get married. You've already got me reeling."

Jane gave a light laugh, as if she found his comment humorous. She supposed marriage made sense to him. It made sense to her, too, but she was reluctant to admit it. Maybe because it made too much sense. She kept telling herself she wasn't going to die, but if there was the least bit of doubt, marriage to Rider would solidify the boys' futures. She admitted to a partial truth. "The reason I placed the advertisement was not to gain a husband. I got sick a while back and it started me thinking about the boys' safety. What if I died? Where would they be?—all alone, small and helpless. I think I'm fine and the doctor can't find anything wrong with me." Well *that* part was the truth. "But you never know."

Jane retrieved the rest of the potatoes and turned toward the slop stone resting atop the table against the far wall. She dropped them and glanced at Rider to gauge his reaction to her words. His face held a somewhat bemused expression.

"Why don't you just take a look around, Mr. Magrane? Get to know the place and find out what you're in for. Be back at the house in an hour for dinner. Tonight you can sleep in the barn loft, if you can find any room." She shook her head in disgust. "You'll see it's as bad as the rest of the place."

"All right." A thoughtful smile turned up the corners of his mouth as he clapped his hat on his head. "See you later, boys. You, too, ma'am."

Like an angry bee buzzing around her head, Jane's chores hounded her. She stepped outside to take the clothes from the line before fixing dinner.

Duty called, but one word kept popping into her head. *Marriage.* Marriage to a stranger, a stranger with warm blue eyes and a beguiling smile. A stranger who was even now walking the perimeter of the yard, occasionally squatting to take a better look at something on the ground or scanning the sky overhead. She couldn't help wondering what was going on in his mind.

She didn't want to think about this unknown man who'd wandered into her life, but she couldn't stop. He was willing to marry her. It was almost more than she could understand. Not only was he willing to take on the responsibilities of the farm and the children . . . but he was willing to take her, too.

Or so he said. She had to wonder why. Maybe all he really wanted was the farm. She watched him stride behind the barn. Whatever was he doing? Changing his mind most likely—about the farm, about her, about the boys. *Dear Lord, please let him want the boys.*

She gathered her clean laundry and ducked into the house before he spotted her.

While wandering the farm's premises, Rider found a narrow, slow-running creek a scant quarter mile from the house. He squatted on the bank and watched as gold-edged leaves floated down the stream or hung up in the shallows along the embankment. He picked up a knuckle-sized quartz rock and tossed it into the clear water. It plunked softly, then dropped and settled on the bottom. He could see it clearly nestled atop the rotting leaves.

He sat down on the grassy verge, well away from a thick clump of blackberry brambles, then leaned back on his elbows and closed his eyes. The sun overhead gave off little heat but still warmed his face. He sighed, knowing he would never again take for granted the intoxicating feel of sunshine upon his flesh.

When he opened his eyes, he spotted a doe and a young buck across the creek. They both stood still and seemed to be staring back at him. Suddenly their ears perked and on spindly legs, they sprinted away, their white tails the last thing he saw before they disappeared in the brush.

Rider plucked a blade of grass and stuck it in the corner of his mouth. He idly wondered if Jane would miss him if he didn't return for supper. The quiet, the solitude, this idyllic setting kept him rooted to the spot.

Idyllic setting? God, he sounded like a lovelorn past-her-prime schoolmarm.

Rider shook his head in disgust, then stood and dusted off the seat of his pants. At the sound of wild thrashing in the brush behind him, he whirled around, searching for whatever caused the commotion. His pulse pounded, his stomach churned. He cursed aloud for not having the forethought to bring a weapon with him. He didn't own a gun, but at the very least, he should have brought his knife. With his hands fisted at his side, and his legs spread wide, he waited.

With a quick rush and a growling snort, something barreled through the undergrowth and struck him hard in the shin, throwing him to the ground and knocking the wind from his lungs. He grabbed for the first thing he could and surprised himself to come up with a leg—hairy, short and . . . cloven? The creature squealed in his ear like a locomotive's steam whistle and struggled for release.

Rider rolled over on top of a stout body and slammed its porcine head to the ground. It kicked once, then lay senseless. He stared at the prone body and shook his head.

He'd wrestled a full-grown, domesticated pig to the ground and laid it out cold.

Rider fell to his back on the ground and gasped for air. Blood pounded in his temples and his heart threatened to burst from his chest. He couldn't remember the last time he'd been this frightened . . . and by a mere farm animal. He felt like a supreme idiot.

Unfortunately, the damned animals seemed to roam in a pack, for soon two more well-fed hogs trotted through the brush and stopped at his side. He jumped to his feet, ready for another set-to. They, however, seemed content to just look over their fellow porker. They sniffed, snorted and then shuffled away. Blue blackberry juice stained their snouts and dripped from their jaws. How the hell did they find blackberries this late in the season?

"Well, hell," Rider muttered. He sat up and stared at his catch, suspecting that Jane and her boys hadn't eaten meat other than chicken for one hell of a long time. He hoped she would appreciate his effort.

He had a bit of twine in his pocket, which he tied around the pig's legs. He stood up and hoped the beast would stay unconscious long enough to get him back to the farmstead.

Rider caught movement from the corner of an eye. Where the deer had recently poised across the creek, a hunter now hunkered down on the bank. He cupped his hands for a drink of water. When he lifted his head, water dripping from his grizzled beard, he spotted Rider. He waved and grinned, then picked up a shotgun. Surprisingly, he started wading across the creek. He carried a bulging burlap bag over a shoulder and cradled the gun in the crook of one elbow. An old slouch hat shaded his eyes.

Rider gave him a hand up as he reached the bank.

"Thanks, stranger. McCampbell Smith's the name."

Rider backed up a pace. Upon closer inspection, Rider saw that he wasn't an old man, just gray at an early age. A square jaw jutted forward from an unlined face. He had a full head of dark hair, graying at the temples. Tall as Rider himself, the man had more meat on him and was powerfully built. He had a commanding air of self-confidence that irritated Rider.

From hooded, blue-gray eyes, the stranger inspected the trussed-up hog and then turned suspicious eyes toward Rider and seemed to be waiting for an explantion.

Hesitant to reveal too much about himself, but unsure how to answer without sounding like it was shy of the truth, Rider cautiously answered by giving his name. "Rider Magrane."

The fellow nodded without obvious recognition. "New to these parts?"

Rider heaved a sigh of relief. "No."

Smith nodded again. "My land leans right up next to the Warner farmstead." He gestured with his free hand. "You know you're on Warner land?"

"Yeah."

"Words are kind of scarce falling out your mouth, Magrane. Why is that?"

Rider resented the nosy interrogation. He dropped the heavy hog to the ground and shoved his hands in his pockets. He straightened to his full height. "You ask a lot of questions."

Smith shrugged. "I'm not the poacher here."

"Neither am I. How do I know that what you've got in that bag you shot on your own property?"

Smith rolled his eyes. "Well I did and you can believe it or not. Just what are you doing with Miz Warner's hog then?" He stared long and hard at the stout body. "Is it dead?"

Rider snorted in disgust. "What does it look like I'm doing, waltzing with the damn thing?"

Smith frowned, his eyes level and appraising. He did not reply.

Rider relented. "All right, all right. The hog took me unawares and I knocked him out cold. I plan on taking him back right now and butchering the damn thing for Jane. That fine with you?"

"Jane? You know her well enough to call her by her given name?"

"I do." Rider winced at his unintentional use of the words spoken in a marriage ceremony. What the hell—in for a penny, in for a pound. "We've discussed marriage."

Smith took an abrupt step toward Rider, and leveled a scowl at him. "Has she accepted?"

Rider stood his ground. "Not yet."

"I was planning on courting her myself."

Rider found perverse pleasure in responding to the challenge in Smith's voice and replied in a voice dripping with disbelief. "That so?"

"I just hadn't gotten 'round to it yet."

Rider wasn't sure why he wanted to antagonize this neighbor, but contrariness goaded him on. "What you waiting for? An invite?"

A humorless smile split his strong work-hardened face. "Ain't you as cocky as the king of spades?"

Plain orneriness made Rider throw down one last gauntlet. "I expect you'll have to wait your turn to court her."

"I expect I won't." Smith turned with a meaningful stare on his too-handsome face and headed across the creek. Halfway over, he stopped and yelled at Rider, "You're too puny for her anyways."

"We'll see about that," Rider hollered back. He could learn to hate that man.

He picked up his shackled pig and headed home, a smile firmly planted on his face.

The sound of uninhibited gaiety met Rider as he rounded the barn. Jane's throaty laughter mingled with Gopher's childish giggles.

When Jane glanced up and spotted him, the sound died, and a wary expression drifted across her features.

Her footsteps slowed, then stopped altogether. She held Gopher in one arm and a rug beater in the other. A stray strand of hair feathered across her furrowed brow. She took one look at the tied hog across his shoulder and shook her head. "I see you found Exodus."

"Exodus, as in the great departure?" How in blazes did she know one from the other?

"No, as in Genesis, Exodus, Leviticus. Did you happen to see the other two?" She stepped closer and studied the old ham. "Is he dead?"

Rider shook his head and lowered the beast to the ground. He stuck his hands beneath his armpits and replied with as much patience as he could muster. "I saw two others, and no, this one isn't dead."

"Good." Relief smoothed the wrinkles from her brow. "I turned them all out not long ago when I ran out of feed. I figured they could forage for themselves. How did they look?"

Rider frowned. "They looked like hogs."

"Genesis?"

He couldn't keep the sarcasm from his voice. "Genesis what?"

"How did Genesis and Levi look? Healthy?"

"You named these damned hogs Genesis, Exodus and Levi?"

"Teddy couldn't pronounce *Leviticus*."

As if that explained everything.

"Wevi," mimicked Gopher. He grinned at Rider.

Rider reached out and tousled the youngster's blond head. "Tell me, Miss Warner, does every animal on this confounded farm have a name?"

"Yes," she said, looking surprised by the question. "Of course."

Of course. "The chickens, too?"

She nodded..

"Does it bother you when you have to eat them?"

"Sometimes, but a body's got to eat."

Rider couldn't disagree with that simple statement.

"You will let him go, though, won't you?" she asked. Her voice sounded oddly troubled.

"You don't want him butchered?"

"Not yet."

Was she planning on waiting until they all wasted away from eating left-in-the-ground potatoes and dried beans? The concerned look on her face baffled him. Was she so attached to these animals that she didn't understand the seriousness of her situation? He had an insane urge to take her in his arms and tell her everything was going to be fine. "All right, Miss Warner, I'll release him, but it may be next spring before we're able to catch up with him again."

"That's fine."

"Fine, fine, fine," mimicked Gopher.

Rider winked at Gopher, then picked up the deadweight of the hog and trudged into the barn.

Naming farm animals and then refusing to eat them? The woman was either crazy or too tender for farm life. "I reckon that will be just fine by me, too . . . for now."

Sleep eluded Jane. After tossing and turning the better part of the night, she flung her legs over the side of the bed and got up. She threw a worn woolen shawl around her shoulders and settled herself in the rocking chair. With stockinged feet, she pushed the chair back and forth and stared out the window at the star-dusted night sky. Though the bright moon hung low in the sky like a child's yellow ball, she had no idea of the time.

Her gaze fell to the silhouette of the barn. No light escaped from between the weathered boards. No lantern glowed beneath the double doors. Rider must be sleeping like a contented dog by the fire—unconcerned about what tomorrow would bring. Unlike Jane, who worried and fretted and tried not to think about that quack, Doc Hendricks, and his dire predictions.

She'd bathed John Michael and Teddy, read them a story from the only book in the house, the Bible, and put them to bed, while Rider kept himself occupied in the barn doing who knew what. For some reason or another, all day he'd kept his distance from her, not even coming in for supper. Perhaps her forward manner intimidated him. But just his presence on the farm calmed Jane's fears, and instilled in her a sense of hope and promise for the future.

Near twilight, Rider came up to the house and asked Jane if she needed anything. When she told him she didn't, he bid her good night and told her he'd see her in the morning. He didn't mention marriage again and neither did she, but his disarming gaze followed her as close as her own shadow as she backed into the house and said good night.

His gentle way with her and the boys unnerved Jane. Why, she couldn't say. Maybe it was a guilty conscience about not disclosing to him the full truth, or maybe she was reading more into his disconcerting look than was actually there, but she'd never met anyone quite like him.

Just then, as Jane stared at the barn, she heard what

sounded like a gunshot. Before she could jump to her feet, the barn doors burst open, and shattered into stove-size kindling. She watched in amazement as a torrent of dust and wood splinters flew into the air, then fell from the sky like leaves in autumn. They settled to the ground, and all was quiet. She rushed outside.

Rider stood in the open space in what should have been the door, with a dazed expression on his face. Clad in stockinged feet, his shirt and trousers unbuttoned, and his hair sticking up like a porcupine, he stared at the ground, then looked up as Jane scurried his way. He shrugged his shoulders, blew out a long breath and folded his arms across his chest. "There must have been too much black powder."

She stared at the bewildered expression on his face, and said in a quiet voice, "What were you doing?"

He paused a moment before answering. "When I was cleaning this afternoon, I found several old shotguns and rifles in a crate in the loft."

"David's," Jane explained. "He liked to tinker with firearms that were broken or otherwise useless."

"Ah. Anyway before I went to bed, I fixed one of the shotguns. I cleaned it up pretty good, found some left-over shot and powder, and loaded it."

"But what were you shooting at in the dark?"

He gave her a bleak smile. "A rat."

"Oh?"

"I don't much like rats."

As if that explained everything, Jane nodded and tried to keep from laughing. "That would explain the barn door bursting like a ripe melon."

"I hate rats," he reiterated.

"I don't like them either," Jane admitted. A shiver

ran up her spine. She shuddered, shaking away the crawling sensation. "I know it's foolish, but when I see a mouse in the house, I jump up on a chair and holler like my dress is on fire."

Rider pulled her shawl closer around her shoulder, then left his hand resting there as if it were the most natural thing in the world. "Really?"

His hand, warm and strong where it touched Jane, tingled through the thin layer of her shawl and night rail. She'd never had a man touch her in such an intimate way. She peered up at him. He smelled of hay and something else indefinable, yet compelling. She had a nearly uncontrollable urge to walk into his arms and feel his strength surround her. Her pulse spinning, she barely could reply. "Honest."

He squeezed her shoulder and lowered his hand to the middle of her back. "Then you understand."

Jane released a sigh as her pulse skittered. She tried to speak in a casual, jesting manner to hide her confusion about the way he made her feel. "I do, except for one little thing."

"What's that?"

"How did you shoot the barn door right off its hinges?"

Even though it was dark, moonbeams highlighted his face and she saw the tips of his ears redden. "I'll fix it."

"Mr. Magrane, I'm not the least worried about that darn door. A good gust of wind will likely blow the whole barn over one of these days anyway."

"Not while I'm in it, I hope." A grin split his face.

She returned his smile. "I hope not, too."

"I sorely miscalculated the amount of powder I

needed." He shook his head. Disgust turned the corners of his mouth downward. "It's been a good while since I shot a weapon."

Jane wondered why he hadn't had a gun in his hands for a long time. Was he a city fella? She thought all men hunted regularly. Even on the farm, there always seemed a need for a shotgun. Feeling it was too impolite to ask, she merely nodded. "Will you be all right then?"

His eyes widened. "My God, you make me sound as helpless as a hooked trout!"

"I'm sorry. I didn't mean to imply that you—"

"Makes no never mind, ma'am," he interrupted. He turned and walked back into the barn. "I'll just be going on up to the loft now. I can still catch forty winks before the rooster crows."

"Mr. Magrane?"

Rider stopped and looked at Jane.

"Did you get the rat?"

He shook his head and then chuckled. "I honestly don't know. I sure killed the door, though, didn't I?" He disappeared inside the darkness of the barn.

Jane stared after him, wondering if she could sleep. Her skin still tingled, her heart still thundered in her chest. When he touched her, she'd forgotten her responsibilities, even the boys. She'd forgotten everything but Rider. All she'd wanted was to be held and touched, to be enfolded in the safety of his embrace.

How utterly foolish.

How ridiculously silly.

How totally pathetic.

She was Jane Warner, plain Jane Warner, who had a doctor's ridiculous prognosis and a mysterious illness hanging over her head like a waiting hangman's noose.

Think today and speak tomorrow.
—H. G. Bohn, A Handbook of Proverbs

Chapter Three

Rider woke well before dawn, his body as cold as creek water in January. He shivered all over like an old man with the ague. He jerked a moth-eaten wool blanket over his head and pushed his numb nose deep into the straw-filled pillow. Unfortunately, pulling the blanket over his head uncovered his feet, which felt like solid blocks of ice. Groaning, he pushed himself up onto one elbow, blinking the sleep from his eyes. Hell, he might as well get up because he sure wasn't going to get any more rest. Not with his limbs half-frozen from the cold.

He supposed blowing the barn doors clean off brought in a lot of air, but he couldn't lay this frigid cold entirely on the missing doors. This was winter acoming.

Gingerly he stood and stretched complaining muscles, then waited for the tingling in his toes to diminish before he climbed down from the loft. He yanked his boots on, then walked over to the barn's entryway where the door *should* have been and gazed out at the purple horizon.

He leaned against the frame as he buttoned up a new flannel shirt over his bare chest. Since money had been in short supply when he received his prison release, he'd foregone the long johns. Now he was sorry.

Frost sparkled on the grass and the few remaining leaves on the trees. A light coating of ice glimmered on the remaining windowpanes in the house. He wondered if the house was any warmer than the barn. He hoped so, but regardless, his next task would be replacing the glass in those broken windows.

He lit a kerosene lamp and hurried to the pump. His exhaled breath fogged the air in white cloudlike bursts. He broke through the thin layer of ice in the bucket and splashed the frosty water on his face. A bar of lye soap lay on the pump's wooden base. Picking it up he soaped his face with one hand while pumping water with the other. He quickly rinsed his face and hands, and after wiping his face with the tail of his shirt, headed toward the still-dark house.

Rider stepped up onto the porch and stood, uncertain. The light from the lantern wavered as he hesitated. Should he just go in the house or did he need an invitation?

The baby's high-pitched wail decided him. It pierced the quiet predawn, jolting Rider into action. He dashed inside and down the hall following the sound of the caterwauling. He found John Michael standing in his crib, his mouth wide, his eyes shut tight, fat tears falling down his cheeks.

"John Michael, what the devil is wrong?" Rider croaked. He cleared his sleep-roughened voice, hoping to soften his tone. He set the lamp on a small table crammed with unknown baby items and reached out his arms. ‘‘Come here, Gopher.’’

And that’s exactly what Gopher did. He leaned so far forward that Rider feared he would fall from the bed and crack his head on the hard, uncovered floor. Rider dashed across the room, slipped on a rag rug and crashed to the floor just as the baby fell. Rider hit the floor hard, his head striking the wooden boards with a resounding thud.

Luckily the toddler landed atop him. Gopher’s elbow connected with Rider’s left eye. His head battered Rider’s chin.

Gopher’s crying stopped, and he stared at Rider.

Blinking back tears of pain, Rider lay flat on his back, and tried to clear his head. He stared upward and saw stars. And not in the damned sky.

His head throbbed like the tail of a pleased puppy. He leaned up on one elbow, and winced at the headache forming in the back of his skull. He turned Gopher over to make sure he’d received no injuries.

The baby smiled. His two front teeth gleamed like a harvest moon. ‘‘Wide,’’ he crowed.

Rider put his forefinger to Gopher’s mouth. ‘‘Not so loud, pal. You’ll bring down the house.’’ Slowly, Rider sat up. A wet warmth seeped through the front of his flannel shirt. He grimaced and pulled the damp material away from his stomach. ‘‘Thanks, pal.’’

Rider lurched to his feet. Finding a clean diaper, he changed the baby, feeling slightly more comfortable doing so than on the previous day. As he left the room he shot a glance at Teddy, who slept quietly across the room in another small bed. How could Jane and the boy sleep through such a ruckus?

"She probably didn't," he grumbled aloud. He grabbed the lantern and tiptoed down the hall toward the kitchen. When the baby's cry first startled Rider, it seemed more like the middle of the night, but now he noticed the eastern sky lightening. Jane would be getting up soon and wondering what he was doing in her kitchen making himself at home. "She'll come after me with that shotgun for sure now."

"Wide," John Michael gurgled.

"Gopher, it's Rid*er*." As he searched the kitchen for something the baby could eat, Rider wondered how he thought he could ever manage to take care of one spunky woman and two young boys.

Although he thanked God every day for just being able to walk in a space larger than four by eight, and to breathe fresh, clean air, he hadn't forgotten his long-held promise to himself to help out David Warner. Child care just wasn't what he thought he'd be doing. Long days in the fields—certainly. Daily chores around the house and barn—of course. But not changing soiled diapers before dawn.

He glanced at the bundle in his arms. Gopher grinned, then pinched Rider's nose with a chubby thumb and forefinger. "Ouch," Rider complained good-naturedly. He tweaked the child's nose, causing him to giggle in return. This child was something all right, he admitted. Both boys were.

Rider shook his head, questioning where all this female sentimentality was coming from. He was immediately sorry for the gesture.

His head hurt like a son of a bitch, and he could scarcely see out of his swollen eye.

Rider plopped Gopher in his high chair with a hard

biscuit he found in a tin. He placed the lamp on the kitchen table. Tossing several pieces of kindling into the stove, he started it going. Rider stood in front of the stove, rubbing his hands together, then up and down his arms. Heat slowly seeped into his body. Feeling himself finally thawing out, he turned around to put water on for coffee.

He then remembered there wasn't any.

"What have I gotten myself into?" he moaned, dropping into a kitchen chair and cradling his aching head in both palms.

"So this is what it's come to."

Jane's laughter brought Rider's head up so fast, he saw stars again.

"Letting yourself into my house, talking to yourself and, smelling like . . . is that what I think it is?"

Rider shot her a tight-lipped smile. "The baby wet on me, and more . . ."

She gave a light laugh, and then, her eyes widening with concern, she stared at Rider's face. "What happened to your eye?"

Jane, still dressed in her nightclothes, leaned over him, bringing with her the warm, provocative scent of a woman newly risen from bed. He watched, his heart in his throat, as her unbound breasts swayed beneath the thin fabric of her gown and the thin shawl thrown around her shoulders. She placed a finger beneath his chin and tipped up his head. Her loosened hair brushed against his chest. Her thigh grazed his.

Rider immediately became aroused. The tips of his ears burned and his pulse pounded. A new ache, much lower, tormented his already-tormented body. He had trouble finding his voice. "I, uh," he croaked, "fell."

"And blackened your eye? Was that after you blew away the barn doors?" With a light touch, she stroked his left brow and around the curve of his eye. Her breath caressed his cheek, then her nose wrinkled. "Take off that foul-smelling shirt and let me wash it."

Oh, boy. If he stood to take off his shirt, she'd see his . . . *interest.*

He took a deep breath, and awkwardly pulled it off over his head after undoing the top three buttons. He extended it to her. She stared at his bare chest. "Aren't you about as cold as an icicle sleeping in that drafty barn? Where are your long johns?"

"Haven't got any."

"No?" Jane rushed from the room, giving Rider time to compose himself by reciting the alphabet. He'd gotten to the letter *m* when she returned bearing a red union suit the likes of which Rider hadn't seen since his boyhood days.

She gave him an apologetic smile. "David left these behind. I guess they're kind of old-fashioned but they will keep you warm. If you like you can go in the bedroom . . ." Obviously embarrassed, her cheeks pinkened. "I mean, the other room, and put them on while I start breakfast."

Jane's gaze left his face and lowered to Rider's bare chest. A rosy flush colored her face as she stared. Goose-flesh rose on Rider's arms and his nipples pebbled. Whether from the cold air or Jane's stare, he couldn't say for sure, but he escaped the room before she lowered her gaze further and noticed his other *interesting* features.

Jane couldn't believe she'd stared at the man like a ninny schoolgirl, practically chasing him from the room, but she couldn't help herself. Before she'd seen him unclothed, she thought he was thin. He was definitely not thin, just lean and rangy. His chest was covered with a dusting of crisp black hair, and his upper shoulders flexed with rope-like muscles every time he moved. His copper-colored nipples puckered before her very eyes and seemed to strain against his body. Thin? She couldn't have been more wrong.

John Michael pounded on his tray, effectively bringing Jane back to earth. She *was* acting like a ninny. Rider Magrane was just a man like any other, with all the same parts and all the same notions.

She shook her head, then gave John Michael another biscuit, the last one in the tin.

She started cooking oatmeal for the boys' breakfast when Teddy stumbled into the kitchen, his eyes bleary and squinting, and his hair falling into his eyes.

"Morning," he mumbled. He pulled out a chair and scrambled up into it. He propped his chin on his arm and watched Jane as she worked.

"Good morning to you, Teddy Warner." Jane glanced at him over her shoulder. "You look about done in. What's the matter?"

He shrugged, not an easy task when seated. "Not awake yet."

"No?" Jane turned back to the stove. "What about Emmett? Suppose she's awake yet?"

"Probably."

"You going to want milk with your breakfast?"

Teddy lifted his head and offered Jane a hopeful expression. "I thought maybe Rider, that is, Mr. Magrane, might do it, since he's already in the barn."

"It's your chore," she reminded him.

"Yeah, but it's cold as hell out there."

Jane shook her spoon at the boy. "You watch your language, young man. Mr. Magrane has better things to do than take care of Emmett and besides, he's already in the house."

"Who's Emmett?" Rider asked as he strolled back into the room.

She looked up to see Rider's masculine chest now safely covered in red flannel. "The milk cow."

"Emmett?"

"Uh-huh."

Rider's brows rose. "I reckon you already figured out that Emmett is a she-cow."

Teddy giggled.

"What's so funny?" Rider asked, as he pulled out a chair, turned it around backward and sat down. He rested his chin on his folded arms and looked expectantly at Teddy.

Jane listened with interest.

"A cow *is* a she," Teddy explained.

"So who gave her a name like Emmett?"

"I did," Teddy admitted, "but I was just a little kid then and I didn't know the difference between boy and girl cows."

"Ah-ha. That explains it." Rider smiled. "Maybe we could go do it now while Jane rustles . . ." Rider hesitated a fraction before continuing, "uh, cooks us up some breakfast. Then we'd have milk to go along with it."

"Together?"

Rider stood and carefully replaced the chair against the table the way he'd found it. "Sure."

With a holler, Teddy leaped up.

John Michael clapped his hands and gurgled.

Rider glanced at him and smiled, then turned back to Teddy. "But you'd best put on some warmer clothes. That nightshirt isn't going to keep the wind from whistling up your a—"

Jane cleared her throat and gave Rider a cautionary frown.

Rider's mouth twisted in a wry expression. "Up your anatomy."

"Be right back." Teddy ran down the hall and out of sight.

Jane nodded her head. "Quick recovery, Mr. Magrane."

Rider cocked his head in acknowledgment. "Why, thank you, Miss Warner, and thanks again for the long johns."

He was out the door before Jane could reply, so he didn't hear her burst of laughter.

Rider stared at the unfamiliar mystery in his arms—Gopher, a bright-eyed, curious bundle of stuff and nonsense.

After breakfast he and Teddy checked out the cornfield. He was pleased to find ears worthy of sowing. He'd have to do it by himself, but heck, he wasn't going anywhere soon. Teddy soon grew bored with the field, and ran off to play.

Rider had been minding his own business, sitting in a sunny spot on the back porch steps pondering life's mysteries. The sun warming his face, he'd allowed his eyes to drift shut, laid his head back against a post and was close to falling asleep. The next thing he knew Jane startled him into wakefulness by thrusting a wriggling Gopher into his arms. He looked up as she brushed past him with a wicker basket full of washed laundry, including his flannel shirt.

He shifted the child to a more comfortable position in his lap and stared into a grinning, drooling face. Big green gumdrop eyes gazed back. The sweet scent of milk and oatmeal tickled his nose. Rider laughed, and Gopher gurgled a contagious reply.

"Hey, Gopher." He took one of the child's hands into his own. How fragile and warm it felt. He marveled at the child's strong grip as it wrapped around his index finger. He considered the hand—little wrinkled fingers, chubby and perfectly formed with tiny all-but-invisible nails. The hand so contrasted with his own; the child's small and smooth, creamy-white without a single spot or speckle, his tough and tanned, scarred and leathery. His own nails were ragged and worn, and not, he noted grimacing, all that clean at the moment.

Saliva trickled from the corner of John Michael's mouth. With the tip of his finger Rider reached to wipe the drop away. John Michael pushed Rider's finger inside his mouth where he proceeded to chew on it like a fresh-from-the-oven biscuit. Actually, gum it was more like it. Rider was at first startled, then he laughed at the surprisingly pleasant sensation. The sharp point of a tooth just beginning to push through rasped against Rider's finger. He gently rubbed the gum. Gopher's eyes drooped and his head dropped onto Rider's shoulder. The toddler gave a gurgle of contentment and fell asleep drooling down the top of Rider's long johns. Rider just smiled.

What was he doing? He knew next to nothing about children. He could count on one hand the times he'd even been in the same room with one—of any age. Of course, he'd seen them in church, at barn raisings or other occasions where the townsfolk came together but he'd been a young man, and what young man really noticed younguns? He had no interest in children, only the opposite sex.

Babies mystified him. When they talked, which to him was seldom, you couldn't understand them. They could hardly walk. Most of the time, they took a few steps and fell down. And to top it all off, most of them couldn't eat solid food because they had few or no teeth.

They still soiled their drawers, which also meant the person holding them had to change clothes often. He seemed to be finding this out with regularity.

All in all, Rider felt ill-prepared. He shook his head and glanced up to find Jane staring at him over the top of a long line of clean diapers. She quickly looked away so all he could see was the hem of her careworn skirt and the tips of her boots.

What did she think? The woman was almost as big a mystery to Rider as Gopher. Actually all women were a mystery to Rider. He had little opportunity to mingle with them while growing up. Not that he hadn't wanted to, but a combination of shyness and his older brother, Chance's interference kept his inner yearnings pretty much to himself.

"Whatcha doing?"

Rider put a finger to his lips and Teddy nodded.

"Whatcha doing?" he asked again, this time in an exaggerated whisper.

"Getting an education," Rider said in a low voice. He patted the step and Teddy sat down, frowning.

"What do you mean? Like in school?"

"There's more to getting an education than reading, writing and ciphering."

"Like what?"

"Like learning about little Gopher here."

Teddy snorted in disgust. "He's a pest."

"I reckon you were, too, at his age."

Teddy scuffed the toe of his boot in the sandy soil at his feet. "Nope," he said, shaking his head, "I never was."

"That so?"

"I reckon."

"You ever heard of the birds and the bees, Teddy?"

"You mean like crows and bumblebees?"

Rider chuckled, causing Gopher's head to loll forward. Rider shifted the little one so he lay more comfortably in the crook of his elbow. "I guess you're a tad young for this conversation."

"What's a con'vation?"

"Can I join this con'vation?"

With a smile on her face, Jane sat down on the step below Rider. Her gaze softened as she glanced at little Gopher asleep in his arms. She reached out and stroked the downy fuzz atop his head, then patted Teddy's cheek.

Teddy hopped up and ran off to chase after a rabbit running across the cornfield. Jane watched him, then leaned her head back against a post and closed her eyes. "I know I've got chores to do, but this surely feels nice."

She rubbed the back of her neck and stretched her head back and forth, easing the ivory skin of her neck with one hand. She placed three fingertips across her mouth and sighed.

The feminine gesture tightened Rider's throat. He swallowed hard and tried to think of something safe to discuss. "You should enjoy this nice day. I reckon it'll be the last of the warm sunshine until next spring. I even had to break ice in the water bucket just this morning to clean up."

Her eyes flew open. She frowned, causing a deep furrow to form between her brows. He had the urge to smooth the tight expression away with the tips of his fingers. It took all his control to keep his hands securely around the baby.

"Oh, I should have thought . . ." She lifted her hand from her lips and clasped her forehead. "I should have warmed some water, I . . ."

He placed a consoling hand on her shoulder, more for his own benefit than hers. He needed to touch her. "Whoa, slow down. I've washed up in cold water before. It's never killed me."

"That's not the point. I should have remembered. My God, you must have about froze last night. Did you get any sleep at all?"

"I slept fine, ma'am."

"I don't know how," she muttered, shaking her head. "My mind's been elsewhere lately."

"Running this farm is too much for a woman alone."

"That's not it."

"No?"

"I'm just worried about the boys' future is all." She sighed again and with heavy steps trudged back inside the house.

Rider glanced up to find Teddy returned from his rabbit-chasing adventure. His face held a much-too-serious look for such a little tadpole. "What's the matter, pal?"

"She's worried about the curse," he said in a matter-of-fact tone.

Rider nearly choked. "Curse?"

Teddy sat down next to Rider and looked up at him expectantly. "This scary man in town said Jane had a curse."

"What scary man would that be?"

"I don't know. He asked Jane a lot of stuff and read out of this big black book and that made Jane mad. She told him to beware of hobble-gobbles."

He gazed up at Rider with his big brown eyes and asked, "What's a hobble-gobble, Rider?"

"Teddy, I don't have the faintest idea what you're talking about." But, by damn, he was going to find out.

He who holds the ladder is as bad as the thief.
—German proverb

Chapter Four

Gopher didn't appreciate Rider's sharp tone; he nearly jumped out of Rider's arms, hollering like a calf for its mother. Jane came back out on the porch and Rider handed the squirming, squalling child to her. She lay the baby on her shoulder and assured him by stroking his back with the palm of her hand. Soon his cries turned to mild hiccups, then a resounding, blessed quiet.

She smiled over his head at Rider. "You've got to keep your voice down around sleeping children."

Rider nodded in agreement. "I guess I'll learn that one eventually."

Her lips turned up in a knowing expression. "It generally only takes once."

"I reckon."

Jane stood up and headed back inside the house, leaving Rider wondering if he'd ever get the hang of this child-rearing business.

* * *

Several hours later, Rider came full circle and stepped up onto the porch to better survey his surroundings. A cornfield, long overdue for harvesting, lay waiting off to his left. The brown dried-out husks and knife-edged leaves waved in the breeze and rasped against one another like sandpaper on dry wood. Off behind the barn was a pasture of spiked sunflower stalks, long since gone to seed. A flock of geese flew high overhead—a vee of honking, long-necked Canadians.

The smell of coming winter, sharp and tangy, tickled Rider's nose. He took a deep breath, tipped back his head and closed his eyes. A rainbow of colors danced behind his eyelids. His spirits stirred as he pondered the complicated circumstances that had brought him back to his hometown, and to this farm.

Still, it was good to be alive . . . and free.

Rider opened his eyes. He removed his hat and placed it on the porch rail. Even though a mite chilly, he shrugged out of his shirt, carefully folded it and left it atop the Stetson. The hot sun, unusual this late in the season, beat down relentlessly, and he knew he would soon be glad he'd discarded his hat and shirt. Both would be soaked in sweat in no time. The hat was new and he was a mite partial to it, and he had only one other clean shirt.

He began cleaning up the yard by dragging everything he could carry, push or curse, from the yard and into the barn. The hens, cackling in irritation, scuttled out of his way. He found three rusted tin cans, colored glass fragments, a broken coffee grinder and a usable bucket with its handle missing. An ax head, a bent spade . . . the list went on and on. He wondered how any one family could accumulate so much useless and broken equipment.

However, he'd noticed earlier that the furnishings inside the house, though sparse, were neat, tidy and well-cared for. In the kitchen, jars, canned goods and utensils stood at attention like toy tin soldiers on the shelves and countertops. He'd seen for himself that Jane gave little time to outdoor work but all of her love and attention to the boys and the house.

Rider pushed the last piece, a busted plow, into the shadowy barn. He knew he would need it next spring if he was still here, and realized with a grin, he had all winter to fix it. He had enjoyed clearing the yard so the boys would have a safe place to play, and time passed almost without notice.

He dusted off his hands and stepped back to stare at the accumulation. He sucked in a tight breath when the unmistakable killing end of a double-barreled shotgun nudged his back.

He raised his hands, dared a glance over his shoulder, and saw no one. Shocked, he then lowered his gaze. There stood a woman—an ungodly old, wizened woman, who was so short, she'd need a ladder to kick a grasshopper's ankle. She wore men's serge trousers tucked into knee-high boots and tied with a rope around her skinny waist. A black leather vest hung straight down over a nonexistent bosom. Atop it all, she sported a visored cloth cap favored by young boys. The belligerent look on her face told Rider all he needed to know . . . it wouldn't be wise to laugh at her outrageous costume.

"What are ye doing, boyo?" she asked in an unmistakable Irish lilt that snapped Rider's head around to take a better look. The old crone's angelic voice could have melted butter, and sure as hell belied her tough-as-cow-leather exterior.

"I'm helping out Miss Warner."

"Oh, aye? By pilfering her farm equipment?"

"Why would I steal this broken-down gear?" He gestured to the pile of rusted equipment stacked against the inside of the barn wall. The old bat poked the cold double barrel further into his ribs. "Hey, watch what you're doing with that thing."

"Turn around, slow-like."

As requested, Rider turned, keeping his arms wide and his hands loose. He had no weapon on him but she wouldn't know that. She kept both barrels pointed at his belly.

Her eyes widened, and she stepped closer, peering into his face. "Why, you're that young Magrane boy."

Rider's stomach plummeted to his boot tops. Damn. He knew someone would recognize him sooner or later. He'd been hoping for later. "Damn."

"Is that all you can say? What in the name of God are ye doing? Most of the townsfolk would as soon string you up if they knew you were here-abouts."

Rider shrugged his shoulders. "What can I say? I did my time. I came back to make amends and that's what I'm trying to do."

"Does Jane know who you are?"

"I gave her my name."

"And your past accomplishments?"

Not only old, but a wise-ass, too. "No," he admitted.

"Were ye planning on enlightening the gal?"

Rider planted his hands on his hips. "Not right away."

Twin eyebrows arched above a pair of twinkling gray eyes. "Ye've got some gumption, boyo."

"Thanks, ma'am, but—"

She lowered the gun and cradled it in the crook of her arm. Giving him a sidelong look of consideration, she said, "It's Smith, young Mr. Magrane, Evelina Smith."

"Well, I'd best be getting up to the house, Miz Smith. Miss Warner's expecting me for dinner."

"Call me Evie."

"All right . . . Evie."

"I stop out this-away whenever I pass by just to check on things. I 'spect Janie'll be wanting to fatten me up, too, even with what little she's got and those wee babes to feed." She started out of the barn beside him, her short legs outpacing his.

"She hasn't much, huh?"

Evie gave him a calculating look. "I guess ye would know that just about better than anyone now, wouldn't ye, boyo, seeing as how ye've been trying to make off with the place."

"I wasn't doing any such thing . . ." Rider stopped, seeing the smile on the old woman's face. He thrust his fingers through his hair, then scrubbed his face with both hands. "I do see what you mean, though."

Evie rocked back on her heels and gave Rider an openly amused grin. "Ye know, I admired Chance for having the gumption to arrest his own brother. Showed a lot of grit, he did."

Rider stopped in his tracks. "I reckon you'd have known him if you lived here awhile."

She kept on walking, not slowing her stride. Rider trotted to catch up. "Oh, my, yes. Quite the handsome lad, but ye ain't the ugliest colt that ever foaled yer own self."

"Thanks, I think," he said under his breath. "And it's Rider, Miz Smith."

"Aye, I remember now. Rider Magrane. That bunch you rode with was always just two whoops and a holler away from trouble, weren't ya?" They came to the house and she stopped at the base of the porch. "Whatever happened to those two Ferlin brothers?"

"They were arrested same as me."

"And that poor young kid? What was his name?"

Rider swallowed hard. How could he ever forget? Just his name aroused gut-wrenching guilt. "Chauncey Carlisle."

"Fancy name for a two-bit thief."

"Miz Smith, begging your pardon, but he was only fifteen years old and that's a mite too young to die."

"For sure and it was a pity, but what were you—an old man of nineteen, twenty?"

"Yeah, nineteen."

"Just trying to be big and tough like young boys will do, but it's a crying shame. You should've done what I do. Pull freight instead of pulling six-shooters."

Rider stared, openmouthed, at the diminutive woman. He couldn't imagine her wrangling a team of oxen. "You're a bull whacker?"

She cackled, the sound as tinny as Monday's washtub, then she pounded him on the arm. Rider held his breath instead of yelping. With that punch she could probably take down a good-sized man.

"I know what you're thinking. I may be a wee one to take on the freighting business, but it don't take muscle, boyo, as much as brains."

Rider reached for the shirt he'd left on the porch, furtively rubbing his shoulder. As he shrugged into it, Jane stepped outside. Her face flushed as she looked at his bare chest. He quickly did up the buttons, leaving the tail hanging outside his trousers. She turned her gaze away and saw the old woman standing behind him. Her eyes widened with obvious delight.

"Evie!" As Jane ran down the steps, Rider saw tears glistening in her eyes. Before they could fall down her cheeks, she dashed them away and threw her arms around the tiny woman. She hugged her close. "How lovely it is to see you again! You're just in time for dinner."

"Sounds grand. So, Janie, how's life treating you and those clever little fellas?"

Rider watched closely as Jane's face clouded with uneasiness, or perhaps, unhappiness. He couldn't be sure. Almost as quickly her expression brightened and Rider questioned if he'd seen the sad expression at all. "They're wonderful, growing like weeds and full of mischief."

Evie gave a knowing nod. "As they should be."

Jane turned back to Rider. "Have you met Mr. Magrane, Evie?"

"Aye, that I have." Evie winked at Rider, making him think that just maybe she'd keep his secret. "I found him in the barn."

"And did he tell you that he proposed?"

Evie eyed Rider with suspicion. "Proposed what?"

"Marriage," Jane simply replied, as if she were speaking about a change in the weather.

"Saints!" Evie stepped back and perused Rider, her gaze slowly sliding down his chest and his legs to his booted feet, then back up to his face, which was heating like an overloaded wood stove.

"You're about as subtle as a rattlesnake, Miz Smith."

"Evie," she reminded him. A playful grin turned up her thin, parched lips. To Rider, she looked like a devious, plotting leprechaun.

Rider snuck a peek at Jane. Her lips twitched and she ducked her head, finding a sudden interest in the ground at her feet.

Rider threw up his hands. "All right, so I misunderstood Jane's advertisement. I thought she was looking for a husband. It could happen to anyone."

One of Jane's thin brows rose in amusement. "Not if anyone actually *read* it."

Rider knew it was useless to argue. He could only shrug his shoulders.

"Lean down here," Evie ordered.

Rider complied, bringing his face close to her leathered features. She rose up onto her toes, and kissed his cheek. The kiss, though short, was as dry as an old possum hide. It so startled Rider that he stumbled backward.

Evie stared him straight in the eye, nodded her approval and swung around to Jane. "I'd marry him, Janie." Stomping up the steps, she hollered a hearty "halloo" to the boys and disappeared inside.

Rider stood speechless, staring after her. He was certain now that Evie wouldn't be telling Jane about his past.

He bent his head forward to look at Jane. Her deep brown gaze met his. She bit her lower lip, and her eyes watered. She brought her hands up to cover her mouth but not before a stifled giggle rippled from between her fingers. With a springy bounce, she turned, bounded up the steps and followed Evie inside.

Rider shook his head. His mouth itched with the need to smile—a smile that quickly turned to a chuckle.

Jacob Ferlin stood on the walk outside the Winged Horse Saloon and took a deep breath. He stared down the familiar, dusty road—a street teeming with activity. Wagons loaded with split wood, hay bales or shucked corn competed for space with strutting cowboys on sweat-stained, lathered cow ponies. Tired housewives dodged horse droppings and corralled running children. Old men sat on low wooden benches and gossiped. In five years nothing had changed. Drover, Kansas, looked and smelled like it always had . . . just like home. Jacob glanced at his brother, Martin. The boy hadn't wiped the mile-wide smile off his freckled face since they walked out of prison two days ago.

"Ain't it good to be out?"

Martin grinned. "I feel like startin' this day with a good fight and endin' it with a bad woman."

Jacob returned the grin, nodding in agreement. "And downing a barrel of beer in between."

Martin smacked his lips. "When do we start?"

Jacob slapped his brother on the back. "Right now is as good a time as any."

They turned around, pushed open the bat-wing doors and entered the cool, hushed quiet of the saloon. Except for an elderly barkeep, the place was as empty as their bank account. The bartender, a skinny man with a towel tied around his waist, stood near the end of the bar humming to himself. With shuffling feet, he seemed to be working on an intricate dance step. Jacob, who knew next to nothing about dancing, stared in shock and wonder.

The man twirled an imaginary partner, then spun her back into his waiting arms. He glided a few more steps, bowed and walked behind the bar. Without even looking up, he started wiping down the counter. Then in a conversational tone, he asked, "What'll it be, boys?"

Jacob choked back his astonishment. He glanced at Martin who merely shrugged his shoulders as if it didn't matter to him what the crazy old codger was about. Jacob guessed it really didn't if the man did his job. "Beer to start."

"Coming up."

They sat down and didn't wait long. The barkeep brought over two mugs. Jacob dropped a few coins in the man's hand and swallowed his first taste of alcohol in five long years. Beside him, Martin took a long swallow and released a sigh of obvious pleasure before he relaxed against the back of his chair. Jacob followed suit. His gaze wandered to the mural of the nearly naked woman above the bar as he recalled better days spent carousing in The Winged Horse. Before they'd all wound up in prison or dead, he, Martin, Rider Magrane and Chauncey Carlisle spent many an evening in this very same saloon drinking, playing cards and teasing the barmaids. There had been no two-stepping bartender back then, but there had been no trouble with the law either.

Before they got it into their heads to make some easy money by rustling cattle, life had been simple and uncomplicated. They were just plain stupid to get caught by the law. He met a few old-time cons in prison and he'd wised up. Now he considered himself smarter. Rustling cattle could be a right lucrative prospect in the hands of a man who knew what he was doing. That man was Jacob Ferlin.

He turned to Martin. "Wonder where Rider is."

Martin appeared to be studying the tips of his shiny new boots. He took his time before he answered. "Heard he went to Grand Fork after his release."

"What for?"

"That's where Chance moved when the good folks of Drover sent him skedaddling."

"Is Chance the lawman there?"

Martin took a long swallow, then wiped the back of his mouth across his sleeve. "Don't know."

"What else you know, little brother?"

He shook his head. "That's it." He called to the bartender, "More beer."

"You reckon Rider went there to kill him?" Jacob asked.

Martin sputtered on the beer he'd just swallowed. Choking back laughter, he barked, "Rider Magrane?" Wiping his mouth with the back of a hand, he gave Jacob a derisive grin. "Rider may be weasel-smart, but he don't have the gumption for killing, especially not his own kin."

"He should hate that hard-ass for what he did—arresting him and sending him to prison. As I recall, they didn't part on the friendliest of terms. If it weren't for that damn Chance Magrane, we wouldn't have spent the last five years doing time neither. He ain't exactly on my dance card."

"We'll find Rider. It'll be good seeing him again,"

Martin said, nodding his head. "And maybe we'll find Chance, too."

"Yeah, but first I want a taste of those bad women you were speakin' of."

Rider slowly stood and, pressing his palms against his lower back, straightened up one painful inch at a time. He shaded his eyes against the westerly sun and scanned the barren cornfield. His shoulders ached. His blistered hands hurt like hell. Perspiration poured down his spine. But he couldn't have been happier, nor could he wipe the grin from his face.

He'd harvested the last of the corn, and a full wheelbarrow sat beside him, waiting to be stored in the barn.

Some could be made into hominy and pudding; the rest ground into flour. Though not as tasty as flour ground from wheat, corn flour could be used for baking biscuits and flapjacks, even cakes and cookies. Or so Jane informed him. Rider didn't have a notion about any of that.

He just put himself to use the best he knew how, or however Jane wanted, and he was as happy as a flea in a doghouse. He swore even one slight grin on Jane's face, or a tiny chuckle that worked its way from her lips, made his day brighter and his heart speed up. He was such a sucker when it came to the attentions of this woman. All she had to do was say "please" and he was all over himself complying. Even when he knew he was acting like a fool, he couldn't seem to stop himself. He rubbed his forehead and shook his head. He needed a break from the farm, from her, from his own ridiculous self. First thing in the morning, he was going to town to do some trading. If he had to trade his horse, his saddle, even his soul, he wasn't coming back until he had coffee. No man worth a hill of beans could be expected to start his day without a scalding-hot cup of coffee.

Across the field the Three Little Pigs—no, not little—the three fat, greedy, obnoxiously cantankerous hogs Rider ever had the misfortune to know, were rooting among the stalks for leftovers.

The sows, or more precisely, two sows and one boar, took it into their feeble pea-sized brains to follow Rider around the farm like ducklings after their mother. He kept them at a distance by pelting them with pebbles, but the damnable beasts always kept Rider within sight. As if farm chores and child-care duties weren't enough, now he had hogs shadowing him. Genesis, Exodus and Levi were fast becoming the bane of Rider's existence.

Almost like a curse, Rider mused. He chalked it up to coincidence. He trudged toward the house shaking his head. He needed a good hot meal. He needed a strong cup of coffee. He needed a decent night's rest.

He badly wanted a woman. He badly wanted Jane.

"Up, up," Gopher said. He stared at Rider, his chubby cheeks reddened and his little mouth pursed in a stubborn line. He held up his arms and repeated, "Up."

Rider plucked the child off the floor, scattering wooden blocks and tin solders across the braided rug. He glanced at Jane who stood in front of the stove, stirring something mouthwateringly tempting. She nodded her head and he seated the child in his high chair before seating himself. Teddy crawled up onto his chair and stuck his tongue out at Rider, then gifted him with an ear-to-ear grin. Rider snuck a quick peek at Jane to be sure she wasn't watching, then did the same. He then stuck his thumbs in his ears and waggled his fingers. Both boys collapsed into giggles.

Rider kept one eye on Jane as the boys made faces at each other. The boys loved it, giggling like they had feathers tickling their toes. Gopher hadn't quite caught on to the subtlety of face-making maneuvers but his laughter proved he was having a good time watching.

"I'm not at all sure that's a good thing you're teaching those boys."

Whoops. Caught in the act.

"I don't know what you're talking about," Rider lied.

"Aww, Jane," whined Teddy. "It's fun."

"Aww, Jane," repeated Rider, imitating Teddy's whine. He winked at her when she glanced his way.

A startled expression crossed her features. She tilted her head, her hand stopped stirring, and then began another slow turn around the pot. He could have sworn a smile threatened to turn up her lips.

Determined to make her smile, if not laugh outright, Rider continued, "Aww, Jane, it's fun."

She pursed her lips before saying, "It's foolish tomfoolery."

"Say, Janie, sounds like you're repeating yourself," he drawled.

One hand went to her hip. If possible, her lips pursed tighter than an old-maid schoolteacher. An urge to brush those lips and soften their expression crossed Rider's mind. He swallowed hard and focused on her liquid-brown eyes.

"You know what I mean," she said in a voice that wiped that idea clean out of his brain. Now she *sounded* like an old-maid schoolteacher.

"What *do* you mean, Janie?" His gaze steady, he studied the subtle softening of her mouth. "I don't understand." God, he loved baiting her, and how he wanted to kiss those unyielding lips.

She blushed, a bloom of color that began at her hairline and worked slowly down over her cheek, her nose, her chin. When it slid along her throat, and into the vee of her dress, Rider's heart stopped. Without realizing it, the shoe was on the other foot. She was now baiting him without even trying.

What was that Rider Magrane up to? wondered Jane. If his gaze was any indication, what began as playful teasing was something altogether different now. She thought she knew the difference between friendly teasing and provocative flirting. If she wasn't mistaken Rider was flirting with her. Actually, his heated gaze left little doubt.

"Stop looking at me like that," she ordered. "If those boys weren't sitting right here, I'd say exactly what I should. You're a bright young man, and you know what I mean and you understand perfectly."

Teddy's glance bounced between Rider and Jane, his expression confused.

"Wide," hollered John Michael. He pulled at Rider's sleeve until he turned to look at him.

Nothing like a child to divert the attention away from her. Jane smiled to herself as she brought the pot to the table and set it down, clear of John Michael's outstretched fingers.

"Saved this time," whispered Rider. "We'll talk after the boys are in bed."

"I don't think I'll have time."

"Then I'll just wait around until you do, even if it takes all night."

"Mr. Magrane, it will take a lot longer than that."

Good or bad fortune usually comes to those who have more of one than the other.
—La Rochefoucauld

Chapter Five

Late in the afternoon, the azure sky disappeared behind a bank of sullen gray-bellied clouds. Scudding across the horizon, they formed a foreboding ashen wall to the west. The wind died, the trees stood as still as soldiers at attention. A metallic smell permeated the air and eerie quiet settled over the farm.

Jane opened the back door and called to Teddy, trying not to sound frightened while her heart thudded like a hammer in her chest and her throat tightened around each and every swallow she attempted. She hurried him up the porch and into the house.

She then picked up a sleeping John Michael, snuggled up tight in a blanket, and carried him into a small windowless room wedged between the back porch and the kitchen. A room useless except for storage until today. She lay the baby down amid a pile of discarded flour sacks, then gave Teddy a peppermint stick she'd been saving for just such an emergency and promised him the whupping of his life if he so much as glanced out the door of the small, airless room. She closed it behind her and ran to fetch Rider from the barn.

She found him bent over a broken plow, sweat darkening his shirt. Damp hair curled over the back of his collar. He glanced up as he wiped a hand across his forehead, concentration creasing his brow, his tongue just grazing the corner of his mouth.

"Hi." His gaze relaxed then shifted to the open door. "Sorry you had to come out to the barn. Didn't know it was so late. I'll wash up and be right up to supper."

"It's not late."

He looked at her, then frowned. He rose to his feet, reached for her hands and pulled her close. "What's wrong? You're as pale as a ghost."

One hand still in his, she pulled him out of the barn. He followed without question, though a quizzical expression etched his features.

"We've got to hurry." Her voice caught, and she had to swallow before continuing. "There's a storm coming."

As they started toward the house, his eyes searched the sky. "You sure?"

She pointed off to the west, where the charcoal-colored clouds shifted and reformed, ominous and oppressive. With a sudden gust, the wind swirled around them and lifted Jane's skirt.

She heard Rider's indrawn breath. His step picked up, his fingers tightened around her own. Now *he* led her up to the house pulling her alongside.

"Where are the boys?"

She heard a tremor in his voice she took for simmering fear not unlike her own. "They're safe in the house."

"Where in the house?" he asked, his voice gentle, yet edged with steel.

"I'll show you." They hurried inside, through the kitchen and stopped outside the door to the small room.

Rider lifted her hand to his mouth and with a touch as soft and light as a moth's fluttering wing kissed her knuckles. Jane's stomach flip-flopped. Their eyes met and something intangible passed between them. He pulled her into the circle of his arms and whispered, "Nothing is going to happen to you or the boys. I promise."

"It's just a thunderstorm," she insisted. She tried pulling away but he held her close to his chest. His broad hands, splayed against her back, warmed and bolstered her quaking body. His heart beat against her ear with a reassuring regularity.

He kissed her then. His mouth, warm and gentle, grazed hers with a surprising tenderness. His lips caressed her own so sweetly tears formed in her eyes. She never knew a kiss could be one of reassurance, one of comfort, and not just one of desire.

"I promise," he vowed. His lips brushed against hers as he spoke. He opened the door and they stepped inside together.

Rider picked up Gopher and sat down in the corner of the room. He held the sleeping infant against his chest with one hand. Teddy had fallen asleep on the floor next to him. He eased the boy's body next to his own and gestured to Jane to sit down on his other side. He placed the toddler in her arms and wrapped his arm around her shoulder. With his other arm he kept a tight grip on Teddy.

The rain began with a flash of lightning followed by a burst of thunder.

Rider ran a trembling hand through his hair. He glanced at Jane and prayed she wouldn't notice. If she did maybe she would attribute it to the coming storm, not the panic coursing through his veins like a runaway team of horses. He was terrified this would happen once he got out. He had hoped he would be alone when it did.

During his stint in prison, he developed a pulse-pounding, near heart-stopping fear of enclosed spaces. He told himself, time and again, it was irrational but his body refused to listen, as it did now.

His heart raced, his skin twitched and crawled. Perspiration beaded his upper torso and the back of his neck. Rider took a deep breath, and deliberately slowed his breathing. His vision blurred as the walls closed in. Battling his demons, he slammed his eyes shut and fought for calm. It didn't help. He feared in a matter of minutes he would be embarrassing himself gasping for air and tearing at his throat.

Rather than embarrass both of them, he rose to his feet and in what he prayed was a calm manner placed Teddy close to Jane. Her eyes widened and her arms tightened around the children.

"Where are you going?" she whispered in a shaky voice, misunderstanding his motive for deserting her.

Thank God.

On the spot, he decided one small white lie wouldn't send him to hell. "I'm going to check on the storm."

Rain battered the roof and dripped from the ceiling

onto the floor into three separate bowls that Jane knowingly had placed about the room. Wind whipped at the side of the house, threatening to tear off the loose boards.

"Are you deaf or just crazy?"

Rider would be more than crazy if he didn't get out of this room. Soon. He tried to smile. It must have looked more like a grimace if Jane's face was any indication. She looked as though she'd be shedding tears as big as fists any minute.

Rider cleared his throat, then rubbed the back of his neck. His hand came away slick with sweat. *Now, Rider, now. Before you make a fool of yourself in front of her.*

He backed toward the door. "I'll be right back." He edged closer to his escape. "I need to relieve myself." One more white lie for the sake of his sanity. God would surely understand.

Jane ducked her head. "Be careful."

If his sense of humor were in place, he'd see a joke in her warning. He gave her a stiff nod, too close to choking to speak. He tore open the door and slammed it shut behind him, cursing as he did so, belatedly remembering the slumbering children. Leaning his sweat-soaked back against the door, he closed his eyes, gulped air into his starving lungs and waited for his heart to slow down to normal.

He swore to himself and shook his pounding head. Guilt gnawed at him. It would serve him right if he stepped out on the porch and got pelted with hailstones. Leaving Jane frightened and alone, while he battled demons she had no way of knowing about was unworthy of even the lowliest of men.

Rider stepped to the window and stared out. Rain poured from the sky and whipped through the air like bedsheeting on a clothesline. Just a thunderstorm, strong and lusty, but just a storm all the same. Unusual for this time of year. He reckoned he could go back to Jane now and leave the door open. No worry about a twister, or his own irrational fears.

He found he did have to relieve himself. At least, his story wouldn't be a complete fabrication. Since the rain fell harder against the front of the house, Rider moved to the back door and stepped out onto the porch.

He finished his business, buttoned his trousers and stared out through the downpour. Something looked different. He frowned, unable to place the reason. He wiped the rain off his face and ran his fingers through the dampness coating his hair. He would have to wait until the rain tapered off but that feeling of missing the obvious nagged at his conscience.

Jane couldn't believe Rider left her and the boys just to heed a call from nature. She recognized the lie for what it was—an excuse to leave the room. But why? Before he left, obvious panic shifted in his eyes. His awkward attempt to mask it made it all the more clear. Surely, he wasn't afraid of storms. He'd been reassuring before the weather took a turn for the worse.

No. There had to be more going on that she didn't understand. She ran her fingers over the baby's downy-soft hair and pondered Rider's odd actions. She didn't understand most men, if her brother was like most men. She rather hoped not. Rider, on the surface, seemed different. Kinder. More patient and understanding. But did she know him?

He startled her by yanking open the door. He stood under the lintel, hesitating, his hands thrust in the front pockets of his denim trousers. A light sheen of sweat coated his ashen features. "Are you all right?"

He took the words right out of Jane's mouth. "Of course, we're all right, but are you?"

"Sure. Why?"

Why indeed. She shook her head. "Never mind." It was unkind to mention that he looked like he'd been kicked by a mule.

Rider helped her to her feet then took the sleeping child from her arms. He looked at Teddy, still asleep, curled up like a puppy. "Let him be. He'll wake soon enough. It's safe to go out. It's just a late season thunderstorm, nothing more."

Although questions still bounced inside Jane's head, she refrained from asking them. When Rider was ready to talk, he would. She could bide her time.

Rider rode into Drover the next morning with more than a little worry nipping at his heels. The sun shone bright and cheery overhead, in complete opposition to his mood. The muted clip-clop of the horse's hooves on the muddied road couldn't even brighten his thoughts. The sharp tang in the air reminded Rider that winter would soon be upon him—one of the reasons he found himself heading into town. A town that five years ago threatened to hang him but instead sentenced him to five years' imprisonment. His mood dimmed even more at the remembrance.

His trip to Drover might be a mistake if the townspeople recognized him but it was a chance he had to take. He'd served his time. They might hate him but he owed them nothing more. The farmhouse needed glass in the windows if they were going to make it through the winter without freezing to death and he refused to face another day without coffee. So be it. He intended trading his saddle for coffee beans, sugar, and the glass and anything else he could bargain for. He'd be riding back to the farm without a saddle but that didn't bother him. There were worse problems.

He liked to think things were going well, and his debt to David Warner would soon be fulfilled. Jane and the boys seemed to like him. Especially Gopher. He'd filled the larder with the last of the garden vegetables and he'd cleaned the yard. He even replaced the missing shingles so the roof didn't leak anymore. Though a never ending process, farm life seemed to agree with him. He couldn't have been more surprised.

He trotted into town past the one and only bordello, painted sick-as-a-dog yellow with peeling white shutters and a picket fence that looked like more than one drunk had gone over it than around it. The curtains were drawn and silence pervaded the place like a cemetery at midnight.

He pondered his celibacy as he rode by. He always assumed he could live without a woman's *companionship.* For a time, at least. While he hadn't chosen chastity as a way of life, it seemed to have chosen him. Until now, he had found it somewhat easy to live with. Though not without prurient thoughts from time to time, he'd never met a woman he wanted to bed. Or marry.

When taken under consideration, his five years of imprisonment left little of his adult life to ponder marriage. Until now. Now he found himself thinking about it all the time and his so-called easy celibacy was becoming harder and harder to endure.

"Poor choice of words, Magrane," he muttered.

He pulled his Stetson low as he trotted past the familiar homes and buildings. He stopped in front of the general store, owned by the late Chauncey Carlisle's pa, Gresham Carlisle. Rider still mourned Chauncey, a good friend who'd been shot and killed while he, Rider and the Ferlin brothers rustled David Warner's cattle. Rider doubted he'd be at the receiving end of a warm welcome from Gresham. But he had to face the man.

Rider dismounted and tied his horse to the hitching post. He straightened his shoulders, took a deep breath, and stepped inside.

"Good morning, Gresham."

The man, five years older than when he'd last seen him, stood straight and tall. Gray-haired, sparse mutton-chop whiskers traced his lean facial features. He stopped what he was doing and turned to face Rider. He held a homemade jar of cherries in his hand, getting ready to place it on a shelf overhead. He took a closer look, his eyes widened, and he let out a gasp of outraged shock. The jar hit the floor and smashed into glittering bits of glass and shiny cherries. Thick red juice oozed across the floor and seeped into the cracks. The sweetish scent hit Rider's nose just before Gresham Carlisle's brick-like fist did.

Taken wholly by surprise, Rider fell, his eyes watering, his nose throbbing. As he stumbled back, his arms flew outward. His left forearm connected with the edge of an iron kettle and snapped like a dry twig. The sound, sharp and out of place in the quiet of the store, echoed in his mind. Excruciating, ragged pain exploded up his arm and shoulder. His numb fingers hung lifeless. Oddly,

Rider found himself wondering at the old man's strength as he glanced at his arm.

"I've wanted to do that for five long years, you sorry-ass son of a bitch," Carlisle said grinding the words out between clenched teeth. He leaned over Rider and swore at him. He seemed not to even notice the broken arm. His eyes bore into Rider's with malice.

Refusing to defend himself against the older man, Rider tensed, waiting for the next blow to fall.

Carlisle straightened to his full height, seeming to gain control over his anger. From where Rider lay on the floor, Carlisle still looked like he could hunt bear with a dinner fork.

He glanced at Rider's blackened eye. "By damn, looks like somebody beat me to it." He then shook his fist in Rider's face and walked away, stepping over the broken glass and its contents. Without a backward glance, he returned to placing the rest of the canned goods on the shelf.

Agonizing pain knifed up Rider's arm and soured his stomach. With slow, measured progress he eased himself to his feet. He swayed a moment before his eyesight steadied and he could stand without falling. Holding his punished arm close to his body, he took several deep breaths before speaking. His voice sounded hoarse as a sick crow. "I've got some bartering for you."

Carlisle turned his head toward Rider. "You've got mighty big ballocks, Magrane."

"No, I just need to conduct my business, sir. I mean no disrespect."

"Don't even try to apologize. Nothing you say now matters." He exhaled a long sigh. "Just state your business. The sooner you get out of here, the sooner your stench is gone, and I can get back to work."

"I've come to trade a saddle for panes of window glass, coffee beans and a sack of sugar." Rider took a rough breath, biting back an urge to swear.

"What makes you think this saddle of yours is worth even that?"

"It's new."

"We'll see."

Rider stepped outside. With painstaking deliberation and the use of his one good arm, he began to remove the saddle. With each movement, pain drove through his arm like buckshot through a double bore. Sweat beaded his brow, and bile rose in his throat. He refused to give in to the pain, reminding himself at every turn that he needed the supplies for Jane and the boys. The task took him almost a quarter of an hour, hobbled as he was with the use of one arm, but he finally hefted the saddle off the animal's back and brought it inside.

Carlisle surprised Rider by giving him a decent trade for the saddle. He purchased more supplies than he'd first hoped for. He even had a little something left over to pay a doctor to splint his arm.

He bid the older man good-bye. Carlisle ignored Rider and went back to stocking shelves.

With his one good arm, Rider attached the supplies to the gelding's back with a length of rope and several burlap bags. He then crossed the street to the doctor's office. Thank God it wasn't far. He felt like puking. His arm hurt so badly that his nose felt like little more than a bee sting. And his blackened eye, more yellow and green than black, was a distant memory.

MITCHELL HENDRICKS, PHYSIC, proclaimed the swinging, rusting sign above the door. Rider didn't recognize the name, and hopefully the doctor wouldn't recognize his. Maybe the man wouldn't blacken his one good eye, or knock him six ways into next week.

The doctor himself answered Rider's knock, or so Rider took him to be, since he had a stethoscope draped around his neck. A distinctive and pervasive odor of chloroform enveloped the older man. He took one look at Rider and broke into a dry chuckle. "Looks like you've been in a bit of a tussle, young man."

Rider shook his head. "It has taken a bit of the spit and vinegar out of me all right but I wouldn't call it a tussle exactly."

The doctor led Rider into a dim room lined with medical texts and cabinets filled with colored bottles and steel utensils. The musty room gave off a disagreeable scent, much like a bootlegger's distillery gone bad. Rider's stomached twisted. Shallow breathing seemed the best way to cope. The doc sat Rider down on an examining table and then proceeded to roll up his own sleeves with careful precision. He crossed his arms and stared at Rider over the top of his spectacles.

"If not a tussle, what then would you call it, Mister. . .?"

"Magrane. Rider Magrane." Rider grimaced, recalling his so-called tussles. "I tangled with a little boy and had words with an old man, for two very different reasons, on two very different occasions. Neither was their fault."

The doctor's brows lifted in a questioning glance.

Rider shook his head. "No, Doc, I didn't strike either of 'em."

The physician nodded his head as he helped Rider out of his shirt, bringing a new wave of agony coursing up his arm. He straightened and shrugged the rest of the way out. In the hour or so since he'd broken it, his arm was hot and swollen up like a bellows.

The doc stood back and studied Rider's arm, then he stepped forward to examine it up close. "You've been cursed then. I've been seeing a lot of this lately. I'd wager in the last month I've seen seven patients with a hex on 'em."

Rider stared in shocked amazement at the elderly physician. Though a little long in the tooth, he looked the part. Serious, bespectacled, a man of schooling. But a curse? Where did he get his education anyway? From a fortune-teller's crystal ball? Or a witch's coven?

He recalled his serious conversation with Teddy a few days before. *This scary man in town said Jane had a curse.*

The idiot must be preoccupied with curses. He had no business practicing medicine. He was as crazy as a bedbug and twice as irritating. Rider fought the urge to beat him senseless. Well, all right, he was in no conditon to beat anyone senseless. But he wanted to. "Are you crazy? It's just a damn broken arm."

"No? I've seen this before." The doc walked across the room and opened a cabinet door. He began picking through several lengths of wood, discarding a few, keeping a few others, until he seemed satisfied with what he held. He ambled back to Rider and measured one of the pieces of wood against Rider's forearm. "You know, son, medicine is an imperfect science."

Each time the man lifted the broken arm, pain shot through it, reminding Rider all over again of his useless set-to with Gresham Carlisle. He gritted his teeth against the misery. "Uh-huh. What does that have to do with curses?"

"We don't have all the answers."

You don't have any, you doddering old fool. "Why would you think my broken arm comes from a curse?"

"You said you tangled with an old man and a little boy but neither of them gave you the broken arm or the black eye."

"Right."

"So, how do you explain the broken arm?"

"I fell."

"And the black eye?"

"I fell."

"See what I mean?"

It was like talking to the town idiot. Maybe he was cursed, right alongside Jane Warner and half the population of Drover, Kansas.

Rider trudged home from the doctor, ankle-deep in mud and mad enough to kick his own dog—if he had a dog. He walked his gelding instead of riding him since he'd traded his saddle, and besides the poor horse was heavily laden with supplies like an ordinary pack mule. He didn't care—much—that he was afoot. Just the thought of riding gave him a headache. At the moment, every muscle in his body ached, every bone creaked. Except the one in his left forearm. That one screamed in pain with each stride he took. He just wanted to get home.

After Rider quit trying to make sense of the quack doctor and stopped listening to his inane ramblings, the man quickly patched him up and gave him laudanum for the pain. The doctor might be an idiot but he suggested Rider not take it until he returned home. Rider agreed. It was probably the only sensible thing the man said to him in the hour Rider spent in his company.

Still Rider fumed with irritation and anger. Anger with himself for allowing the situation with Gresham Carlisle to get out of hand, although he didn't know how else he would have handled it. Carlisle hit him before he ever saw it coming. And he supposed Carlisle thought he had it coming. And he was infuriated with the doctor because, well, because the man was a fool who had no business doctoring. Besides he'd upset Jane with his nonsensical talk of curses.

The walk gave him time to ponder his situation with Jane, and to decide how to handle the matter of her so-called curse. He was having trouble remembering why she thought she had one in the first place. Something about her health. He recalled her saying she'd been sick but she didn't explain the nature of the illness. Although on the thin side, she seemed healthy enough to him. He, of course, was no expert. And neither was Mitchell Hendricks, Physic.

Deep in thought he failed to hear the two horsemen until they galloped their mounts up alongside him. As they maneuvered around him, one of them gave a startled gasp. "Holy hell!" he hollered. "It's Rider Magrane!"

Rider's head whipped up and around. Damnation. The Ferlin brothers, loose upon the countryside once again. Could this day get any worse?

They pulled up and, in a jangle of spurs and squeaking leather, dismounted. "You dirty dog," Jacob exclaimed as he jumped to the ground. In his eagerness, he nearly toppled to his knees. "Heard tell you was out, too."

Wide grins spread across their young faces as they ground-reined their mounts and staggered his way, red-faced and glassy-eyed. Rider shook his aching head in disgust. They were so lit they couldn't hit the ground with their hats. It was a wonder they could ride. Luckily, their mounts held a slight lead in the smarts department.

"Rider, long time, no see," Martin said as he slapped Rider on the back, jarring his splinted arm.

"Not long enough," Rider muttered under his breath.

He continued walking. The brothers had no choice but to follow if they wished to converse. Rider would have preferred they took their sorry asses elsewhere but held little hope in that regard. To be found in their presence was about the last thing he wanted. Or needed.

The Ferlin boys picked up their horses' reins and trotted to catch up.

"Whoa, what happened to you?" Martin asked as he angled up beside Rider. He tipped his head to better study Rider's face. A lank of greasy-brown hair fell over one eye. "You look like you were tossed through a bobwire fence with yore hands tied behind yore back."

"And *you* smell like bad whiskey and cheap women."

Martin shook his head, then grinned. "She warn't cheap, but she was worth every penny. Eh, Jake?"

"Can't argue with that, brother," Jacob agreed with a nod of his head. The red in his eyes matched the color of his nose—crimson as a rooster's comb.

"What 'bout you, Rider? Have you had a taste of the lovely ladies yet?"

"Nah, I'm getting married." *Now, why the hell did he go and say that?*

"To a woman?" Martin asked.

"They make the best wives." Rider couldn't help but grin. These two boys were once his best friends but between them they didn't have the sense to come in out of a pouring rain. Heaven help him if he didn't find a way to lose their company before he reached the Warner place. He'd pay hell explaining this long-lost friendship to Jane. Or their so-called marriage plans.

"Congratulations, pardner, or maybe I should give you my condolences. What say you, Martin? You think Rider is jumping the fence a mite soon? How long you been out? A week, maybe two?"

"A little longer."

"And you found a woman willing to say yes to a convicted cattle rustler? How'd you do that? Hog-tie her to a post?"

"No."

The sound of hoofbeats pounded in the distance. Both the Ferlin boys' heads bobbed up and an uneasy look passed between them. By some signal unseen by Rider they quickly mounted. That is, as quickly as two soused men can.

"We got to be going."

"Are you in trouble again?" Rider asked. He could only guess what mischief these two had managed in Drover.

"Nah. Well, not much anyway but we gotta get."

"Good to see you again, Rider. We got some catching up to do. We have some interestin' plans you might want to consider."

"Not if you can't find me," Rider muttered as they tore off down the road.

With a hoot and a holler, their voices faded. The horses rounded a bend in the road leaving nothing but mud clods. The air stank like the inside of a saloon, ripe with perfumed women and boozy men anxious to share their beds.

Rider released a long sigh of relief. He trudged the rest of the way home, just trying to keep one foot in front of the other without falling face-first into the mud and muck. It took all of his willpower.

Health is a precious thing.
—Montaigne

Chapter Six

"What do you see?" Rider asked. He wrapped his good arm around Jane's waist, encompassing her in an intimate, yet somehow very natural gesture. She watched his expressive face as he scanned the yard. His eyes slanted in a quizzical expression before he turned his gaze back to her. "Call me crazy but do you see anything missing out here?"

Before daybreak, Jane had watched Rider amble out of the yard on his smoky-blue gelding. Man and horse rode as one, slow and easy, comfortable with each other. Jane watched, fascinated, as Rider leaned forward, patted the cow pony's neck and spoke a few words to him, which, of course, Jane couldn't hear.

Confused by the way she felt, she wondered where he was headed and if it meant he was leaving her and the farm forever.

And although she didn't see him ride back into the

yard, Teddy informed her that when he went out to milk Emmett, Rider was in the barn. After restlessly wandering around the house for hours, Jane heaved a profound sigh of relief.

She thought Rider spent an inordinate amount of time in the barn, but then he trudged up to the house, his head low, and his step hesitant. Jane stared in dismay. The man looked as if he'd wrestled a bear and lost. The man must be a walking accident.

He carried a sack of coffee beans tucked under his good arm and a burlap sack of sugar and other supplies in his fist. Upon entering the kitchen he didn't explain the broken arm. Nor did he seem in a hurry to do so. He set his packages down, corralled Jane and herded her to the back porch where they now stood.

She didn't understand his urgency or the unspoken familiar gesture of his arm around her. She glanced up at his wan, ashen face. He gazed back at her from sunken blue eyes dulled with pain.

The warmth of his body surrounded hers. She thought she should have been uncomfortable with his closeness. After all, they were little more than strangers. Instead she found she relished his easy strength, his casual reassuring touch. She welcomed it. And what was even more odd, she found herself worried about him.

"Shouldn't you be sitting down?"

"In a minute," he said in a voice impatiently male. "What is missing, dammit? I cogitated on this all the way to town and most of the way back. It's driving me as crazy as a mouse in a milk pail."

Jane tore her eyes away from his and stared out into the yard. She squinted against the sunshine and saw nothing unusual or out of place. Then she realized what he saw, or actually what he didn't see.

A surprised giggle escaped her, then another. And another. She turned her head into his shoulder, her body shaking with laughter. It took all her willpower to stand and not collapse onto the floor in a fit of giggles.

"What? What the hell is it?"

"The privy," she said in a muffled voice. Her mouth against his shirtfront twitched with humor. She stepped out of his embrace and pointed to the back of the yard. "The privy isn't there."

As she watched, Rider's expression changed from one of exasperated impatience to quiet understanding. His expressive lips quirked upward in a slow grin.

"Damned if you're not right."

She wiped her eyes with her apron. "When it rains hard it gets muddy around the outhouse and well . . ."

"Smelly?" he offered.

"Right. So I haven't used it since the storm."

"Me either."

He grabbed her hand and marched out to the spot where the outhouse should have been. They stood together and stared at the wooden seat above the deeper unseen trench in the ground. Surprisingly, the innards of the facility were still in place, but the walls were long gone. Vanished into thin air like soap bubbles at the end of Monday's wash day.

Jane stared at Rider. Rider stared back. Wide-eyed, his brows slanted in a quizzical frown. They turned simultaneously to look at the scene of the crime. For a simple, quiet moment they just stared.

Then uncontrolled laughter consumed them both. They fell into each other's embrace. Jane clutched

Rider's shoulders as tears trickled down her cheeks.

When Jane heard a groan from Rider, she broke away from his embrace, startled and concerned.

"Your arm?"

"Yes. No." He shook his head as if to clear it. "Damnation."

"Rider, what happened in town?"

He just shook his head again and walked away from her, essentially ending the conversation. Jane wanted to call him back but obviously he wasn't ready to discuss it with her. And with a womanly instinct, she knew not to press him for answers.

"Later?" she asked.

As he rounded the house and disappeared from her sight, she heard him say in a muffled voice, "Maybe."

Jane yawned, blinking her eyes and squinting to see in the darkness. She swung her legs over the side of the bed. Before they reached the cold plank floor she pulled on thick woolen socks. Shivering, she wrapped her worn knit shawl about her shoulders, but it did little to stave off the cold seeping into her exposed skin. She stood up, stretching her arms above her head, and glanced out the window at the night sky. The moon hung high on a midnight-black blanket covered in twinkling stars. Frost glittered like a reflection of the stars above on the grass-covered ground below. Tiny webs of frost sparkled on the windowpane.

Although it must be the middle of the night, mouth-watering scents wafting from the kitchen tickled her nose. Unless the smell came to her in a dream, how could she explain the enticing scent of fried potatoes that woke her from a deep sleep? She padded down the hall to find out.

The kitchen beckoned, warm and cozy, and lit by a single kerosene lantern placed on the table. Rider stood at the stove, barefoot, his red flannel-covered back to her. Denim trousers hung low on his lean hips, and he wore an apron tied around his narrow waist. His tousled black hair curled around his ears and neck and stuck out in endearing clumps on the top of his head. A melancholy tune of unrequited love whispered from his lips. He kept the beat of the music with the tapping of one foot.

Jane stood still just outside the circle of light, savoring the homey scene. How right and how comfortable Rider looked in her kitchen. And how alluring, she thought. Without knowingly doing so, he had released a tiny place in her heart previously under tight lock and key. She shook her head. Her reaction to him never failed to surprise her. She found herself wanting to marry him, even with all the secrets he kept locked inside his own heart.

She listened for a few more bars from Rider's rich, deep musical voice before she spoke. "Midnight snack?"

The singing abruptly stopped. Rider pivoted to face her, dropping a fork on the floor as he turned. He gifted her with a boyish grin, then bent to pick it up. In his usual gentlemanly manner, he walked to the table to pull out a chair for her. She sat down, as he pushed it back in. He went back to the stove, poured her a hot, steaming cup of coffee and brought it back. He set it in front of her so she could savor the smell.

He stood facing her close enough she could see black

stubble on his cheeks and along his jaw. His lovely blue eyes, no longer quite so dimmed with pain, sparkled like gems in the low light. He stood near enough to touch, but kept one hand on the back of her chair as he spoke. "Did I wake you?"

She swallowed around the thickness in her throat that just being this close to him caused. "Not any noise that you made, just the enticing aromas."

"I apologize but only a little bit." He grinned. "I was near starving, so I scared up these vittles. Had to wake up some angry hens. But I couldn't wait to taste coffee again."

Jane took a sip, savoring the mellow brew. "It is wonderful but I thought you didn't have any money."

"I bartered for it." His gaze grew serious as he lifted a handful of her hair, stroking it between his thumb and forefinger. His eyelids lowered just a bit, and she thought she heard him sigh. He straightened away from her in a quick move that startled her. He was back in front of the stove before she could figure out what sent him away so suddenly.

Finding her voice, she asked, "Rider, can I ask you something, and will you answer honestly?"

He cleared his throat, then gave her a veiled glance. "I'll try."

"What really happened to your eye, first here at the farm and then in town—what happened to blacken the other one and how did you go and break your arm?"

"Would you believe it was just a string of bad luck?"

"I'm serious."

"So am I. Serious as a nest of rattlers."

He turned toward her and leaned back against the stove. He took a long swallow from his coffee cup and seemed to be contemplating how to answer her questions.

In the short time Rider had been at the farm, Jane had learned several things about him. He wouldn't be hurried, whether it was a chore or conversation. When he chose to speak, he used very few words and then only when he was darn good and ready. She wasn't sure he was ready now but she intended to get answers one way or the other. She didn't like secrets.

"Gopher gave me the first one," Rider began.

"What? The baby?"

Smiling in obvious remembrance, Rider shook his head. "That little tyke decided he wanted out of his crib, and right *now.* He leaned forward; I jumped to catch him, and slipped on the edge of the rug. You know the one there on the floor?"

She nodded in understanding.

"I fell head over ass . . . er, pardon me, head over teakettle onto my backside. Didn't really hurt myself 'cept my pride. That was until Gopher landed smack-dab on top of me. One tiny baby elbow to the eye and I got a shiner to brag to my friends about."

Jane couldn't help but smile at the image of Rider falling and the baby landing on him. "I don't mean to make light of it but that's quite a picture."

"You have no notion. That child scared me half to death. I thought for sure he was going to knock himself senseless, and you'd be mad enough at me to kick a cat."

"Well, it certainly wasn't your fault."

"Don't know 'bout that." He reached for a tin plate on a shelf above the stove. "You ready for potatoes and eggs?"

"Thank you, yes."

He took down another plate and began dishing up the food. For an one-armed man, he managed quite well. He grabbed a fork and served her first, then went back for his own.

When he seated himself, she took a small mouthful. Although tasty, the food clogged her throat because she couldn't help but think the boys needed it much more than she. She set her fork down and glanced at Rider. He had dug right in, not even noticing that she wasn't eating. His plate was half-empty before he looked up again.

His cheeks reddened as he carefully set his fork down beside his plate. "Is something wrong with the food?"

"Oh, no." She hurried to reassure him. "I guess I just don't have as much appetite as I thought."

Rider blew air out between his lips, then settled back in his chair. Although he relaxed his body, his eyes were veiled and he seemed to be contemplating her, his expression still and unreadable. A slight pink still tinged his cheeks but he didn't seem the least bit embarrassed or uncomfortable.

"Go ahead. Eat."

"My appetite seems to have flown, too."

"So are you ready to tell me what happened in town then?"

He rubbed a long, callused finger around the lip of his cup, then did so again.

Jane watched in fascination. She'd seen his hands hold the baby with tender care and stack blocks with Teddy on the floor. She'd seen his hands hard at work chopping wood and harvesting corn.

But when he touched her, he did so with a gentleness

she couldn't imagine a man possessing. She found herself wanting, no craving, his touch now. Right now. And in the most intimate of ways. The ways of lovers. Heat began beneath the bodice of her night rail and rose up her throat. She prayed Rider couldn't read her immodest thoughts, or discern the reason for her blushing face. It felt infused with flames, and she knew she must look like a ripe tomato, and not at all desirable.

"I'm not certain you want to know that," he said at last.

"That?" she croaked. She'd completely forgotten the gist of their conversation.

"What happened in town, Janie."

"Why did you call me Janie?" she asked. She couldn't raise her voice above a thin whisper. An emotional tangle the likes of which she'd never experienced had her in a tizzy. Desire. Indecision. She couldn't begin to name them all.

"Just seems to fit. Don't you like it?"

"Yes. Yes, I do." Unable to pull her glance away, Jane stared Rider square in the eye. "Very much."

Rider explored Jane's expressive face. Unless he missed his bet, her high color wasn't caused by talk of his black eye and broken arm. No, her eyes conveyed longing and plain old-fashioned desire. Her hair, tangled and curled from sleep, spread about her shoulders and begged for his touch. She still wore her nightclothes with only a thin shawl covering them, and he knew without being told that nothing but soft, pink skin lay beneath. His heart came to a backpedaling stop, and his groin began a galloping start.

He swallowed hard and couldn't have said what

they'd been discussing just moments before. He couldn't think straight. He couldn't see straight.

He couldn't straighten up. Arousal, as heavy and potent as a Gatling gun, held him glued to his chair, and ready to fire at any given moment.

Jane Warner had no idea what she could do to him.

Fortunately, or not so fortunately, Rider wasn't certain, a pounding at the door startled them both. Jane jumped in her chair, and his erection vanished like a rat deserting a sinking ship.

"Where's your rifle?" he asked when he at last found his voice and could speak in a normal tone.

Clutching the shawl about her shoulders, Jane pushed back her chair as if to stand up. "Oh, that won't be necessary."

Rider reached out and stopped her with a tight grip on her shoulder. She blinked, then her eyes widened in surprise, and settled on his face.

"Good God, woman. It's the middle of the night. Who would be about but someone looking for trouble?"

Jane sighed in exasperation, and tried to shrug off his hand.

He didn't relinquish his hold, instead tightening his grip.

"This is Drover. We don't have that sort of thing."

Whoever was at the door pounded impatiently on it again.

"This is not Drover," Rider said, his voice rising. He lowered it so as not to sound angry, but he couldn't believe Jane's naiveté. "And they do too have that sort of thing." Not so long ago, Drover had the Ferlin brothers, Chauncey Carlisle and Rider Magrane to contend with.

"Oh, all right," Jane said. Reluctantly, Rider lifted his hand and allowed her to rise. She walked to the stove, then bent down beside it. From behind the box of kindling she retrieved a trapdoor Springfield rifle and handed it over. He noticed her hands trembling. "But I think you're being silly."

Rider checked to see that the breech held a cartridge. When he saw that it did, he pulled the block back. "If it's silly why are your hands shaking? And silly or not, you're not answering that door until I have a gun, primed and ready."

Jane eyed the rifle with suspicion. "Well, you do now, but please don't shoot anyone." She then pulled the door open and stepped aside.

Though Rider held the rifle a bit awkwardly, he aimed it chest-high, his finger poised on the trigger.

The courting neighbor, McCampbell Smith, stood on the porch. With shoulders as wide as the door frame, he filled the entryway with his hearty masculine presence. Dressed in a buckskin shirt that looked like it hadn't seen a bar of lye soap in a month of Sundays and snug trousers that molded his rooster, he didn't even smile in greeting.

Rider didn't smile either. He was really beginning to despise the man.

"Saw the light," Smith stated without so much as a blink.

As if that explained why he had the lunatic sense to pound on the door in the middle of the night. Besides, what was he doing so close to the house anyway?

Rider lowered his weapon and stepped forward, blocking Smith's view of Jane clad only in her night things. Smith glared at Rider, his mouth a thin line, his gray eyes condemning. Rider's hackles rose. He now saw Smith for what he was—a contender for Jane's affections. He hoped she didn't notice the prominent bulge in Smith's pants.

Smith attempted to peer around Rider, so riling Rider that he jerked the gun up and stuck it in his groin, daring the man to try it again.

Smith had the good sense to back up and look away. "Unless yore gonna shoot me, I'd rather you pointed that elsewheres, *friend.*" His emphasis on the word didn't sound in the least bit friendly. Behind him, Jane snorted. Rider glanced at her from the corner of his eye, and saw the bemused expression on her face.

"You two know each other?" she asked.

Rider nodded. "Yeah. We met."

"The other day," Smith said by way of explanation.

"You didn't say anything."

"Didn't seem important at the time."

"It weren't," Smith agreed.

"See." Rider turned his attention back to Smith. "What the hell are you doing out here anyway? Do you usually come calling at midnight?"

"Rider," Jane admonished.

"Well, damnation, Janie. I think I have a right to know."

"You do not." She tried to step around him but Rider refused to budge. He didn't like the idea of Smith seeing Jane barely dressed, and began to feel a tad belligerent about it. What was it about McCampbell Smith that brought out Rider's worse traits anyway? His good looks? His cocksure attitude? His attentions toward Jane? Rider figured it was probably all three but the man was fast becoming a jealous thorn in Rider's side.

"Are you accusing me of something?"

Jane's tone pushed Rider out of his musings. He turned to look at her.

"Because if you're thinking what I think you're thinking I want an apology this instant."

Dumbstruck, Rider said, "I'm not thinking anything."

"Hmph." She stuck her nose around Rider's shoulder. "Mr. Smith, come on inside."

When Smith made to do so, Rider barred his entrance with the barrel of the rifle. "Oh, no, you're not, pal."

With a well-placed elbow, Jane jabbed Rider in the ribs.

He smothered a groan, but kept the rifle up.

"Mr. Magrane, the last time I checked, this was my house and I can invite whomever I please inside. Now let him in."

"This clodhopper can't come in. You're hardly dressed for company."

"You've seen me."

"That's different."

"Why is that?"

"Because you and I are getting married," he shouted. "That's why."

"I didn't know that," Smith said. He sounded disappointed to the extreme.

At the sound of his voice, Jane and Rider turned toward Smith. Apparently they remembered at the same time that they weren't alone.

Jane frowned at Rider. "Neither did I. And furthermore, I don't recall agreeing to anything either," Jane shouted back. "You men are all alike, you make me furious."

"We aren't," Rider and Smith said simultaneously.

They glanced at each other and glared.

"You are. You just think you can do whatever you want. Well, I've got news for both of you. Neither one of you is invited into my home or my kitchen. Now, get out before I get really riled and do something *you* both might regret."

She grabbed the rifle out of Rider's hands and shoved it into his belly.

"Careful with that thing." He pushed the barrel sideways. "What the hell did I do anyway?"

She didn't reply to his question, merely brought the gun around and pointed it at the two men. "Out. This minute."

"Can I at least grab my boots?" Rider asked.

"No," Jane answered in a frosty voice. "You can freeze your toes off for all I care."

She gave him a slight push. He stumbled out the door and onto the porch. The door swung shut behind him with a resounding bang.

Rider glared at Smith.

Smith glared at Rider.

"This is all your fault, farmer," Rider said.

"Who you calling farmer? I saw you out in the fields harvesting the last of the corn, and sweating just like the rest of us *farmers.* Whether you like it or not, yore one, too."

"Damned if I am."

"Damned if yore not."

Rider grumbled his reply.

"And I don't like you none either," Smith said, "but like me or not, we're in this together."

"We're not in anything together."

He placed his hands on his hips and gave Rider a

pointed stare. "I reckon we're both vying for Miss Warner's affections. And I reckon you just lost a few points back there, and this here"—he held the feed sack above his head—"is gonna gain me back any I lost in that wee set-to."

Curiosity got the better of Rider. "What's in there, Smith?"

"Squirrels." He pulled out a gutted and skinned creature that no more looked like a squirrel than a once-healthy church mouse. "Got me three of 'em."

"In the dark?"

"Aye. Best time to hunt. Catch 'em nappin' and unawares."

"You can see them up in the trees?" Rider couldn't keep the astonishment from his voice. The man must have the night vision of an owl.

"Aye."

"And these would be . . . courting gifts?" Rider questioned, not bothering to keep the sarcasm from his voice.

Rider's tone passed right over the farmer's single-minded brain. He grinned. "You betcha. They're gonna get me inside Miss Warner's front door, and standing together in front of the parson before long."

"Not if I have anything to say about it," Rider said under his breath. He shivered as the cold night air swept inside his clothes and penetrated the soles of his bare feet. His arm ached, his head pounded and his toes were beginning to lose any feeling. He stepped off the porch and strode away.

"Where are you going?" Smith asked.

"Back to bed."

"What about the squirrels?"

As he rounded the corner of the house, Rider told

Smith in no uncertain terms where he could stow the damned rodents. He then pushed up the boys' bedroom window and, cursing under his breath, awkwardly climbed inside. He hoped McCampbell Smith tripped in the dark on his way home and shot off his conspicuous personal parts. Of course, that wouldn't happen, thought Rider morosely, since the handsome neighbor had eyes like a bat and could see as well in the dark as in the light of day.

Jane smiled as she leaned back against the door. The men's voices barely penetrated the walls but it didn't sound as though they were arguing. Thank goodness. She didn't believe they would do bodily harm to each other, but you just never knew with men. Rider was in no shape for a row and she didn't want to see him hurt anymore, despite everything she said.

She didn't know where all her cantankerous back talk came from but she felt good about it anyway. Men were always telling her what to do, and by God, she was sick to death of it.

Sick to death. Poor choice of words, Janie.

She cleaned up the kitchen and went back to bed but she couldn't sleep. For all her talk of independence, she found herself thinking about Rider, and wondering if he'd gone back to the barn to sleep. Guilt pricked her conscience, but only a little.

It no longer mattered that he kept secrets to himself. She did want to marry him. She told herself it was only for the boys, but she knew in her heart that just wasn't true anymore.

* * *

With Teddy squeezed up tight to his side in the narrow bed, and Rider's toes hanging out the end of the bed-coverings, Rider couldn't sleep. It didn't have anything to do with the meager space they shared. It had everything to do with Jane and her effect on him.

He stared at the rafters above his head, not really seeing them. Instead he remembered Jane in the moonlight with her golden-brown hair down and curling around her shoulders, her eyes bright and inquisitive, full of laughter and downright spunk. He'd seen desire, too. He should come clean and tell her the truth about himself. He knew deep down that he should but he didn't know how without ruining the relationship they were building together.

He did want to marry her. He told himself it was only for David Warner and what he still owed the man, but he knew in his heart that just wasn't true anymore.

Men have a thousand desires to a bushel of choices.
—Henry Ward Beecher

Chapter Seven

With quiet deliberation, Jane pushed the door to the children's room open an inch and peeked inside. Dawn light filtered through the curtainless window and filled the room with golden light illuminating those inside. John Michael slept soundly on his side, his thumb tucked inside his mouth, his bedding snuggled around him.

But Teddy no longer slept alone. Rider lay beside him on the narrow cot meant for one small boy. So this was where he went when she kicked him out of the house.

Jane smiled. How adorable he looked. He lay on his back, his injured arm across his bare chest. His other arm fell over the side of the bed. While the sheet and quilt enfolded Teddy like a mummy, not even a thin blanket shielded Rider from the cool air. Only the red flannel bottoms of his underwear covered his long legs and lower body. His feet stuck out over the end of the bed and he lay so close to the edge of the mattress, she wondered how he managed to stay put without falling.

His bruised and battered face contrasted sharply with the relaxed, almost boyish expression of sleep. She fought the urge to take him into her arms and cuddle him against her breast. She pushed the foolish thought aside. Instead she dropped to her knees and with the fingertips of one hand brushed them gently across his chest. His torso was covered in a light dusting of springy, sable hair. At her touch, her fingers tingled from the cool yet silky texture of his skin. She glanced at his taut belly and saw that the hair followed a thin dark wedge and disappeared into the waist of his loose flannel underwear. Her fingers itched to follow that line. She battled curiosity and excitement as heat washed her face.

She turned and fished an extra blanket from the chest by the bed and spread it over him, careful not to jostle his arm. Her fingers brushed against his collarbone as she pulled the blanket to his chin.

Rider groaned in his sleep, then whispered in an agonized voice, "No, not me, I didn't, I didn't . . ." Jane's gaze rushed to his face but he slept on, seemingly unaware of his strange nighttime ramblings. She leaned against the mattress and brushed his cheekbone with the tip of her finger. She stroked his temple and his forehead, and marveled again at his skin's smooth texture. She never imagined a man's skin could be as soft as a child's but so hard with muscle beneath. Pushing back a lock of his sable hair, she stared into his face.

His eyes fluttered, then opened and captured hers in a heavy-lidded gaze. "I thought I was dreaming," he said. He gifted her with a heart-stopping smile. "Or maybe I'd died and gone to heaven."

She smiled back. "No," she whispered. "You seem to be very much alive."

"I do at that."

His free hand cupped the back of her head, and tenderly, yet firmly, he brought her face close to his. "I'm laying claim to you, Janie. You can forget about that good-lookin' Smith fella," he murmured in a hoarse whisper. "I should have done this before now. I waited until I thought the time was right and that appears to be now."

With the tip of his tongue he wet his lips, then surprised Jane by drawing her closer and doing the same to hers. Jane watched his eyes lower as the delicious, dizzying sensations raced through her body. His tongue continued to caress her mouth with velvety warmth, spreading that warmth lower and lower until it settled in her abdomen. Then his lips parted, he tilted his head and drew her into an undeniable, tantalizing kiss. With featherlight strokes, his lips brushed hers back and forth, and then again with delightful determination. She heard his breath hitch before he lifted his head. He leaned his forehead against hers and in a choked voice he said, "Janie, Janie. We need to talk about getting married."

"Now?" She didn't understand. Why did he stop kissing her? Her heart pounded in her chest and she wanted more of his drugging kisses. Yet, he sounded miserable, almost in pain.

He didn't reply, simply reclaimed her lips once again. He swept her into his embrace, then covered her mouth with his own. His tongue darted in and out, first slowly, then quickly, then slowly again. His heart quickened against her own. Mesmerizing heat pooled in Jane's womanly parts and she squirmed, trying to ease her body closer to his.

He moaned and deepened the kiss. His hand lowered, molding her back. Cupping her bottom, he lifted her so she lay almost on top of him. Beneath her stomach she felt him move against her.

At that very moment Teddy grunted in his sleep and rolled over.

Rider gave a startled yip, and jumping up, he had them both out of bed and onto their feet in one lithe movement. He backed away, staring at her, his eyes wide. His voice tight he said, ''Damnation. We were almost making love with that child right there in bed with us.''

Jane stared at Teddy, then at Rider's face, which was turning as pink as a summer rose. Her gaze fell. His arousal was intimately apparent. He lowered his hand, and half turning away, tried to cover it from her view. She glanced up, her own face heating and saw his blush as his vivid blue eyes swept her up and down, and then again. His eyes widened and settled on her face.

She tried to dispel his embarrassment as well as hers. ''We didn't even wake him.''

''I don't know how,'' he said, his face turned partially away.

She, too, had completely forgotten the boys. How could she be so stupid? Where had her common sense gone? Flown in a moment of selfish longings. ''I guess I'd better start breakfast.''

''Yeah, and I'll go milk Emmett. The cold air will take care of my . . . my, damnation.'' He groaned aloud and if possible blushed even redder. ''I mean, it will help my . . .'' He glanced at her over one shoulder. She saw him swallow. Still cupping his manhood he nodded toward the door. "Are you going?"

"Yes. I'm sorry if I embarrassed you."

He shook his head, but his voice quivered a bit. "You haven't done anything wrong, Janie. I'm the one at fault here, but what were you doing leaning over the bed like that?"

"I saw you were cold and was just covering you with a blanket."

"You don't mind that I snuck back to the house to sleep?"

"No, I shouldn't have kicked you out. Besides it's too cold to sleep in the barn."

Keeping his body turned away, but his eyes on her face, he said, "Thank you for the concern, Janie, but would you please go now."

"I truly am sorry."

"I'm sure you are, honey, but did you know you can see clean through that gown of yours? Now scat!"

Jane glanced down. She wore her oldest nightgown, once white and warm, now gray and threadbare. Her nipples pushed against the fabric like pearl buttons and displayed the dusky pink aureoles of her breasts for Rider's avid, though, uneasy stare. The dark cleft between her legs was all too obvious even to her own eyes. Covering her mouth to keep from crying out in abject humiliation, Jane ran from the room.

Displaying herself like that. What must Rider think of her now?

Jane was magnificent. How had he ever thought her thin and plain? Rider corrected his thinking. Rounded in every place she ought to be with ample hips that curved down to long, slender legs, she met his every expectation of womanhood. The shadow between her legs hinted at wondrous mysteries Rider found himself wanting, no needing, to explore. With plump, firm breasts just ripe for holding and caressing and kissing and . . . that part of his anatomy that he held cupped in his hand twitched and throbbed to life. He moved his hand away from his body and drew a deep breath. Blowing it out slowly and unsteadiy, he closed his eyes and waited for his over-heated body to calm.

Emmett waited in the nice, cold, freeze-your-ass-off-in-a-minute barn. For a one-armed man, Rider dressed in record time. For a change, Emmett had no complaints because this morning Rider milked her with warm fingers. Emmett didn't notice his racing heart or the blood thrumming through his veins.

"No eggs," Rider pronounced as he pushed open the door. Cold air swirled around him and drifted into the kitchen. He stepped inside and slammed the door behind him with the heel of a boot. He placed the bucket of steaming milk just inside the door.

"Wide," crowed John Michael when he saw Rider step into the room. Clapping his hands, he repeated, "No weggs."

Rider stopped long enough to tug on John Michael's ear, making him babble in delight. Then he reached across the table and pinched Teddy's nose. Though he grinned, Teddy pretended to fight him off by batting at his hand.

Rider left the boys and walked across the room to warm himself in front of the range. Crowding Jane just a bit, he poured himself a cup of coffee. He took a cautious sip, then leaned over the stove top and peeked into the skillet where corn fritters fried in hot lard. He frowned, wrinkled his nose, then turned and glanced at Jane with a steady gaze.

"Good morning, Janie," he murmured in a bold, seductive whisper. "You're looking *well* this morning." What he left unsaid filled the room with a sexual tension that skittered across Jane's jangly nerve endings.

Without trying to be obvious, she edged away from him. He stepped closer. She swallowed hard and clenched the fork she'd been using to turn the fritters. His nearness sent her senses spinning. She tried without success to forget their earlier exchange. It was nigh impossible. Standing so near to her, his scent overwhelmed her, a clean scent of soap and potent masculinity, and very much Rider.

"We need to talk," he whispered in her ear. Gooseflesh blossomed up and down her arms. "About things."

Jane couldn't seem to find her voice. She opened her mouth to speak, but all that came out was a squeak.

"Cat got your tongue?" Rider murmured in a hushed voice meant only for her ears.

Jane stared at him. Lazy amusement reflected in his blue-eyed grin. He seemed to be feeling no ill effects from his broken arm or his abused face or their aborted lovemaking this morning. In fact he seemed in fine form and as cocksure as a rooster. After the liberties she'd allowed, ones that made her feel like a wanton harlot, she'd best put him in his place. She wasn't that kind of woman, and she needed to make that clear.

"You'd do better to use you own tongue to explain how you broke your arm and blackened your eye while you were in town. I want an explanation before we ever discuss 'things'."

His confident grin vanished. He replaced it with an affronted frown. "Sometimes, Janie, you can be a real stick-in-the-mud."

She ignored him. "Why aren't there any eggs?"

"Because the hens aren't laying?"

Jane bit her tongue to keep from being as rude and obnoxious as he was being. What happened to that sweet gentleman of only a few days past? Maybe it had all been an act to get her to accept him on the farm. Maybe he had no real interest in the boys or their welfare? Maybe she had misjudged him. She decided it was high time to find out. "Sit down."

His sable eyebrows slanted at her abrupt order but he obliged without a word. He took another drink of his coffee and sat down staring at her over the rim of his cup.

"I've decided," she said, pointing the fork at his flannel-covered chest, "to give Evie's son, McCampbell Smith, an opportunity to court me."

"That . . . what?" Rider jumped to his feet, his eyes wide and his lips parted in surprise. "Damnation, those two are related?"

"Sit," she ordered again.

"Shit," John Michael said.

"I agree," grumbled Rider.

Teddy giggled, then covered his mouth when Jane warned him with a reproving glance.

Rider's mouth curled in a wry grin as he leaned toward John Michael and chucked him beneath the chin. "That's sit, Gopher. S-s-sit."

"Shit," the baby repeated.

Teddy giggled and John Michael gurgled, obviously pleased with the reaction.

"Teddy, please don't encourage him unless you want to find yourself with a few extra chores."

"Yes, ma'am."

"Jane, maybe you should rephrase that to 'take a seat, Rider.' "

"Wide."

Jane sighed as she wiped her hands on her apron. Scooping the fritters onto a plate, she said, "At least he's saying something else."

"For now," Rider said. He leaned toward the toddler and growled, "*Rrrr.* Rider."

"Wide."

"Someday that boy is going to get my name right." He turned his attention back to Jane. "What do you want with Smith anyway? An opportunity to court you? He's already got the means to win you over. I sure don't."

She settled the dish on the table in front of Rider. "What means are you talking about?"

"He's a good-looking fella and *you* probably think he has a sterling character. The damned fool can see and hunt in the dark, no less, so he'd be a good provider. He's also your nearest neighbor. You could double your farm land by marrying him."

"That may be true, especially the handsome part," she said catching Rider's grimace, "but does he like the boys? Or me?"

"I reckon he could like you just fine but I thought you were beginning to like me."

"*I was.*"

His thumb traced the rim of his cup as he replied, "I see."

Give him time to think about that. ‘‘So what are your plans today?’’

‘‘I thought I’d impress you by rebuilding the privy. What do you say, Teddy? You any good with a hammer and nails?’’

‘‘Don’t know.’’

‘‘Now’s as good a time as any to find out. After breakfast and chores, we’ll start impressing your Aunt Janie with our skills. Later I’ll try working on her with my charm.’’

God, what a muck up he’d made with Jane. Rider figured he must have honestly scared her with his amorous leanings. He sure scared himself. When he kissed Jane, he didn’t know he could become so aroused that he’d forget where he was, who he was or what the hell he thought he was doing. Talk about curses!

Now he found himself standing in the loft of the rickety barn. He stared at the stack of mismatched pieces of oak, maple and walnut. He rubbed his forehead and rolled his shoulders. His neck gave a loud crack in the early-morning stillness. Dust motes floated in the air and glimmered like fairies. Fairies who put spells on unsuspecting men. He sighed.

What he really would like to do is lie down on a bed of straw here in the loft and just plain forget. For the first time since he’d come to the farm, doubts about his abilities assailed him. Did he have what it took to protect the boys’ interests? Could he manage the farm? Could he redeem himself or would he just make matters worse? He wasn’t at all sure anymore. And what was worse, did Jane believe in him at all? Or did she think he was a self-serving, lusty lout?

How in the name of Sam Hill was he going to rebuild the outhouse with one working arm and the doubtful help of a six-year-old boy? And a stack of wood, no two pieces alike?

Well, however he managed it, it wasn't going to take place in the loft. He yanked on a pair of gloves and dragged the wood one piece at a time to the edge. He pushed them over the side of the loft where they landed with a thud on a bed of straw below. He put Teddy to work finding nails he'd seen earlier in an old, rusted tin.

Together, they managed to get the wood out to the privy without a whole lot of trouble. That is, aside from a splinter in Teddy's thumb and a whack on Rider's hurt arm that brought tears to his eyes.

When they stood staring at the sorry sight, Rider leaned toward Teddy and confided, "It's been a mite embarrassing sitting out here doing your business with God looking over your shoulder."

Teddy stuck his hands in his pockets and rocked back on his heels. "I didn't like it much neither."

"Either," Rider corrected. "I been using it at night mostly."

"Me, too," Teddy agreed.

"Still anyone who might come ambling by could take a peek at you with your trousers down around your ankles."

"Like Mr. Smith."

A bit startled, Rider glanced at Teddy. "Yeah, like Mr. Smith."

"You don't like him much, do you?"

"Sure he does. He just has a peculiar way of showing it," came a voice that set Rider's teeth on edge.

To protect Teddy's tender ears, Rider forced back the

vulgarity that jumped immediately to his lips. He would recognize that voice in a dream, or more like, in a nightmare. He didn't need to turn around.

McCampbell Smith. Come courting. Again.

Why did Smith show up every time Rider turned around? The man was as irksome as a boil on Rider's butt.

"Looks like you could use another hand, Magrane." Smith threw back his head and roared with laughter. "I made a wee joke, didn't I?"

"Wee," mumbled Rider. "In a pig's ass."

Smith's blue-gray eyes twinkled with confidence. "You just got no sense of humor."

"Not at the moment, no, I don't."

Rider couldn't help but notice that Smith had cleaned up, presumably for Jane, with a clean-shaven jaw and his dark hair combed. He'd polished his boots to a high sheen and he wore a clean flannel shirt. All of this just irritated Rider even more since he hadn't taken the time to clean up, shave or comb his hair after he had to skedaddle out to the barn this morning in such a rush. He'd just thrown on his clothes from the day before. "Don't you have somewhere you have to be, Smith, that's far away from here?"

"Nah," he answered, missing Rider's blatant sarcastic tone or simply dismissing it. "I stopped by the house to give those dressed-out squirrels to Miz Warner and she said she thought you'd welcome the help." He held out his hand, palm up. "Give me that hammer, boy. Let's get to work."

Teddy handed over the tool without a word—the traitor.

Rider couldn't keep the irritation from his voice. "She said that, did she?"

"Aye." Smith knelt before Teddy and stuck out his hand. "My friends call me Mack. What's your name, boy?"

Solemnly, Teddy shook his hand. "Teddy Warner."

"Teddy, do you know where your pa keeps the buck-saw?"

"Sure."

"Run and fetch it for me."

"You be careful with it, Teddy," Rider warned him as he ran off. He turned back to Smith. "Just taking charge, eh, *Mack*?"

Smith straightened to his full height, then folded his arms across his considerable chest. He regarded Rider with disdain. "What's your problem, Magrane? Can't take a little honest competition?"

"This isn't a game. Besides, I don't trust you."

Smith shrugged his impressive shoulders. "I don't trust you either."

"Looks like we're at a standoff."

"Looks like it."

Rider turned and walked away. "Damnation."

"Giving up that easy, Magrane?"

"Not on your life, Smith," Rider shot back over his shoulder. "I'm just going to help Teddy find the saw and sawhorses."

"Need any help?"

"Not from you," Rider grumbled. The thing was he did need Smith's help. He just hated admitting it. He just hated hearing him offer it. He just hated Smith.

Rider's patience snapped like a fiddle string. He turned on his heel and stomped back. He stopped in front of Smith and glared at the man. Smith glared back, refusing to back down. They stood nose to nose. Although the same height, Smith outweighed Rider by a good fifty pounds. All of it solid muscle.

"Can't you find some other woman to court? Why has she just now become the object of your regard?"

Smith's mouth turned up in a grin. "I like Miss Warner. I'm not interested in any other woman."

"I don't want some rutting stag like you sniffing around her."

Smith stabbed a finger at Rider's chest. "Who you calling a rutting stag? Just what were *you* doing with Miss Warner last night and her in her nightclothes?"

Rider brushed Smith's hand aside. "That's none of your business."

"What is your concern here, Magrane? That I might win her over or make you look bad?"

Both. "Neither."

"Ha." Smith stepped back and threw his arms wide as if to encompass the farm. He began walking in ever-widening circles, his eyes skyward. With each step, his feet came closer to the privy's exposed seat. "This is what you want."

One more step, Smith. Just take one more step back so when I take a swing at you, you'll already be sitting down. "Yeah, what's that?"

"You want—" Smith caught the toe of his boot on the corner of the privy seat and toppled sideways, abruptly cutting off his next word. Rider heard him swear, saw his hands scrabbling in the air. The last thing he beheld was Smith somersaulting, his long legs disappearing over the back. Rider heard a squishing thud, then Smith's voice turning the air blue with a string of vulgarities worthy of a mule skinner. Worthy of his mother.

Rider grimaced but then couldn't keep the grin from his face. He leaned forward and, biting his lip to keep from braying like a jackass, glanced behind the privy. As he did so, Smith's frowning face appeared and seemed to be coming right out of the hole.

Rider took one look and burst into laughter.

A dark expression twisted Smith's handsome features into a mask of annoyance. "You could have warned me," he growled.

Rider wiped tears of mirth from his eyes before he answered. "Not on your life, farmer."

"What is going on here?" Jane stood on the back porch shading her eyes against the sun. She picked up her skirt, scrambled down the steps and ran across the yard. A look of concern crossed her features as she gazed from Rider to Smith, and back again.

Although Rider knew better, he guessed from her look of horror that Smith's body must appear to be inside the privy with his head popping out above.

She released a loud sigh when Smith scrambled to his feet.

Rider glanced at Smith who wore an expression of guilt, which he knew he wore himself—like two boys caught trying to steal a freshly baked apple pie cooling in a windowsill.

And nothing had been done on the outhouse except that a stack of wood now lay on the ground beside it. Jane certainly wasn't going to believe that nothing but hard work had been taking place before she showed up.

When Smith walked around the exposed outhouse seats, Rider saw that the back of his shirt and trousers were covered in brown muck and he smelled like, well, he smelled like a privy.

Jane wrinkled her pretty little nose. "What were you two doing?"

"Nothing," they replied simultaneously.

"Smith fell," Rider began. "He—"

"Did you push him?"

Giving her a tight-lipped smile Rider waved his splinted arm at her. "With this?"

Jane stared daggers at him.

"All right, all right. No, I didn't push him, Miss Warner." He shuffled a booted foot in the dirt, quirking an eyebrow and giving her a mischievous grin. "No, ma'am."

She didn't even smile, apparently not buying his aw-shucks attitude.

"Where's Teddy?"

"He went up to the barn for the saw." Rider pointed behind her. "Here he comes now."

"How about you, Mr. Smith? What's your version of the story?"

"I tripped." He lifted the back of his shirt away from his skin and grimaced. "I'm headin' on home to change clothes now, but I'll be back later to put up that blamed outhouse."

"You're welcome anytime," Jane assured him.

"Yeah," murmured Rider beneath his breath. "Anytime."

Smith strolled up to Rider. He patted his shoulder and left a muddy, foul-smelling handprint. "Now don't you be aggravating that arm, Magrane. Wouldn't want you to become incapacitated."

"Can't hardly believe you even know the meaning of the word, farmer."

"You'd be surprised 'bout what I know," he said. He left the yard whistling.

Rider studied Jane as she stood with her hands on her hips watching Smith walk away. By the way she pressed her lips together and the angle of her jaw, he reckoned he was about to be on the receiving end of a little set-to.

Children and chicken must always be picking.
—Sixteenth-century proverb

Chapter Eight

"Teddy, the chickens and Emmett need to be fed."

Teddy hesitated, a wooden bucksaw clutched in one hand and dragging in the dirt. He held a tin can of nails in the other.

"Right now."

He dropped them where he stood. "Yes, ma'am."

Teddy much have recognized Jane's angry expression though the boy had done nothing wrong. Seemed he also knew better than to argue with her when she spoke to him in that tone. He scampered around the side of the house and disappeared.

"Come with me." Jane took Rider's hand and started back to the house. He glanced at her with a bemused expression on his face, but with long, determined strides followed without a word.

For some unfathomable reason, Jane was perturbed with Rider, McCampbell Smith, and for that matter, the whole male species. She wanted to speak to Rider. Now.

Once inside the house he poured himself a cup of coffee. He held up the pot and when she shook her head, he settled himself at the kitchen table. He glanced at John Michael curled up in the corner of the settee napping, and smiled. He didn't speak but waited for her, his body relaxed, his face intent.

She turned away and stood with her back to him, to collect her thoughts. She stared out the window at the bleak fall landscape. With a fingernail, she scratched at the frost that clung to one corner of the window glass, pondering how to tell him what was on her mind without sounding nosy, presumptuous or insolent. Or all three.

"I get the feeling you want to say something but don't know how. I'm not good at this sort of thing either, but I've got a few things I'd like to get off my chest, too."

She heard him take a deep breath.

Shocked, Jane swiveled to look at him. Cold desolation swept through her like the prairie wind in February. She feared he was getting ready to tell her he was leaving. She hid her hands beneath her apron so he couldn't see how they shook, and bit her lip to keep from crying. *Please. Please, don't say you're leaving,* she prayed.

"About five years ago I lived in Drover with my brother. I didn't leave under the best of circumstances. I'm surprised you haven't heard of me."

Jane swallowed around the lump in her throat and tried to appear unconcerned. Inside, though, her stomach tightened and her breath caught in her throat. "I . . . I don't get to town often and when I do I don't pay attention to the gossip, and besides I haven't lived here long myself. I only know a few people."

"Jane, I—"

"Honestly, Rider, I don't care about your past. I care about my nephews' future. About my future." *About our future together.*

Jane wondered what thoughts passed through his head. He stared at her, a pensive gaze on his face, his vivid blue eyes flickering with doubt. "Don't you want to know what I've done?"

"Not unless it concerns the boys' welfare."

He cocked his head to the side, his eyebrows raised. "It might."

"How?"

"I'm not certain."

"Are you trying to tell me you're running off?"

Rider jumped to his feet, sloshing coffee on the table. "Hell, no. Why would you think that?"

Thank you, God. Jane closed her eyes. Tears welled in the back of her eyes.

"Are you all right?" Rider started toward her but she waved him away. He sat back down, a look of concern on his face.

"I don't worry about the past because I have plenty to fret about with the here and now. Putting food on the table. Making sure the boys have a decent roof over their heads and a warm bed to sleep in at night."

Rider nodded. "I understand."

"Then what's the problem?"

Rider's face colored a bit. "What about Smith?"

Perplexed, Jane asked, "What about him?"

"Where does he come into play? Are you planning on sharing a warm bed with that *farmer* on your wedding night?"

Jane sat down and folded her arms on the table. She

smiled at him, her emotional turmoil subsiding. "You're sounding a mite jealous, Rider Magrane."

He actually blushed, right down to the roots of his thick, black hair. "I am," he admitted. "I just don't want him—"

"Now don't you go ruining my good temper by putting your foot in your mouth. I'm not angry at either of you. I just think we need some guidelines, I don't know, maybe a clear direction. To know that we want the same things for the boys. I need to be sure about what you're thinking and that you'll be staying."

Rider frowned, as he traced the rim of his cup with his thumb. Finally, he looked up at her. "Jane, I—"

"I know. I know men don't talk about their feelings."

"Uh-huh."

"Try."

Jane began to think he wasn't going to reply. He kept his head down. He held his hand around his coffee cup while his thumb rubbed back and forth across the rim. Finally he spoke in a tentative voice. "I like the boys, honestly I do, and I have only their best interests in mind." His head came up and he stared at her. "But it's you that I'm having problems with."

Jane froze, her heart in her throat. "You don't like me?"

Rider groaned. "That's not quite the problem." His earnest gaze sought hers. "I like you all right, I like you plenty."

"I don't understand."

Rider stood up to refill his coffee. He leaned against the table and took a sip, eyeing her over the rim. "Janie, what were you thinking when I kissed you this morning?"

Now it was her turn to blush to the roots of her hair. Her skin tingled in remembrance of her heated response to his ardent kiss and how he'd stoked the growing fires within her. She didn't know how to respond to his intimate question without sounding either forward or inexperienced. Both of which she felt.

"Did you think it was terrible?" he asked.

"Sort of."

"Sort of?" He snorted, his bruised male pride obviously offended. "What does that mean?"

Jane ducked her head. "I dón't wish to speak of this."

"I guess this kind of brash talk makes you skittish as a newborn calf, but I have to know."

"Why?"

Rider reached across the table and clasped her chin in his calloused hand. Her head tipped up so she found herself staring into his bright blue eyes. He searched her face, keenly probing, his discerning eyes questioning. "Janie, if you find me wanting in any way, tell me so I can fix it. I want to be here. I know you don't understand why, but trust me, I do, and I don't want to wait around while you dillydally between Smith and me."

"Wait around for what?"

"For you to make up your mind! Damnation. I can't be charming, I don't know how. I can't court you with flowers or fancy talk. I only know one way to do things. Work hard so I can build a decent life for your boys . . . and for you. If that's what you want."

A warmth flowed through her. It was what she wanted, wasn't it? A good man to make a good life for the boys. A promise for their future just in case she wasn't around to provide it. Why, then, did she feel like crying? Did she honestly expect a flowery speech about undying love and devotion?

"I want you, Janie, and I want you in my bed."

But was *this* what she wanted to hear? What about love? *Don't be silly, Jane,* she admonished herself. She was a plain woman who never had expected much anyway. Certainly not love. Love didn't matter, the boys did. She swallowed past the lump in her throat, and brushed aside the tears welling in her eyes.

"I think you want me, too," Rider said in a hoarse whisper.

She did want him with a heart-deep yearning, but she couldn't admit to it without admitting to the other feelings she had for him. Feelings of comfort and protection. Feelings of caring and friendship. What she thought might be the first stirrings of love. She shook her head. "What we did this morning was wrong."

"Dammit, it wasn't wrong. It was only wrong to do it with Teddy in the same bed with us." His voice held a slight tremor as he continued. "We just have to get married to make it right for the next time that we . . . um, kiss and such."

"Oh, I don't know . . . about a next time, that is."

His eyes grew openly amused and he chuckled. "There will be a next time, Janie. Sure as I'm standing here, you can count on it."

Since Rider left to work on the outhouse an hour ago Jane had been in such a state she couldn't remember if she was supposed to knead the bread dough and wash the breakfast dishes, or wash the bread dough and knead the breakfast dishes. The only thing she'd managed was to stir up a pan of hoecake and get it baked.

She glanced at John Michael. He sat in his high chair chattering at Jane and munching on a warm slice of hoecake just out of the oven, oblivious to her or the fact that she couldn't string a coherent sentence together if her life depended on it.

You can count on it.

Whenever she thought of Rider, her knees wobbled and her heart pounded in her chest. Jane sat down at the kitchen table to settle her nerves with a cup of hot chamomile tea, a cherished supply that she only used on rare occasions. Among her other intimate concerns, marriage to Rider weighed heavy on her mind.

"The chickens are acting funny," Teddy hollered as he dashed into the kitchen, his nose pink from the cold, his knitted scarf flapping around his neck. An oversized felt hat that once belonged to his pa tilted sideways on his head.

"They won't eat the corn I set out for 'em, and they are chasing one scrawny old hen round and round. They are like to make her life a misery."

"Well, we won't let that happen," Jane promised. She plucked Teddy's hat off his head and kissed his forehead. "She'll just be today's dinner. A nice stew, perhaps."

A worried look crossed Teddy's wind-whipped, reddened face. "Why do you reckon the other chickens are pestering her?"

She helped him out of his jacket and pushed him toward the chair across from her. "Sit down, honey, and have some hoecake, it's just hot out of the oven."

"Cake," repeated John Michael. His expectant smile sought Jane's. Crumbs lay about the tray of his high chair and scattered across the floor. Yellow bits dotted his chin and cheeks, a clear sign that he'd devoured his piece already. Jane spread honey over another slice and handed it to him. She did the same for Teddy.

"What do you say?"

"Thank you," Teddy said.

John Michael licked the honey off the cake but managed to leave a sticky mess on his fingers. He single-mindedly bit into the piece and ignored Jane's question. Maybe he was a little young yet for her to be teaching him his pleases and thank-yous. She shook her head and turned back to Teddy. "Now, about those chickens."

Teddy, quietly munching, glanced at her with an expectant expression.

"What else are they doing?"

He shrugged his thin shoulders. "That's all, they won't eat and they're just chasing that one old hen around."

Jane stood and pushed back her chair. She grabbed her jacket off the peg by the door and put it on. Unwrapping Teddy's scarf from around his neck, she wrapped it around her head and tied it under her chin. "I'll go check on those chickens myself. Please keep an eye on John Michael. If he wants another cake, give it to him, but only one small piece. That boy's going to be as round as a pumpkin by the time he's your age. When I get back he should be about ready for a nap, so just try to keep him out of mischief until I can put him to bed."

Reaching for another slice himself, Teddy nodded.

Jane heaved a sigh and walked out onto the front porch. A brisk northerly wind tore at her skirt and whipped it around her legs. Tugging her scarf tight beneath her chin, she stepped off the porch, and took a look at the chickens. Her heart plummeted. Teddy was right. The stupid birds were chasing one old hen. Before long the poor dear would just drop over from heart palpitations and then the chickens would be onto another one. If she knew chickens at all, the whole brood would be dead before another month was through.

If those stupid chickens died, they would have to butcher one of the hogs to get through the winter and she hated to do that. For some odd reason she was unreasonably attached to the ugly threesome. Her own three little pigs. All right, so they weren't little but they owned a special place in her heart. It was at times like this that she wondered if she was cut out for farm life. She hated butchering, even when that was the animals' sole purpose for being.

"Looks like you got yourself a wee spot of trouble, Miss Warner."

The sound of McCampbell Smith's voice interrrupted her thoughts. She looked up to find him smiling at her, dressed in different, though not entirely clean, clothing. He stood with his hands on his hips, the wind tossing his dark hair over a lowered brow. His broad shoulders stretched the seams of his buckskin shirt taut across his chest and arms.

"I do at that, Mr. Smith," Jane agreed.

He nodded his head at the clucking poultry intent on chasing the old hen into an early grave. "Chicken for dinner?"

"I'm afraid so."

"Would you like some advice?"

"Why, yes."

"I expect that hen has an open sore. If you get any others with the same problem, just put hot tar on the spot. That'll keep the others away. If you haven't got any tar, I can bring some by the next time I come calling."

"Thank you."

"Is there anything else I can help you with?"

Jane shook her head and pointed around the side of the house. "I believe Rider could use your help though."

He grimaced. "He don't want it."

"But he needs it."

"'Tisn't all he needs." Jane heard him grumble as he sauntered toward to back of the house. She couldn't help but smile. It was kind of nice having two men acting as if they were concerned about her. Yet she doubted both their motives. McCampbell Smith hadn't shown her the slightest interest until she posted her advertisement about the farm. And he acted as if the children were invisible. Rider, on the other hand, never admitted to anything other than the obvious, and he seemed to like the children.

Rider was the better choice and she'd been immediately drawn to him, so why was she dithering like a schoolgirl? Maybe because she'd been a plain, shy girl who went without notice all through her growing-up years. She'd never had a beau, never even had a man come courting. And now here she was, Jane Warner, with two men glowering at each other, tossing barbs back and forth, and practically clashing their antlers against each other like a couple of stag deer.

To say she found it exhilarating was too mild a term. Then she looked around and recalled why she was in the yard to begin with. A hen needed to be captured, and its neck wrung. She had two boys inside the house probably making a mess . . . and, well, the list grew with each waning minute.

The point was she was no longer a schoolgirl with stars in her eyes and dreams yet to be fulfilled.

Her woman's chores weren't getting done. According to the doctor she wouldn't be around much longer anyway and men problems should be the least of her concerns.

The boys were her prime focus and she'd do best to remember it.

Rider couldn't move. His good arm lay beneath his body. As he pulled it free, blood rushed to his fingers, stinging as it pumped through his veins. His legs, pinned against the wall, were immovable. He opened his eyes to total darkness. As they adjusted, he found himself staring at the wall, not six inches from his nose. A small body warmed his backside.

Sometime during the night Teddy must have climbed over him because he now lay on the outside of the bed where Rider usually slept. Pressed tight against his bare back Teddy lay like a stone—a stone fence that effectively penned in Rider. And Rider needed to relieve himself in a serious way. He flipped the measly blanket off himself, then awkwardly crawled over Teddy, trying not to wake him. He needn't have worried. The boy didn't so much as twitch.

Rider tiptoed across the room and pushed the door shut with the heel of his foot. In the kitchen, he threw wood into the stove, got it going and stepped out onto the back porch. The frigid night wind skimmed across his bare chest and arms raising gooseflesh the size of small pebbles. Rather than walking barefoot through the cold yard, he undid his long johns and began to relieve himself off the side of the porch. In the quiet night, the splashing sounded overly loud against the normal muted nighttime sounds of skittering animals and rustling naked tree branches.

Muffled whispering behind his freezing butt had Rider finishing up and buttoning his drawers in a profanity-filled hurry. If that McCampbell Smith was calling again in the dead of night, Rider was going to throttle the man. Especially if he brought meat, which the family needed, and which Rider couldn't provide with only one arm. Smith made Rider feel as useless as a bucket in a dry well.

Instead of Smith, though, Rider turned to find two young women gaping at him like they'd never seen a half-dressed man before. If their astounded expressions were any indication, they hadn't. One had her gloved hand covering her mouth while her eyes, wide as pie plates, stared at a spot just south of his navel. The other girl, younger by several years and shorter by a good foot, smiled shyly, giggled, then ducked her scarf-covered head.

Rider's face heated at not only getting caught pissing off the side of the porch but wearing nothing but his gaping, low-slung long johns. He finally found his voice. "Evening, ladies." It came out sounding like a dog with a porcupine quill lodged in its hind end. He cleared his throat.

"Kind of late to be calling, wouldn't you say?" He glanced at the eastern sky where a blush was just pushing its way above the horizon. "Or maybe kind of early." He had the urge to fold his hands in front of himself, but refrained. No point in drawing attention to something, that young ladies had no business noticing in the first place. It was a little like closing the gate after the cows were loose.

Somehow the older of the two women managed to draw her scandalized eyes above Rider's waist and up to his face. He couldn't help but notice the pink in her cheeks, and the sour pucker of her lips. Something about the shape of her face and her chocolate-brown eyes seemed very familiar.

"We're not calling," she stated. "We're here to help Jane. Who are you, if I may be so bold to ask, and why are you dressed in your underwear? Have you no shame, young man? And doing that"—she waved her hand like she was shooing away a pesky fly,—"in public. What is wrong with you young people today?"

Geez. Unless Rider was mistaken she was younger than he by at least five years, and she was acting like his old-as-God, tyrannical Aunt Tildy. If a man couldn't take a leak off his own porch in the middle of the night, where could he? All right, so legally it wasn't his porch, but still . . .

She continued berating him without taking a breath. "Has that Jane up and married without even a by-your-leave? She never did have a lick of sense. Always with her head in the clouds."

She turned to the young woman standing beside her. "Mary Jo, don't just stand there with your mouth open, fetch our bags."

"I can get 'em," Rider offered.

"You, young man, can go put on your trousers. And I expect an explanation on your return."

He obliged. Bold as brass, she didn't leave room for argument.

* * *

Jane woke to the sound of a strident female voice, and the smell of coffee brewing and bacon frying. Bacon? There hadn't been bacon in the house in a good four months. She dressed in a hurry, ran a brush through her hair and haphazardly braided it. When she stepped into the warm kitchen, her heart almost stopped when she saw one of her two younger sisters standing at the stove. "Sukie?"

"Sukie?" Rider repeated. Jane turned to look at him seated at the table. He stared up at her, one hand wrapped around a steaming cup of coffee. He'd removed the sling and his splinted arm rested atop the table. He wore an expression on his unshaven face that she couldn't quite place. Perhaps irritation, but more like plain ol' befuddlement. His hair needed combing and his flannel shirt was misbuttoned. He wore one gray and one white stocking. Jane recognized the effect Sukie had on people—stunned, dazed and utterly confused.

"Susan Kay," Jane said to Rider, by way of a brief explanation. "Sukie for short."

Jane took her sister in her arms, kissed her cheek, and hugged her tight. The hug she received in return was decidedly cool and much less intimate. Over her shoulder Jane spotted Mary Jo, her baby sister, standing by the door, pensive and unsure, still dressed in her coat and head scarf. Her pale cheeks were flushed and her cupid's bow mouth curved in a little smile. Jane recognized the blue mittens she wore because she'd knitted them herself as a going-away gift six months prior. Jane winked and was pleased to hear Mary Jo's sweet, girlish giggle.

"So, Jane, what is going on here?" Sukie gave Rider

a pointed stare, then turned her austere expression toward Jane.

Jane stepped away from Sukie, but stood close enough to see the disapproving look in her brown eyes. "It's good to see you, too, dear. Rider, my sisters Sukie and Mary Jo. Girls, meet Rider Magrane."

Sukie drew in a deep breath, and if Jane wasn't mistaken, snorted. She didn't bother to acknowledge the introduction. She just huffed an impatient sigh, which Jane knew from past experience would only be the beginning of a lengthy tirade. She didn't have long to wait.

"We came all this way, spent the night in a horribly disgusting establishment the proprietor had the nerve to call a good hotel, and we even had to carry our own bags up two backbreaking flights of stairs. Then we rose before daylight, had to wake the blacksmith to hire a rig, which he wouldn't even drive out here for us. The thankless ogre. On top of all that, I find this disgraceful excuse of a man—"

Rider half rose from his chair, his sapphire eyes flashing, his dark brows slanted in a frown. "Now wait a doggone minute! I—"

Sukie pointed a finger in Rider's direction. "Don't interrupt, Mr. Magrane, it's impolite."

Rider stood there, halfway between sitting and standing, his mouth hanging open. After a second, he sat back down and closed his mouth. His expression remained bewildered.

"As I was saying, I find this person who, by the way, looks like he's been in a tavern brawl, half-dressed and . . ." she lowered her voice to a whisper, ". . . urinating in public. Right out in the open for God and all his simple creatures to see! I was scandalized. Simply scandalized. Poor Mary Jo nearly had herself an enlightened education on the male anatomy. What would Mama and Papa say if they were alive? God rest their souls.''

Jane bit her lip to keep from laughing outright. As if Sukie knew anything about the male anatomy herself. Sukie was as virginal as Jane herself. She glanced at Rider beneath her lashes and found him suffering from the same desire to laugh as she did. He, at least, had his head bent, but she could see his lips turned up in a wide grin and his shoulders shook.

''I imagine they would say I'm doing the best I can with what I've been given,'' Jane said. ''I'm taking care of David's children.''

''What about this man doing that, well, that personal business, on your porch, for heaven's sake?''

''I would guess he had to go.''

Jane distinctly heard a squelched snort from Rider. His shoulders continued to shake.

''Don't you get sassy with me, Jane Warner.''

''Well don't you be bossing me around either. You seem to have forgotten that I am older than you.''

''By fourteen months.''

''That still makes me older.''

''Is *he* living here?''

Jane sighed. There was no stopping Miss High-and-Mighty once she got going. Sukie was younger in years, but older than Father Time in her ways. ''Yes.''

Sukie placed her hand over her heart, and rolled her eyes heavenward. ''Without benefit of marriage?''

''For God's sake, Sukie, we're not sleeping in the same bed.''

Sukie colored fiercely, then set her lips in a tight line. She turned her grim expression toward Mary Jo. In a voice tight with forced lightness, she said, "Dear, why don't you go wake your nephews? And don't forget to change the little one's diaper before you bring him out for breakfast."

"Yes, ma'am."

"You can take off your coat first," Jane said, "and then come over here and give me a hug." When Jane had Mary Jo pressed against her chest, she whispered in her ear. "I've missed you like a mooncalf, sweetie. Now don't you be letting Sukie make you crazy. I sure don't."

"I won't," Mary Jo whispered back. She scuttled out of the room with a smile as wide as the whole state of Kansas on her young face.

To see her family again after so long a period, even bossy Sukie, brought Jane the same wide smile and a feeling of joy she'd hadn't realized she'd been missing.

Even Sukie couldn't ruin her delight.

Sukie turned back to Jane. The look on her face could sour milk. "He has to go. It's unseemly."

Maybe she *could* ruin Jane's good mood.

Jane placed her fisted hands on her hips and glared eye-to-eye at her sister. Sukie glared right back.

"He's not going anywhere," Jane stated. "He's helped me a great deal—on the farm, with the boys, getting ready for winter. I don't know what I would have done without him."

"Then you obviously don't need him anymore. Sounds like he's taken care of everything."

"I do, too, need him and you can't make him go."

"I most certainly can."

Rider didn't doubt Sukie's words for a minute. She looked as stubborn as a Missouri mule. He sat back, laid low and waited for the two women to really warm up.

Rider had never witnessed a fight between two women before. Oh, once he saw two whores scuffling over a hat in the general store but that ended before it even began. As he recalled it, his brother Chance, the sheriff, broke it up with a few well-chosen words and a promise to *visit* each of them later. Knowing Chance like Rider did he doubted Chance visited them but it appeased the women at the time.

Women.

He didn't understand them but as he watched Jane's brown eyes glitter with angry promise, he found himself warming to the confrontation.

Rider glanced at the stove after his nose twitched disagreeably. Black smoke rose from the pan where the bacon was frying. "Damnation!"

He jumped to his feet and rushed across the room. Sukie squealed as he ran past and Jane stared at him wide-eyed. Both women scrambled to get out of his way. He grabbed the pan off the stove and looked down at the burned mess. "We haven't had bacon around here, except on the hoof, in some time." He gave Jane a pointed look. She acknowledged him with a good-humored grimace.

"Now you," he glared at Sukie, "with that burr under your saddle—and you, Janie, you aren't much better—were about to let the whole tasty panful go up in blazes like a wheat field in a strong wind."

He dumped the pan upside down on a plate. It fell in one clump, blackened and almost inedible. "I was just getting into your squabble, too. Damn, I really wanted to see the two of you have a go at each other. I expect it would have been real entertainin'."

Sukie's jaw dropped. Her eyes grew large. Her breath quickened. ''Well, I never.''

''Me either,'' Rider added. ''But I sure was hopin'. Since the fight's gone out of you, did you by any chance bring more bacon?''

Sukie glared at him, straightened her spine and stomped out of the room.

A family is but too often a commonwealth of malignants.
—Alexander Pope

Chapter Nine

"Is she always like that?" Rider asked.

"Yes," admitted Jane, sighing. "Always."

Having sliced off several more slices of bacon, he stood over the stove making sure this batch didn't burn. He wiped his fingers on the apron tied around his waist and turned a dismal eye toward Jane. "She needs a good man in her bed," Rider mumbled. "Someone to put a spur to her stiff butt."

"Excuse me?" Jane glanced up from contemplating her coffee. She hadn't caught all of Rider's statement. Something about her sister's backside?

"No disrepect intended but that sister of yours. Phew." He shook his head. "She has an intemperate disposition. I believe she needs a man to put her in her place."

Jane nodded in agreement. "The love of a good man might soften her at that. But her place has always been to make everyone around her miserable, especially her own family.'' She shook her head. ''Poor Mary Jo, traveling all this way with only Sukie for company. It's a wonder the girl still has her wits about her.''

''I wouldn't worry none 'bout her. She looks to be as smart as a treeful of owls.''

''I'm not worried about her.''

''What's the problem then?'' he asked in a voice edged with concern. He glanced at Jane, then pulled the skillet off the fire and set it to one side. Drawing a chair up alongside Jane, he tipped her chin up so she had no choice but to look at him. She could see the ebony whiskers sprouting along his chin. His thick hair tumbled over his brow. His eyes, alight with life and sparkling with intensity, looked at her with gentle assurance. When he took her hands into his, she relished his strength and allowed herself to relax in his confident hold.

''I know you've got concerns about me but that woman is right about one thing.''

Jane frowned, surprised by his statement. ''What could possess you to say such a thing? Sukie thinks she's right about everything.''

''Well, she's right about this one thing. It is wrong for me to stay under your roof without us being married.''

''Oh?''

''So I reckon I'll ask you again. Are you going to marry me?''

Jane stared at him, his open face, his expressive eyes. She should have big doubts about marrying him because she didn't know him. Not really. He didn't talk about his past in detail, only in generalities. He'd been in some sort of trouble but she didn't know what it was and was surprised that she didn't think she cared.

He didn't ask on bended knee. His stockings didn't match and his shirt was misbuttoned. His hair was mussed and he needed a shave. He didn't declare undying love. Yet in the depths of his cobalt-blue eyes an unquenchable warmth shone upon her. Surrounded her. And touched her heart.

"Yes," she said. For Teddy and John Michael, Jane would do anything, but she wasn't thinking of them at the moment. No, all she could think about, all she could see was Rider. His face was so close she could pick out each sable eyelash, each dark blue fleck in his sapphire eyes. She thought she could drown in his gaze. She touched her lips to his. Soft and magical, their kiss sealed her answer.

Yes, she would marry him.

She heard his sharp intake of breath. Then he kissed her back, his lips opening ever so slowly, his mouth tentatively exploring. The heat of his face caressed hers. She reached for him, hoping for more, but he lifted his head and backed away. She heard him take a short breath and release it through his lips.

"This is the right thing to do," he said with an ever-so-slight tremble to his voice. He whispered the words in her ear, tickling her. Goose bumps broke out up and down her arms and her heart gave a resounding *thump-thump-thump* before it settled down.

"I promise to be a gentleman and—"

"You have to be a man before you can be a gentleman." Sukie's chilly voice broke the mesmerizing spell that held them.

She stood in the doorway to the kitchen holding a

smiling John Michael. Teddy stood behind her, yawning. Mary Jo, as usual, stood back out of the way waiting for the sparks to fly.

However, the insult didn't seem to bother Rider a bit. He merely grinned and nodded his head in acknowledgment of her presence. "Miss Warner, I am a man, as you rather pointedly noticed while gawking at me on the porch just this morning."

Sukie's jaw dropped open. Again. Jane chuckled, drawing Sukie's attention and an immediate scowl.

But Jane couldn't help herself. Twice in one day, she had witnessed her sister's comeuppance at the hands of a man. Jane could hear Sukie now, shortly after the family had received the telegram from David asking Jane to come care for his children and his farm so he could move out West and make something of himself . . .

"I will never marry. No man is going to tell me what to do, where I can go and whom I can see. Why, that James Sturbridge, you know, Jane? The pastor? He even tells Lorena what she can wear, and him a minister and all, for goodness' sake. From what I've seen, men are loud, ill-mannered, despicable creatures. Just look at David—abandoning his children, and his responsibilities. He's so typical, selfish and unthinking. No man will ever do that to me, I tell you."

No, Jane couldn't help smiling. While Sukie might never marry, Rider was besting her at the moment.

"Wide!" John Michael almost jumped from Sukie's arms when he spotted Rider across the room. Despite her frown, Rider plucked the child from Sukie's embrace and tickled him beneath his chubby chin. John Michael burst into giggles of pleasure, kicking his feet and waving his arms about.

"Good morning, Gopher."

"Wide!"

"My stars. You allow *him* to call John Michael that?" Sukie, still flushed from neck to hairline, stood with her hands on her hips and glared at Jane.

Jane glared back. "Oh, Sukie, do be quiet. It's just a pet name, and John Michael is rather a mouthful. I kind of like the name."

"A woman has to draw the line someplace."

"Sukie, please."

"Now, ladies, no arguing," Rider urged. "Pull up a chair, everybody. We have bacon, edible this time around, eggs, and hot biscuits and honey. Don't know how many more days those hens will be laying, so eat up." He motioned to Mary Jo who hung back among the shadows. "Come on, little sis. You, too."

Jane stared at Rider. She'd never heard him so talkative, or so . . . charming. She really didn't know him at all.

Jane took a seat though she was still somewhat unsettled by all the happenings of the morning, particularly Rider's simply-stated marriage proposal. She stared at him as he began to serve breakfast, astounding both she and even Sukie, who seemed to be spending the morning with her mouth open, either in astonishment or embarrassment or both. She barely closed it even to eat. Jane had never known her to be tongue-tied, no matter what the circumstances. Feeling wickedly sinful, Jane enjoyed every minute of Sukie's discomfort.

"We got ourselves a whole passel of work to plow through this morning," Rider stated with a good-natured grin, "so let's get at it."

"I'll clean up the kitchen and do the dishes," Mary

Jo offered, "and keep an eye on Gopher."

"Don't you be calling him that, too," Sukie demanded in her usual chilly tone.

"Thank you, Mary Jo." Sick of Sukie's high-handedness, Jane turned to her and said, "For God's sake, Sukie, let her be."

"Don't you talk to me in that tone, Jane."

"Now, ladies."

All three sisters and even Teddy turned to Rider with surprised expressions on their faces. No one, including Jane, expected Rider to act as peacemaker in this willful family.

Teddy was the first to find his voice. "I'll milk Emmett and fetch the eggs."

"Good. Be sure to let me know how they're faring, son. Need to keep on eye on 'em. Jane?"

"I have laundry to do."

"Sukie?"

"I, I guess I'll unpack and get Mary Jo and I situated."

"All right." Rider swallowed the last of his coffee. "I've got work out in the yard and a few finishing touches on the privy, so I'll catch up with you all later."

He scooted back his chair, chucked John Michael beneath the chin and winked at Teddy as he settled his hat on his head and headed out the door.

Like a whirlwind, he was gone leaving the room oddly bereft of his commanding presence.

"Well, I never," Sukie said.

Rider tossed another forkful of hay out of the loft and watched it scatter over the dirt floor below. Dust particles danced in the meager sun that penetrated the barn's interior. The falling bits of chaff caught and glittered in the slanting rays of morning light.

Emmett stood in her open stall and mooed in contentment since she had just been milked, fed and watered by Teddy. He'd skipped off to check on the chickens. Teddy found their fussing endlessly fascinating and couldn't wait to see the poor hen they chose as their next victim for the stew pot. To him it was just a game; to Rider it was another vexing problem to work out.

Rider leaned on the rake, contemplating his life. How it had changed. In less than a month's time he went from living in a four-by-eight-foot cell block with a number instead of a name, to the male head of an unconventional family on a ramshackle Kansas farm.

Lost in contemplation, he found himself smiling—until he saw Jane enter the barn. For a heartbeat of a moment, her windswept skirt swirled up past her boot tops giving him a glimpse of slender calves. She'd covered her head with a scarf and over her dress she wore a threadbare man's jacket. Jane removed the scarf and stuffed it in the pocket of her coat, then rolled her neck as if it were stiff. When her head came up he saw her eyes close. Then she made an odd sort of strangling sound and sank down onto the three-legged milk stool. Leaning her elbows on her knees, she clasped her hands to her face and appeared to be staring at the ground. Her shoulders shook. Her body trembled.

Janie crying? His gut clenched. He took a step toward the ladder, then stopped, unsure about interrupting her privacy. He stood there, despairing, his heart aching. A thickness built in his throat. His eyes burned. Had he caused her this anguish? He didn't know, but her torment was almost more than he could bear. He felt torn between taking her into his arms and providing comfort, and letting her cry out her pain.

Suddenly, she lifted her head and looked up. Her lovely eyes were heavy with tears but as sure as crows caw there wasn't a bit of sadness in their depths. And she was chortling like a hysterical fool!

Her lilting laughter lightened his spirits like no amount of hard alcohol ever could. He wiped his eyes, and felt like whooping. Instead he started down the ladder all set to grab her up and give her a hug the likes of which she wouldn't forget. With his foot poised on the first rung, he heard someone else enter the barn.

"What's so funny?" the unmistakably charming Sukie asked.

Rider lifted his foot off the ladder and stepped away, moving carefully to avoid detection. He didn't feel the slightest twinge of remorse over eavesdropping between the two sisters. Maybe he would learn why they weren't close, and why Sukie and Mary Jo chose this odd time of year to make a long, uncomfortable trip for an unwanted visit.

"My life," Jane said, wiping her eyes. "If I didn't laugh, I'd cry. It's so pathetic even you might find it laughable."

Sukie folded her arms over her chest, and looked down her pert nose at Jane. Rider shook his head at the domineering gesture, although it didn't seem to have any effect on Jane. She merely chuckled and glanced up, shaking her own head. "Don't try any of your dramatic antics with me, Sukie. I know you and they won't work."

"Humph," came the cool reply. "Now who's being dramatic?"

Jane ignored the question. "You never did say. What are you and Mary Jo doing here anyway?"

"We just thought you might need us."

"You just thought, you mean. You didn't come because you felt like your big sister could use a helping hand?"

"Well, of course that was the reason, too," she answered, a bit defensively, "but we were worried about you and the little ones."

"Oh? And you thought you two could help? How exactly? By bringing in the late corn? Maybe climb up on the roof and replace the shingles that have gone missing? Oh, no, I'll wager that you, Sukie, would want to whitewash the house. Or maybe get Mary Jo to slaughter a cow that, as you may recall, we don't have any of. I don't need help baking bread and washing the laundry. I need a man's help."

"Why are you being so mean and hateful? It's not like you."

"No, that's your duty."

Sukie gasped, then took a faltering step backward. "Jane, how unfair."

Jane jumped to her feet, frustration clearly etched on her fine features. "You want to know what's unfair? David up and leaving Teddy and John Michael. Everyone expecting me to take care of David's family when, maybe just maybe, I'd like a family of my own. Then having to put up with you. You're a cross to bear, I can tell you."

"Jane, honestly, you're exaggerating."

"There's more." Jane took a deep breath, then stabbed a finger at Sukie's chest and spoke in a whisper Rider couldn't make out. "My courses have stopped, the larder is near empty, the house has drafts so bad the children will probably catch their deaths, and, listen to this, the doctor says I'm cursed and probably won't live long."

"What?"

Jane's voice rose, and she said in a bitter voice, "I actually had to advertise for a man to care for the place in case I pass away. So now I'm going to marry a man I hardly know who I certainly don't love. What do you have to say to that?"

Sukie looked stunned. Much the same as Rider felt. He probably bore the same shocked expression. *A man . . . who I certainly don't love.* It might be true, but still it hurt. Deeply. Rider didn't realize how deeply until he heard the words issue from Jane's mouth. He scarcely heard another word of the women's conversation. He swallowed hard, and determined to keep his one true goal first and foremost in his head—to redeem himself to David Warner.

"Did I mention the doctor thinks I'm cursed?" Jane asked.

"I think you're just feeling sorry for yourself."

Jane snorted, then her lips twisted in a humorless smile. The fire seemed to have gone out of her. "I probably am."

"There is no such thing as curses. You aren't going to die, and you don't need to marry that odious man unless the reason your courses have stopped is because you are in a family way."

Jane blew out a slow breath before speaking. "I'm not expecting a child."

"Has he forced himself on you?"

"Of course not."

"I see nothing to be worried about then."

Jane dropped onto the stool, hugging her knees and staring at the tips of her boots. In a voice devoid of feeling, she said, "I should have known I'd get no sympathy from you."

"Oh, good night! You don't need sympathy. What you need, girl, are just an extra pair of hands."

"Male hands, calloused, experienced farm hands, and Rider's are quite sufficient, thank you. Besides if I lived to be a hundred, you would be reminding me every single day about how you helped me when I most needed you. You'd play the put-upon sister to the hilt."

"I wouldn't."

"You have before and you will again. You'd let me know at every opportunity. I've got enough on my plate, thank you very much. Why don't you go home to embroider pillowcases and wait for your knight in shining armor?"

"I'll just leave you to wallow in your misery then," Sukie declared. She lifted her skirt and marched out of the barn.

"Fine." Jane's voice choked as she spoke the single word.

Rider stared at the top of Jane's bent head. His heart ached for her and for himself. They were quite a pair.

In his bewildered and somewhat rattled state, he momentarily forgot his one-armed status and hurried to descend the ladder. He grabbed for the side piece, and remembered too late that his arm wouldn't extend completely. His foot missed the second rung, slipped past the next six, and he ended up on the straw-covered earthen floor flat on his back. The air rushed from his lungs and he lay there gasping for breath.

When the stars circling his head dissipated, and he could breathe normally again, he opened his eyes to find himself staring into Jane's concerned face as she leaned over him. "Are you all right?"

Although humiliated by his ungraceful descent, he found her nearness distracting. The scent of roses tickled his nose and sent his reeling head spinning once again. He couldn't take his eyes off her parted lips. It took a moment for him to collect himself, find his voice and speak coherently. "Jim-dandy."

Jane put her hand on his back to help him sit up.

"Quite an entrance," he said. "You must think I'm the clumsiest man in the entirety of Kansas."

"Not at all," she replied, shaking her head.

He quirked a brow in question.

"Well, maybe just in Drover," she said, with a slight smile.

"I guess I asked for that. Seems I've done nothing but trip over myself since the day I arrived at your place."

She sat back on her heels. She eyed him closely, then she must have decided he was going to be fine. "You really were quite rude to eavesdrop like that."

He grinned. "I know."

"Did you hear everything?"

"Not quite." His smile widened. "Sound doesn't carry all that well up to the loft."

She smiled in exasperation. "And you gave me quite a fright. I didn't know you were up there or I wouldn't have said those things."

"You were just being truthful."

"No. Sukie's right. I was being hateful."

"I guess I could have made myself known earlier but I'll admit I was curious about your family. That doesn't explain my tripping down the ladder to tell you that, though."

"You're probably suffering from the same curse or hex or whatever it is that the doctor says I have."

"Come on now," he said as he stood and brushed the hay off his sore backside. "You don't really believe any of that nonsense."

She rose, to stand beside him. "I don't know what to believe."

She stared up at him with those honest brown eyes of hers, her lips parted, her attraction undeniable. Rider so wanted to kiss her but her own words deterred him. She didn't love him. It wasn't a revelation but it stopped him cold.

She placed her hand on his arm, as though to offer an apology. "Despite what you heard me say before, I'll still marry you if you'll have me."

"*Have you?* I haven't changed my mind." How could he? He wanted her whether she felt anything for him or not, and he still needed to settle his debt to David Warner. He swallowed his bruised male pride and answered honestly. "If anything I'm more determined than ever to help out."

"I'd not want to die and leave those little darlings in Sukie's tender loving care," she said in a sarcastic tone. She shivered as if the thought brought a chill to her body. "They'd probably become so desperate to leave her, they would resort to cattle-rustling, or bank-robbing, double-dealing outlaws on the run for the rest of their natural-born days."

Rider struggled to keep from flinching. "I'd wager you're overstating Sukie's influence. Besides they're a mite young to be robbing banks."

"Sukie could drive them to it."

"She is a mite pushy," Rider admitted.

"How diplomatic you are. Sukie is high-handed, high-minded and high-strung."

Rider snorted. "Much like a good racehorse."

Jane dropped her hand from his arm. "She's a Warner, not a thoroughbred."

Rider shrugged, then started up the ladder to the loft. "I still say she needs a good—well, let's just leave it at that."

Jane glanced at him, a gentle look of contemplation on her face. "Are you sure you're all right?"

His pride might be bruised, as well as his backside, but determination kept him from saying anything more. He looked at her over his shoulder. "I'm fine. You go on. I've got work to do."

She gave him a puzzled look but left the barn without another word.

A woman. A gentle, soft-spoken woman with silky, flowing hair, and skin as smooth and white as satin. A knowing, hot-blooded woman with seeking hands. One who could warm his bed, stir his blood and appease his lusty cravings. McCampbell Smith's randy thoughts fixed on the vision as he wandered his property hunting just after daybreak. He stopped to adjust the tightness inside his buckskin breeches when he spotted two strangers camped alongside the creek he shared with the Warner homestead.

On foot and somewhat less than attentive, Smith didn't even have time to lift his hunting rifle when he heard two guns cock simultaneously. He stared down the barrels aimed at his belly, which cooled his heated blood and eased the discomfort within his trousers as effectively as a dousing with a bucket of icy-cold water.

"Ain't you a big one," one of them observed. He sat on the ground tending a cook-fire.

The other one nodded in agreement, never taking his eyes off Smith. "Big as a lead-bull in a cattle herd, I reckon." He stood leaning against a cottonwood tree, one ankle crossed over the other, the thumb of his left hand tucked inside a belt loop. A seemingly casual stance with one small difference—an ivory-handled Colt revolver held steady in his hand and pointed at Smith. A lank of greasy dark blond hair fell over one hooded eye. His glance dropped to Smith's belt as if to see if he too were carrying. One eyebrow rose a fraction. He turned to his younger companion, who had lighter, but just as dirty, hair. He gave him a lurid wink. "And purty darn well equipped, I'd say."

They both snickered. The first man, sitting crossed-legged on the ground, tossed another log onto the blaze, keeping his own revolver leveled on Smith as well.

Irritation, then anger boiled up inside Smith. "What is going on here? This is private property you're on."

"That so?"

As cozy as you please, they had a pair of rabbits skewered and roasting. Fat droplets plopped into the flames and sizzled. Coffee brewed in a pot next to the fire. The tantalizing smells and the men's sarcastic tones irked Smith no small amount. He bit his lip to keep from saying something that might stir their ire.

Smith glanced about. Despite the bite in the air, hats and heavy coats were strewn about. Two horses, unsaddled and hobbled, munched late-season weeds. Bedrolls lay spread across the dew-laden grass. It appeared as though they'd spent the night and were in no hurry to leave this morning.

"You planning on shooting us or can we let up on our trigger fingers, mister?" asked the man sitting on the ground. He cocked his head and gave Smith a squinty-eyed stare.

Smith snorted. "For God's sake, I'm not gonna shoot anyone. I just want some explaining. Holster those damn weapons."

Smith was somewhat surprised when the two men eased the hammers back on their revolvers and holstered them as he requested.

The man standing spoke. "We needed a spot to spend the night. This place looked right comfortable so we bedded down, and this morning we scared us up a couple of rabbits for our breakfast. Any other questions, mister?"

"It's Smith. McCampbell Smith. And you are?"

The one lounging against the cottonwood asked, "I reckon you know these parts purty well, eh, Smith?"

"Well enough."

"You know of a Rider Magrane?"

Smith should have suspected these two trespassing poachers who refused to give their names would be friendly with that no-good stranger. He shrugged his shoulders. "And if I do?"

A secretive looked passed between the two men. One of them replied, "We might be lookin' for him."

"You bounty hunters?"

A hoarse bark of laughter erupted from the man sitting on the ground. He quickly composed himself. "No, siree."

"Is he wanted by the law?" Smith asked.

Again a stealthy look passed between the two men. "Nah. I don't rightly think so."

Smith wasn't so sure. Something about these two not only put Smith's hackles up, but made him doubt every word they said. Maybe they weren't telling him blatant lies, but they were obviously experienced at lying.

"Try the Warner farm just down the road a piece," he said. "I heard tell Magrane's helping out there."

The man leaning against the tree stepped forward, his eyes bulging and his brows raised. "At the Warner farm?"

"Yeah."

The two men turned to look at each other, then burst into laughter. The one on the ground slapped his denim-clad knee as tears of merriment spilled down his cheeks. "The Warner farm!"

"Don't that beat all! And him telling us as how he was getting hitched. That damn weasel was just putting us off his trail."

"I never knowed him to be so wily. Makes me wonder what he's got up his sleeve, eh, big brother?"

"It sure does."

"What are you boys talking about?"

The man who had been standing sauntered over to the fire and joined his companion on the ground. He gestured for Smith to join them. "Why don't you have a bite of breakfast, Mr. Smith, and tell us all about this Rider Magrane fella. We'd be most obligin'. We might even scare us up a bottle of whiskey to add to this awful coffee my brother's brewin'."

To add insult to injury.
—Latin proverb

Chapter Ten

It had been one long, miserable week.

Seven straight days—and nights—of Susan Kay Warner proved to be as hard on Rider as on her own family. She had the Warner household, particularly Rider, on a short rope, with an even wider loop.

Rider thought he could almost feel a raw spot on his own thick neck. There was definitely a raw spot on his temperament. He wanted nothing more than a moment to himself without that witchy woman telling him what to do, how to do it and where and when he should be doing it. Since she arrived she'd scolded, corrected and criticized everything he did.

From sun up until sundown he devised excuses, however flimsy, to get away from the demanding woman. Even one-armed, he chopped wood until his shoulder ached so bad it felt like it might detach itself from his body. He cleaned out the barn on a daily basis. He talked to Emmett, the milk cow, the chickens and even the hogs who continued to follow him around like faithful hound dogs. In fact he found himself in the barn so much he was beginning to wonder if he wouldn't start mooing one of these days.

To make matters worse Sukie kept Rider away from Jane at every opportunity. It was obvious to both him and Jane that Sukie didn't want them to spend any time alone until they decided to marry. They still managed to find a few minutes here and there where Rider could steal a kiss, but it was not enough to satisfy him. He was determined to show Jane he was the man she needed for the boys and the farm. He was getting mighty frustrated at not being able to prove himself.

Tonight he sat outside, again, alone, because Sukie'd shooed him from the house so the women and children could bathe. He was more than happy to oblige, though the thought of seeing Jane, naked, wet and slippery, sent his senses reeling.

Rider blew out a long breath and relaxed against a porch pillar. He cradled a cooling cup of coffee in his hands and stared out across the shadowed yard at the henhouse.

What was left of Jane's paltry brood of hens was dwindling, slowly but surely, and soon would be as scarce as his Aunt Tildy's chocolate cake at a church picnic. Whatever ailed them seemed unlikely to stop before there were none left—to be eaten, to lay eggs or to just plain ol' frolic in the sunshine or whatever it was chickens did.

Rider knew he needed to slaughter one of the three little pigs. It would kill Jane as well.

What really chapped Rider's hide was that he'd have

to ask that cocksure McCampbell Smith for help.

The door creaked open behind Rider and he glanced over his shoulder. Silhouetted against the light coming from inside the house, Jane stepped outside.

She stood in the doorway looking like an angel in a floor-length flowing white nightgown. Though wrapped in a faded quilt against the cool night air, she wore nothing on her feet to protect them from the cold. As she stepped forward and leaned against the opposing porch post, a hint of rose tickled Rider's senses. Her hair, still damp from her bath, spilled over her shoulders and down her back in waves of shimmering dark chocolate.

It took all of Rider's willpower to keep from pulling her into his arms to run his fingers through those beckoning strands. He could almost taste the sweetness of her throat and feel the rapid thud of her pulse against his mouth. How he wanted to gather her close and claim her lips with his own. His whole being ached with wanting.

Jane smiled, a weary, yet still irresistible smile. "Some week, huh?"

He nodded in agreement. He tried to return her smile but found he couldn't. He answered in a voice thick with contained passion. "You shouldn't be out here. It's damned cold."

She gave him an aggrieved glance, apparently misunderstanding his harsh tone. "It's not that cold, and I needed to get out of the house. The boys and Mary Jo are bathed and down for the night . . . at last. Besides, it's always so peaceful and quiet out here in the yard at the end of the day."

"That it is." To take his mind off Jane's state of

undress, he changed the subject. ''Where's that evil sister of yours?''

Jane grinned. ''General Warner is taking her bath.''

''Maybe she'll drown,'' Rider muttered under his breath.

An arched eyebrow and a twist of her lips indicated Jane's amusement but she didn't reply.

''Sit down,'' he suggested with a wave of his hand. He dropped down to the wooden porch, and extended his legs out in front of him on the steps. He watched her movements, glad of the darkness that hid his frank searching gaze.

She sat down, pulling the quilt tight around her shoulders. As she lowered herself, her hair swung forward. Rider watched, mesmerized, as she pushed the unbound locks out of her face. She leaned her head back against the post and stared out into the yard.

Rider reached across and drew her bare feet into his lap. Startled, she sat up straighter. Her head swung around to stare at him, her eyes wide with uncertainty. She tried to pull her feet away but he held them in a firm, yet tender grip. ''I'm just going to warm them,'' he said. He wondered if she detected the pent-up desire in his unsteady voice or the longing to touch her in any way, even if only her feet.

Although she nodded, he heard her swallow as she watched his hands.

He started with a gentle touch, one foot at a time. He ran his fingers under the arch of her foot, while rubbing his thumb over the top. His hand massaged, caressed, grazing the smooth skin, soft at first, then harder, making tiny circles with his thumb. He stroked his fingers up and down the length of her slender foot, then moved to her ankles where the bones felt small and delicate in his large hand.

He looked at her small pink feet enfolded in his work-roughened hand and something elemental passed through him. His whole body filled with wanting.

A groan rose from deep in Jane's throat, though it easily could have come from his own. Inch by inch, her body relaxed. She sighed, then closed her eyes, a whisper of eyelashes sweeping down, in a final surrender to his soothing manipulations. Once again she leaned her back against the post, exposing her ivory throat to his unwavering gaze. "That feels heavenly," she whispered in a languid voice, warm and rich as honey.

Since Jane seemed unaware of him watching her, Rider studied her contented features. A smile, feminine and mysterious, creased her slightly parted mouth. As he watched, the tip of her tongue escaped to trail across her lower lip. It was more enticement than he could stand.

Rider leaned forward and folded Jane into an awkward embrace. Her unfettered breasts, soft as the moonlight, pressed against his chest and thundering heart. As he stroked her back, she snuggled her head into the crook of his neck. A feminine fragrance and the soft scent of summer roses surrounded him, heady and inviting. She felt so right in his arms. He reached beneath the quilt to massage her slender back and press her close.

With a timid touch, Jane grazed his face, her cool fingers lightly splayed against the late-day stubble on his cheek. He hissed through his teeth as her knuckles brushed along his jaw then down the column of his throat. Her fingers skimmed along the nape of his neck. She stopped to knead the taut tendons she found along his shoulder muscles. And all his reasoning, his sanity, drifted away in the frosty air. "My God."

"Ahh," she whispered just before he lowered his head and placed his mouth on hers. Her lips parted and her eyelids drifted shut.

Rider kissed her then with all the passion and hunger he'd been denying himself. Rampant desire flowed through his heated veins. He didn't know if there was a correct way to go about courting a woman. He didn't know what she expected from him. And he, for damn sure, didn't know if he was pleasing her. He wanted to, with a desperation bordering on obsession.

As his tongue met hers, a shiver coursed up Rider's spine. She, too, trembled in his arms. She returned his kisses timidly at first, then exploring, then probing. As her mouth began a more aggressive assault, he allowed her to take the lead and discover her own passionate nature. He couldn't help but gasp for air when he at last lifted his mouth from hers.

Jane stared at him with wonder. The stars above seemed to twinkle in her stunned, wide-eyed gaze. Her lips, wet and swollen from his kisses, glistened. Her rose scent beckoned. He wanted more.

He lowered his head and nibbled her lower lip before gathering it into his mouth.

McCampbell Smith stopped dead in his tracks. Beneath a full moon and bright shining stars accenting the suggestive scene, Rider Magrane, the scoundrel, held Jane within the circle of his arms. They were locked in a tight embrace, all right, and if Mack wasn't mistaken, they were doing more than a wee bit of spooning. To his keen eye, it looked a whole helluva lot like lovemaking. Mack watched, hidden at the edge of the woods, and regarded the pair. Painfully aware that what he was doing was not only spying, but somehow wrong, he still couldn't stop himself.

He may be beaten by that damnable fellow in the courting game, but he wasn't going to let Magrane make love right out in the open to the woman he wanted. Not while he stood there with a mess of squirrels in his hand. Out of sheer spite and stinging male pride, he approached on light feet.

When he stood not five feet away he stopped and stared at the couple. They continued kissing, their hands roving over each other, exploring, and caressing. Finally it was the sounds of their lovemaking—the soft sighs, the panting breaths—that embarrassed Mack. He cleared his throat.

Rider lifted his head and stared right into Mack's eyes. He muttered a rather obscene vulgarity, then turned and twisted his body as if to shield Jane from Mack's gaze.

Slowly Jane glanced about, her features soft and radiant, her lips rosy and moist from Magrane's kisses. For a brief moment she looked confused. Then she stiffened and scooted backward, her hand pressed to her chest. Her cheeks flushed as she pulled the quilt, fallen to her waist, up around her shoulders. Her fisted hand held the ends together beneath her chin. She looked close to tears.

The no-account varmint. Mack wanted to strangle Magrane for putting Jane in such an uncomfortable position.

"Smith, what the hell are you doing here this time?"

Mack placed his booted foot on the lowest step, and leaned his elbow on his knee. He glanced from Jane's guilty countenance to Magrane's belligerent one. He stared him straight in the eye and said, "I could ask you the same thing, Magrane. You been taking advantage of Miss Warner?''

''No, no, it's not like that,'' Jane said, clearly discomfited by the situation. ''I wanted—''

''No offense, Miss Warner,'' he said, interrupting her, ''but I was asking Magrane here.''

''What Jane and I do is none of your business. Why don't you take yourself back to that rock you climbed out from under.''

''Rider!''

Mack grinned. ''No, that's all right. I expect Magrane is just staking his claim on you, Miss Warner. I understand, but I don't have to like it much.'' He inhaled a long breath and released it slowly. He gave Magrane a marked stare. The man acknowledged him with a slight nod of his head. ''I did bring you a mess of squirrels, though, seeing as how Mr. Magrane is still incapacitated, what with that broken arm and all. Would you like me to take them inside? They're dressed out and ready for the frying pan.''

With a mocking smile plastered across his face, Rider stood up and with a sweeping motion of his hand beckoned Mack to go inside the house. ''How kind of you, Mr. Smith. What with me being incapacitated and all. Why don't you just go on in and drop 'em there on the kitchen table. Help yourself to the coffee. I believe it's still hot.''

''Rider, Su—''

''Would you mind refilling mine while you're at it?'' Rider asked, interrupting Jane. She gave him an odd look then suddenly smiled and ducked her head. Mack thought he heard her giggle.

As he straightened and started up the steps, Rider

shoved a tin cup into his hand. "Thanks, farmer. And go in quiet-like, so as not to wake the boys."

The back of Mack's neck always tingled right before something bad happened—like now. He shook his head. He was acting foolish, probably an after-effect from seeing Rider steal the woman he wanted right out from under his own nose. What could possibly be inside the house aside from a couple of harmless, sleeping little boys?

Mack quietly opened the door and stepped inside.

"That was a mean thing to do, Rider Magrane," Jane said as the door swung shut behind them.

"I know."

"Wish I'd thought of it."

His eyebrows raised and his eyes widened, then Rider threw his head back and roared with laughter.

Jane placed her hand over his mouth. "Shh," she whispered. "You'll wake the boys."

Rider covered her hand with his. He kissed the middle of her palm, then gently nipped it with his teeth. She started to draw her hand away but he held it in place, his thumb tucked beneath her chin. With his tongue, he lapped the sensitive flesh with a gentle, soothing motion.

Jane sought his gaze and found him staring at her. His blue eyes sizzled with implication but there was no mistaking his desire or his intent.

He clasped her hand, entwining their fingers together, and lowered them to rest on his knee. In a voice ripe beatenwith innuendo, he asked, "Now where were we, Janie?"

As Mack's eyes adjusted to the shadowed room, lit only by the banked fire in the fireplace and the meager light of a lantern, he saw a figure moving in the kitchen.

Startled, he stopped, stunned into utter silence. A full-grown woman, naked as the day she was born, stood in a bathing tub. Looking like a sea nymph, tiny droplets of water shimmered and glistened all over her pale golden skin. She'd piled a thick mass of brown hair, as dark and sleek as an otter's, atop her head, giving him a glorious view of her slender neck and the graceful curve of her back. His gaze lowered to a narrow waist, nicely rounded hips and the cleft of her buttocks, each side of which would fit exactly into the palm of his hand. He swallowed hard and found he couldn't speak.

When she bent to pick up a towel, Mack thought he might die the way his breath caught in his throat. He could barely breathe.

She proceeded to lift one long leg from the tub, then the other. She turned slightly giving him an unimpeded view of the side of a full, round breast, gilded by the lamplight. He thought his thundering heart was going to climb through his chest. His throat closed, his head spun. Again he tried to speak but all that came out was a frog-like croak.

Lowering the sack of squirrels to the floor, he inched his way toward the door. Just as he'd about made his getaway, a floorboard creaked beneath his heavy booted foot.

The woman swirled and saw him. She clasped the towel against herself and let out a shriek that must have pierced the eardrums of every person in the four neighboring counties. "You contemptible lout! You debaucher of women! You . . . you, vile wicked . . . lust-monger! Get out! Get out before I fetch the shotgun and fill you full of lead!"

Before Mack could draw a breath, she was across the room and beating him about the head and shoulders with a straw broom. He wasn't sure how to stop her but did throw up his hands to try to protect his head. He made a grab for the broom and got whacked upside the face.

Since she was delectably bare-ass naked, he was afraid if he tried again he would place his hands on her in an intimate location. One that would surely further upset the enraged madwoman. He found he didn't mind being beaten—too much—she gave him a sight that left his eyes entranced and his ears ringing. That might be the broom's doing, he reasoned, but didn't have anything to do with the tingle growing in his belly.

Each time she lifted the broom above her head to give him another wallop one uncovered glorious pink-tinged breast rose and fell. He couldn't take his gaze from the deliriously wondrous vision.

"Out! Damn you!" With one last whack, she persuaded him, somewhat unwillingly, to back out of the door. His last view of her was with the broom held high in one hand, the towel clutched against her chest with the other and her eyes as wild and untamed as the Kansas wind. And screaming at the top of her lungs. Magnificent!

"I expect we'll be hearing Sukie soon, hollering like a—"

"You . . . you, vile wicked . . . lust-monger! Get out! Get out before I fetch the shotgun and fill you full of lead!"

"Lust-monger?" Rider questioned. His eyebrows waggled in an exaggerated fashion. "I don't believe I've heard that particular expression before."

"How about 'fill you full of lead'? You suppose Sukie's been reading those dreadful dime novels?"

"Sure sounds like it."

Jane grinned. "I'm shocked."

They looked up as Mack stumbled out the door and onto the porch, mumbling beneath his breath. Jane scrambled to get out of his way.

She needn't have bothered. He jumped over the three steps and landed in the yard like he was running from a burning building. He gaped at Jane and Rider, his blue-gray eyes wide, his mouth gaping. Taking a deep unsteady breath, he stepped back.

He'd ripped his flannel shirt at the shoulder and lost the top two buttons. His hair stood up in wild disarray. A slight scratch trickling blood marked his left eyebrow. "Saints alive," he said in a voice shaking with emotion. "I ain't never seen the like."

Jane looked at the bewildered man and tried in vain to hide her amusement. She supposed by his exasperated expression that she was doing a mighty poor job. She gave up and grinned. "Welcome to the Warner madhouse."

"You might've warned me."

"Nah," Rider said in an aggravating, calm voice that Jane guessed was intended to irritate poor, flustered Mr. Smith. "We couldn't do that. How else would you get to know Jane's favorite little sister?"

His eyes widened. "That was no *little* sister."

Jane nodded. "Maybe he should have said younger sister. That was Susan Kay, Sukie for short. What did you think of her, Mr. Smith?"

"Beggin' your pardon, Miss Warner, she's a fine specimen of womanhood, but that wildcat nearly took my head off."

"Oh?" A glint of humor danced in Rider's eyes. "Why would she do that?"

"You know damn good and well why, Magrane. She was taking a bath." His voice lowered toward the end.

"And what did you see?"

"Every last wondrous thing," Mack answered in an awe-filled voice. His eyes gleamed as if he were visualizing the scene all over again. His whole being took on a wistful expression unexpected in a simple country man, particularly one of his size and strength.

When Mack looked at Jane, catching her exchanging a surprised look with Rider, a deep red flush started up his neck. "By all that's holy, she didn't have on a stitch of clothing. It may have been wrong for me to look but, by God, I couldn't help myself. She was a sight to see, that's for certain."

"Is that right?" Rider replied.

"That's right, Magrane, but I suspect you knew that already. When she commenced to beat me with that darned broom, I didn't know what to do. I couldn't stop her and I couldn't touch her, not while she was in the altogether like that. I did the only thing a decent man could; I turned tail and ran."

"A smart call, Smith."

"I agree with Rider, Mr. Smith. Sukie might've killed you. I heard her threaten you with a gun."

"Aww, she was just bluffing." Smith grinned. "She's a skittish, high-strung filly, though, and a fine-looking woman."

"I believe you said that already," Rider said.

"Did I?" That look of wonderment crossed his face again. "I may have, it's true, but it bears repeating."

"Seeing a naked woman can make a man a mite forgetful, I reckon."

"You have no idea." Mack stood with his hands on his hips and stared at the door as though willing her to appear before his eyes.

It must have worked. The door banged open, and out flew the oddly quiet shrew, otherwise known as Sukie. Mr. Smith smiled cordially, took one look at Sukie's angry countenance, and lost the smile. He took several hesitant, slow steps backward, his eyes wary, his hands outstretched.

Sukie had quite obviously dressed in a hurry. The fabric of her gown clung to her in several damp spots and Jane saw bare skin between gaps in the thin, misbuttoned cloth. To her chagrin, Jane realized that Sukie had thrown on her dress without bothering with underapparel. Her breasts not only bounced like rubber balls every time she gestured with her hands but the nipples were disconcertingly evident. She held Mr. Smith enthralled with the display. So incensed was she that she didn't even notice his avid gaze never lifted above her chest. Jane's face heated. How embarrassing. How funny. Although she should have been mortified on her sister's behalf, Jane wasn't in the least bit. She chewed her lip to keep from laughing outright.

Sukie's usually sleek and fashionably styled hair, now tangled and looking wind-whipped wild, danced about her contradictory flushed cheeks. She attempted to brush the knots out of it with a hairbrush using short, angry strokes but it was proving ineffective. "You still here?"

"Yes, ma'am, I apologize for—"

"Don't take that tone with me, young man."

"No, ma'am."

"I should go get the shotgun." She turned as if to actually retrieve the weapon.

"I don't think that's necessary." He made the mistake of stepping forward.

She shook her hairbrush at him as if it could do mortal damage. And in Sukie's hands, Jane thought, it probably could. "Don't you move, and for heaven's sake don't even think."

He obliged, stood stock-still and regarded her bobbling breasts. "I—"

"You hush."

"Yes, ma'am." His voice sounded as if he were strangling.

Rider glanced at him with a suspicious expression. Thank goodness he wasn't watching Sukie. Jane didn't know what she would do if he, too, caught the daring display Sukie was putting on for Mr. Smith's avid gaze. As it was, Mr. Smith looked close to apoplexy. His eyes were mere slits and a muscle quivered at his jaw. His lean face, suffused with pink, shone bright under the cloudless night sky.

She should have felt guilty for not taking Sukie aside and telling her. She didn't . . . not in the least. She just let her rant and rave, and bobble.

"Who are you and what gives you the right to go marching into someone's house without even knocking? What were you doing sneaking around in my kitchen?"

"My kitchen?" Jane repeated.

Sukie rapped her on the head with the hairbrush.

"Ouch!"

"Don't interrupt, Jane."

With a grin on his lips, Rider reached over and rubbed Jane's head.

"Don't you have the sense God gave a goose? I might have taken you for a robber, a thief in the middle of the night, for heaven's sake."

"Ma'am," Mr. Smith said, when Sukie stopped to take a breath.

She didn't let him continue. "What was in that smelly sack you dropped on the floor? What's your name? Are you a friend of Mr. Magrane here?" She nodded although he hadn't answered any of her questions, just stared at her dumbfounded. "I should have known you would be in cahoots with the likes of him. He's led Jane astray. While I was inside bathing, these two were out here sparking sure as God is in heaven. Can't leave them alone a minute."

"Drat this hair!" she stormed, as the brush tangled in a thick, snarled lock. The brush stood out of the side of her head like a branch on a tree.

"Let me," Mack said, as he bounded up the steps. He had his hands on the brush before Sukie could naysay him.

She backed away pulling the hair he held in his outstretched hand. She winced. Mack clasped her upper arm and pulled her nearer. Still she held him at arm's length and gave him a withering look that left no doubt what she thought of him. "This is highly improper. I don't even know your name."

"It's McCampbell Smith, Miss Warner. I'm your closest neighbor. Right pleased to meet you."

"I don't know . . ." Sukie said, trailing off.

Mack, with natural slow, easy strokes, brushed through her hair like he'd been doing it for years.

Jane thought she heard Sukie sigh.

Rider chuckled. He leaned over and kissed Jane on

the tip of her nose. "I'm for bed. A man needs his beauty sleep. Besides I suspect Sukie here will have me cooking oatmeal, changing diapers and shining her boots before sun up tomorrow. You take care with Sukie, Smith. Just remember her bite is as bad as her bark."

Sukie sniffed as she scowled at Rider.

He returned her disgruntled look with a grin. "I'd say you're in good hands, Sukie. Good night all."

Rider stood and winked at Jane. He surprised her and even more, Sukie, by kissing Sukie on her ever-reddening cheek. He started to walk inside whistling a merry tune beneath his breath when Mack pulled him aside.

"By the way, Magrane, I met a couple of real close friends of yours today."

Rider's face paled and the tune died on his lips.

"They might come calling," he said and then lowered his voice to a soft whisper. "If I were you, I'd steer clear of 'em, if you know what's good for you."

Rider nodded, and Jane thought she heard him say "thanks." His head lowered, his steps slow and measured, he walked inside the house and shut the door quietly behind him.

Jane sat a moment more contemplating Mack's words before realizing she was hardly needed on the porch. She got up to go inside herself.

"You can't leave me out here with this man," Sukie said. Her voice wavered with uncertainty as she tried without luck to disentangle her hair from Mack's hands.

"Why ever not?" Jane agreed with Rider. Sukie couldn't be in better hands. She needed someone to corral her wayward tongue and lofty manner. Mack seemed a likely choice.

"Good night, Sukie. Good night, Mr. Smith." As she stepped past him to go in the house, she caught his gaze and whispered, "Good luck. I believe you'll be needing quite a bit of it."

Keep your eyes wide open before marriage, half-shut afterward.
—Benjamin Franklin

Chapter Eleven

"You and me are going into town today."

Jane looked up from her breakfast and glanced across the oilcloth-covered table at Rider. Although he had yet to escape to the barn, he must have risen early for he'd shaved and washed up. She saw a small nick just below his earlobe where he must have cut himself shaving. His glossy black hair, still damp and neatly combed, gleamed. Staring out the window, his intent gaze riveted on the bleak early winter landscape, he didn't glance her way even as he spoke. His bowl of oatmeal, half eaten, sat before him, cold and congealing. How odd, thought Jane, since his enthusiastic appetite had become something of a joke. Baffled, she watched as his thumb traced the lip of his coffee cup. His mind seemed miles away.

"Me?"

He nodded, still gazing outside.

She turned to stare out the window herself, but saw

nothing out of the ordinary. Swinging back to face him, she couldn't keep the exasperation from her voice. "I simply can't take the time today. I have way too much work to do right here on the farm."

He propped his elbow on the table and rested his chin in his hand. His expression serious and unnervingly calm, he gave Jane a speculative frown. "Nothing that can't keep." His thick eyebrows slanted and his eyes darkened as he spoke again. "It's high time we had a little chat with the parson in Drover, Jane. You may not cotton to the idea of marrying me, but you've got to think of the boys now."

Torn between conflicting emotions, confusion waged war in Jane's spinning head. He didn't understand. She did want to marry him, not only for the boys' sake but for her own as well. His kisses heated her blood, and she was powerless to resist his embraces even had she wanted to. Although she'd confided in him about the curse, and he said it was just so much nonsense, even Rider couldn't explain the things that had happened to him since he'd arrived at the farm. Shooting the door off the barn, little John Michael blackening his eye, the man in town who broke his arm.

Not to mention her own problems. She still didn't have her monthly cycle. And after more than six months, there was still no word from David.

In all honesty, there really was no decision to make. David might well be dead. John Michael and Teddy needed a father. The farm needed a man to tend it.

"I agree with Mr. Magrane," Sukie added, smiling at Jane over her coffee cup. Her skin glowed a lovely golden color this morning, and her brown eyes twinkled. Her back didn't seem as stiff as a fence post, and her voice didn't grate like a dull knife blade against a grindstone.

She couldn't have shocked the adults sitting around the table much more. Each turned to stare at her. Mary Jo gaped, her mouth hanging ajar. Rider, who had been teasing John Michael, stopped and gaped at her beaming face. Sukie simply smiled back.

"Can I go, too?" Teddy asked. He glanced from Rider to Jane and, with obvious reluctance, at Sukie.

Sukie patted his head affectionately. "I have plans for you and John Michael, my boy."

"What's that?"

"You'll see," she said with a mischievous grin. "Right now it's a secret."

"I like secrets," Teddy admitted. His mouth curled in a tentative smile.

"Everyone likes secrets," Rider said, winking at Teddy.

"Sekwets," John Michael echoed. He waved his arms about his head and kicked his stocking feet against the table.

Rider laughed at his antics and easily plucked the giggling child from his seat. He bounced the baby on his knee and talked to him, nose to nose, rolling his eyes, and smacking his lips. The baby giggled and tried to imitate his actions. The growing affection he showed toward John Michael and Teddy warmed Jane like the first spring breeze after a long winter. Rider was well on his way to being a good father. She had a feeling he would make a good husband, too. Patient and caring, hardworking and determined. He seldom raised his voice or lost his temper, except with McCampbell Smith.

Still she foresaw several problems in marrying him.

Mostly with herself. She didn't want to believe the doctor's dire predictions of her early demise but should she tell Rider? How much of that conversation between Sukie and herself had he heard? And what about future children? For that matter, could she even have any?

Marriage and most particularly the marriage bed terrified her. What kind of wife would she make and what would Rider expect from her in bed? She knew nothing of what went on between a man and a woman, and the whole idea of relations with a man scared her half to death. Since theirs would be a loveless marriage, perhaps he wouldn't expect that of her. She hoped not. She enjoyed his kisses but the rest . . . well, she wasn't so sure.

It didn't matter. Only the boys' welfare mattered.

As Jane watched Rider with John Michael, she noticed that he had removed the splint from his arm, although it had been little more than two weeks since he'd broken it. She thought he should still be wearing the darn thing, especially after seeing how he moved his arm in an awkward manner. It was none of her business what he did, she told herself, and refrained from saying anything.

"We can take Gopher to town with us," Rider offered, interrupting Jane's musings, "if it'll give you a free hand."

"Oh, no, that won't be necessary," Sukie said in a voice as sweet as a plump, ripe strawberry. "You need time alone with the minister."

Jane's jaw dropped and Rider choked on his coffee. Who was this woman? Was there such a thing as a good curse, and could it possibly have transferred from Jane to her sister? "Sukie, are you feeling all right?"

Mary Jo patted Rider's back until he stopped coughing, but his eyes watered as he stared at Sukie, quite obviously flummoxed by her behavior.

"Of course I am," Sukie said. "I'll help you get dressed."

"I don't have a decent dress."

"You look fine," Sukie said, "but you can borrow one of mine if you like."

"We'll have to walk," Jane warned, hoping that might deter Rider.

He glanced at her askance. "It won't hurt me if you don't mind."

"I have a heavy package I need to take with me and trade in town."

"Fine. I can carry it."

"I don't know the minister. Actually I don't even know if Drover has a minister."

"There's one," Rider replied, scowling. His voice took on a mocking, bitter edge as he continued, "If I know the upstanding citizens of Drover, they couldn't go a single, solitary day without having a parson to tell them how to live their pathetic, little lives."

An awkward silence fell over the room. Even John Michael quieted. Teddy broke his biscuit into crumbs, and watched the pieces fall onto the table. Mary Jo stared at her plate. Sukie stared at the ceiling. Disconcerted by his harsh words about Drover and its people, Jane sought Rider's gaze, but she lowered her eyes when he scowled at her.

At last Sukie spoke, breaking the uncomfortable hush. "You've lived here before? I guess I didn't know that."

"No need for it to come up in conversation, but yeah, I lived here a long time ago." His gaze turned back to the view out the window. "There are people who won't like me coming back."

"I'm sure they've forgotten your transgressions, whatever they might be," Sukie said. "I find most people are forgiving."

"Not in this town, they aren't," Rider said. He placed his hand atop John Michael's head. "This little feller likes me, though, don't you?"

"Wide!"

"I just don't think today is a good day, that's all," Jane persisted. She knew she was beginning to sound petulant but she couldn't seem to stop herself.

"What's wrong with you, Jane Warner?" Sukie asked in a voice much more like herself—annoying and shrewish. "The man is being obliging as can be. I thought this was what you wanted. Besides he can't stay here any longer otherwise. It's not right."

"Sukie, you don't understand."

"I think I do. Mary Jo, why don't you take John Michael and Teddy to the henhouse and collect the eggs. Then you can show John Michael how to milk the cow." She shooed them out of the house and waited until they were gone before she continued. "Since we don't have Ma with us anymore I'm going to take her place, and give you some motherly advice."

"*Please,* Sukie, you're only seventeen. What do you know that I don't?"

"So? I can give advice. Just pretend I'm Ma. You, too, Mr. Magrane."

Rider shook his head, frowning in exasperation. "I don't think so. Maybe I should go on out to the barn with the kids. This sounds like a female matter to me."

"No, you stay. I'm trying to help. You'll be the groom."

He leaned back in his chair and folded his arms over his chest. A skeptical look crossed his features. "What are you up to?"

"Do you know what comes after the wedding ceremony, Jane?"

"The kiss?" Rider asked, as a wry grin played about his lips.

Her eyes narrowed. "Be serious now. Jane?"

Jane hesitated before answering. Where was Sukie taking this? "No, what?"

"The honeymoon, silly. The honeymoon."

"So far, so good," Rider added in a rush. "But I think I can take it from here, Sukie. If you haven't been on one yourself how would you even know of such things? Anyway, Jane and I won't be going on a honeymoon. We'll be spending our wedding night right here on the farm. The only difference is that from now on, I'll be sharing my bed with Janie instead of Teddy. Hopefully she'll give me a little more room than he does."

Sukie blushed scarlet at the mention of the word *bed,* certainly not polite conversation in mixed company, but she continued on undaunted. "Now I know you're still a maiden, Jane, but—"

"Susan Kay!" Jane sputtered, bristling with indignation. "Enough is enough." Her cheeks heated at the blunt conversation. She looked at Rider to gauge his reaction. Exasperation lit his eyes.

Rider jumped up from his chair, toppling it over in his rush to get to his feet. His tin coffee cup toppled, rolled off the table and bounced once before rattling to a stop against the toe of his boot. Quite obviously provoked, he kicked it away. A muscle twitched in his jaw as he gritted out, "We're not about to answer any of your damn fool questions. Our personal lives are none of your business."

"If your ill-mannered reaction is any indication, you must be innocent, too."

"I am not innocent!"

"If you say so, Mr. Magrane."

"How the hell would you know anyway?" Rider turned to stare at Jane. "This, from the girl who was disgusted when I took a piss off the back porch. Who said I was—what was your damnable turn of phrase—a 'disgraceful excuse of a man'? Tarnation! This is one man who's not going to stand here and let some know-it-all girl preach to him about the facts of life. I didn't just fall off the turnip truck, for God's sake.

"You ready to go to town, Janie?"

She stood up, surprised by Rider's vehemence, and even more surprised by Sukie. Acting like she knew even the first thing about marriage. What had gotten into her? "As soon as I fetch my scarf and coat and the . . . the package I want to trade for."

He snatched his wool jacket and black Stetson off the peg by the door and glared at Sukie.

She smiled back, oblivious to his frown.

"I'll be outside waiting."

Jane found him standing in the yard, his back to her, his hands on his slender hips. He turned when he heard the door slam shut. He held a hand out to help her down the steps and took the package from her.

Shaking his head as he tucked it under his arm, he said, "I can't figure out that sister of yours."

Jane placed her mittened hand in his. "Don't fret about it. None of us have."

"One minute she's cantankerous as an old mule, the next minute she's sweet as can be, though I admit I haven't seen that side of her much."

"I've *never* seen that side of her before," Jane confessed.

Rider started down the road, taking short measured steps so she could keep up with his longer stride. He seemed glad to be going to town. A cheerful grin turned his lips up and brightened his handsome face. A splendid clear blue sky and bright shining sun disguised the crisp cold air. As they talked, their clouded breaths mingled, then danced away on the wind.

"I can't believe Sukie had the gumption to try and give you marital advice. Maybe my Aunt Tildy, but your little sister?"

Jane shrugged her shoulders. "I don't understand her either. You think something happened last night between her and Mr. Smith?"

"Who the hell knows? She was right pleasant there for a few seconds this morning."

"I think she's lost her mind."

Rider snorted. "Can't argue with that."

Jane turned to look up at Rider. His cheeks and nose, and the lobes of his ears, where they stuck out from beneath his broad-brimmed hat, were red from the cold. He caught her glance, smiled and squeezed her fingers. Jane's heart thudded against her chest. Was he really as calm about this big step as he seemed? She didn't see how he could be.

"Rider, I heard you speak of your brother before but you have an aunt, too? Living?"

Rider's mouth twisted in a slight grimace. "Very much so. She means well, I think, but she's a contrary, nosy old woman. I expect Sukie will be the same way when she reaches a certain age."

"I'm sorry if Sukie embarrassed you."

He laughed aloud, a deep, rich resonating sound that warmed Jane. He didn't laugh often enough, she thought. Always a kind of sadness enveloped him, even though he was careful to mask it with sarcasm or humor. Like most men she knew he tried hard to disguise his emotions but his beautiful blue eyes gave him away. They glowed with an inner fire that seldom reflected in his conversation. "She's seen me at my worst, so to speak, with little left to her imagination."

Jane could imagine. His handsome face and virile body left her breathless when she looked at him, and caused her to toss and turn in the dark of night with thoughts of her attraction to him.

He glanced at her, then ran his hand down the side of her face. His calloused fingers warmed her cold cheek. "Janie, don't worry about me and your sister. There's not much that can embarrass me anymore, but getting caught by two young gals with your pants down around your knees can still do it."

Jane remembered Sukie and Rider's initial meeting. Her face heated. Jane was such an innocent, just seeing the man without a shirt set her pulse racing. She couldn't think what she would do seeing him without his trousers. She'd probably make a fool of herself by fainting or worse.

He must have seen her blushing features. He stopped walking, turned her to face him and placed one hand on her shoulder. "You look like you're heading to the slaughterhouse. I'm not that bad, am I?"

She tried smiling but feared it wasn't working. Inside her mittens, she clenched her hands into fists to try to gain control over her uneasy emotions. "It's not you, Rider."

"This isn't the wedding you dreamed of as a young girl, now, is it? With a pretty new dress and flowers and all the fancy trappings that go along with it?" His eyes widened in alarm. "Say, you don't have a young man waiting for you back home?"

"Oh, no."

"That's good."

She did manage a thin smile at that.

"I know you don't love me," Rider stated in a resigned voice.

Jane's heart plummeted. He sounded so sad. She shook her head as a tear escaped her eye. "You don't understand."

Rider cupped her chin in his fingers. His warm breath caressed her face. She turned away, afraid to see the hurt she'd thoughtlessly placed in his eyes. "Look at me, Janie," he murmured, his voice patient and calm.

She lifted her head and gazed into his beautiful blue eyes. He stared back, giving her a bittersweet smile, so sweet and caring in its intensity tears filled her eyes.

"Janie, honey, don't cry." He took her into his arms and held her close. "If you don't want to marry me, we won't do it. I'll just find another way to help you out."

"But I do want to marry you." She gulped hard as another hot tear escaped and slid down her cheek.

"Oh?" he asked, a trace of laughter in his voice. "Then why are you crying?"

"I'm not."

"You could have fooled me. Are you afraid, Janie?"

"A little."

"Don't be," Rider reassured her. "In no time at all you'll get used to sharing your bed with me. I promise I won't hurry you into lovemaking or make you uncomfortable. At least I'll try not to."

"I'm afraid for the boys," Jane lied. She just couldn't hurt him with the truth. No, she wasn't at all sure whether she loved him, but she liked him a great deal. She admired and respected him. She thought in time she could learn to love him. Maybe she even did a little bit right now. Should she say that or would it make matters worse? Confused, she said nothing more.

He stepped back and looked at her, a frown of concern etching his brow. "Why are you afraid for the boys? That I can't take care of them?"

"No! Not that. You're wonderful with the boys. You've managed everything, even the farm, just fine."

"I wouldn't say that exactly. I did shoot off the barn doors. Remember?"

How endearing he looked. She couldn't help but smile. "I remember. It's just that I worry."

"Well, you can stop worrying now. From here on out, I'll do it for the both of us."

He tucked her arm in his and strode forward. They continued to town, trudging uphill the last mile or so, in relative silence. Jane lost herself in her own thoughts—of the future, of the wedding, of the marriage bed. Despite his calm reassurances, just the thought of sleeping with Rider sent a shiver up her spine. He didn't notice her discomfort, seemingly lost in his own thoughts, a deep frown etching his features.

When they reached the edge of town and could see the huddled rooftops of the ramshackle buildings and the white smoke curling from the chimneys, he stopped and pulled her to the side of the well-rutted road. With a grim look on his face, he said, "I'd better warn you about what you might hear about me in town. Things that won't be too, uh . . . well, too flattering."

Jane placed her hand over her heart and smiled. His worried face—yes, he was already worrying for her—bore such a serious expression she'd do whatever it took to relieve his anxiety. "For my future husband, I promise to ignore everything I hear while we're in town."

He smiled in obvious relief, picked up her mittened hand and kissed the back of it. "Thank you. And for my future wife, I promise to give you a big, wet kiss if you do."

She laughed, her spirits lightening. "You don't have to do that."

"Janie, darlin', that's something I'd enjoy doing."

Rider hated Drover. He hated the memories invoked by a town that had sent him to the penitentiary, and where Chauncey Carlisle had been killed. A town that chased off his blameless older brother, Chance. For five long years the memory of this town tormented his brain and ravaged his body. He'd never blamed his brother for arresting him or even killing Chauncey, who drew down on Chance first. He blamed the upstanding Drover citizens for thinking the worst of their sheriff, and dismissing him.

A bad taste settled in his mouth as he once again stood on the main street and surveyed the irregular board sidewalk, the one-story square-fronted buildings, and the respectable townsfolk going about their business. He searched for the church, not quite recalling its location.

While Drover had never been a thriving cowtown like Abilene or Ellsworth, the Atchison & Topeka passed through with regularity. Rider eyed the red-painted station and the long platform. Fenced stockyards with cattle milling about stood beyond the rails separating the small town from the endless miles of open prairie. The town smelled of cattle manure, and always would.

He took Jane's arm and glanced about looking for a white church steeple or bell tower. He spotted one in the distance. They'd have to pass every saloon, every gambling hall, the post office, even the hotel and restaurant to get there. Some days Lady Luck was with you. Most days she wasn't.

They had just passed the Winged Horse Saloon, a drinking establishment Rider knew all too well, when a shot rang out from inside its walls. He pushed Jane and her package into a nearby alley as a screaming woman rushed out of the batwing doors. Her short red skirt and plunging neckline left little to the imagination. Nor did it leave anyone wondering what she did for a living. She flew across the street, shrieking, and ducked into a dress shop.

Right behind her came a swaggering fool, spurs jingling and boots thumping. He held a revolver high above his head and discharged it again, howling at the top of his lungs. Frightened women and angered men scurried out of his way in every direction, leaving the street as quiet as a sleeping babe.

Rider stepped up behind the drunkard, reached around him and relieved him of his gun. When he turned on Rider, spittle flying from his mouth, Rider hit him upside his head with the weapon. Damnation. It was Martin Ferlin, drunk as a cowboy after a long, hot, dusty cattle drive. He hit the boardwalk like a fifty-pound sack of grain, and he didn't get up. Rider hoped the fall didn't break his nose.

When Chance was sheriff, things in Drover were much quieter, even with Rider and the Ferlin brothers causing mischief at every turn.

Rider shook his head, then handed the gun to Jacob Ferlin, who came sauntering out of the swinging doors, a look of benign tolerance on his young face. Though his eyes were glassy, Jacob didn't seem quite as inebriated as his brother. He glanced at Martin laid out at his feet, then stuck the revolver inside the front of his trousers. He inclined his head. "Rider."

"Jake."

Jacob looked up and down the deserted street, then spat on the boardwalk. "I take it you didn't kill him."

"I doubt it."

"The damned fool pup. He never could handle his whiskey."

"I recall that about Martin."

"He was pestering Sally, one of them saloon gals, something fierce to take him upstairs for a poke."

"And she didn't take kindly to his interest?" Rider asked.

The felled man groaned, lifted one hand and then dropped it. He grew quiet again.

Jacob looked down, and kicked him none too gently in the ribs. When he didn't move, he said, "Nah, she didn't like his manner. I reckon it was the way Martin kept on sticking his hands down inside the front of her dress. When he pulled out his gun, then threatened to pull out something else, she hightailed it out of there.''

When he heard a gasp, Rider belatedly remembered Jane waiting in the alley behind him. He glanced over his shoulder. He noted her arched brows, the unconscious biting of her lower lip. Rosy color dotted both of her cheeks.

Jacob saw her at the same time that Rider did. A genuine look of surprise crossed his face. Her embarrassed reaction seemed to amuse him. His mouth spread open in an unpleasant grin. ''Well, what do we have here, Rider?'' As his grin widened, he nudged Rider in the ribs. ''Would this little lady be your intended?''

Reluctantly, Rider took Jane's hand and pulled her forward to stand beside him. He kept his free arm around her waist. ''Jane, this is Jacob Ferlin, an old . . . uh, friend of mine. Jake, this is Jane Warner.'' Over the top of Jane's head he glared at Jacob. ''You remember David Warner, don't you, Jake? This is one of his sisters.''

Jacob jerked his hat from his head and brushed back his greasy hair. ''Is that so? Miss Warner, my pleasure. Warner, eh?''

Jane gave Rider a questioning look before her good manners took over. ''Mr. Ferlin, how are you? It's good to meet a friend of Rider's. Have you known each other a long time?''

Jacob winked at Rider. ''Well, we haven't seen other in a coon's age, but, yeah, we've known each other since we were boys growing up right here in Drover.''

''How nice.''

''Miss Warner, you must be new to town. I'm sure I would've remembered a purty gal like you.''

Jane flushed and gave Jacob a slight smile. ''I've only

been here six months. I live on my brother's farm, and seldom get to town."

Jacob nodded. "That would explain it."

"Explain what?" Jane asked, obviously perplexed.

Rider shot Jacob a warning look.

He grinned in return. "Oh, just that we hadn't met before. How is ol' David these days?"

"I'm afraid he isn't around right now, but if he contacts me, I'll be sure to tell him hello for you."

"That won't be necessary," he rushed to say. "I reckon he's got better things to concern him."

Jane opened her mouth to say something, then must have decided against it. Instead she glanced down at Martin, unmoving on the wooden walkway. "Do you know this poor gentleman?"

Jacob shook his head in disgust. "He ain't no gentleman. That's my sorry brother, Martin."

Rider thought the conversation had gone on far too long already. He'd best get Jane away before Jacob said any more and spilled the beans. He took Jane by the arm and swung her around nearly pulling her off her feet. She gasped in surprise, then frowned at Rider.

"Good to see you, Jake, but we've got business to tend to." He walked away pulling Jane alongside him.

"That was rude. Aren't you at least going to say good-bye?" she asked, hurrying her pace and huffing a bit to keep up.

Unwilling to stop, he did slow his steps to accommodate her. "No."

Jacob shouted to their retreating backs. "Be seeing you, Rider. I guess I know where to find you when I need to, and I hope that'll be darn soon." Jacob raised his voice as the distance between them widened. "Nice to meet you, Miss Warner.'' The sound of raucous laughter echoed down the street.

Jane looked over her shoulder and waved. ''I thought you said you were friends.''

''We were. Now where's that damned church?''

Jane jerked on Rider's arm, then dug in her heels, pulling him to a stop before they stepped off the boardwalk and into the street. ''Rider!'' She stared up at him, a look of blatant displeasure on her face. ''What is wrong with you?''

''I'm sorry, Janie. I'll slow down. Just trying to remember where that gol'darned church is.''

''Try Church Street.'' She pointed around the corner. Sure enough, he spotted a church with a tall spire reaching into the bright blue sky. As he recalled, the parsonage was just next door.

He heaved a sigh of relief.

Until he spotted Evie Smith slowly driving a team of oxen and a loaded freight wagon down the road. He pulled Jane around the corner.

Damnation. Rider was beginning to think there was something to this curse.

Nothing is so burdensome as a secret.
—French proverb

Chapter Twelve

Overjoyed to see her friend and confidant, Jane thrust her package at Rider and waved her hands above her head. Tugging on Rider's jacket sleeve, she pointed far down the street. "Look! Evie's home again."

Jane wondered how she would ever capture Evie's notice. Now that Rider's so-called friend was no longer shooting up the town, the streets bustled with foot traffic and wagons alike. Evie, focused on driving down the congested street, seemed oblivious to Jane's frantic attempt to catch her attention.

"Wonderful," Rider muttered. His mouth twisted in a frown. "That woman scares the hell out of me."

"Oh, don't be silly. She's just a bit blunt, is all." The wind caught Jane's scarf and threatened to blow it away. She yanked it free and waved it above her head.

"Yeah, I've felt the blunt end of her shotgun, all right, and I didn't much care for it."

Jane waved her scarf again, her eyes on Evie. Although Rider wasn't anxious to see her again, Jane could scarcely contain her excitement. "She really is harmless."

"About as harmless as scaring up a skunk in the dark of night," Rider said. "And now that I know she's McCampbell Smith's ma, I'm not sure what to make of her."

"Evie!" Jane called.

At last Evie heard Jane and waved back. A wide grin graced her lined features as she guided the oxen team to the side of the road. Dressed in her usual man's attire of trousers, leather vest and high mud-encrusted boots, Evie could easily have been mistaken for a man, thought Jane. That is until she climbed down from the wagon. Much too diminutive for a man, and far too old to be a bull whacker, she certainly drew attention. Not only with her unseemly clothes, but her salty language, lilting Irish brogue and snapping gray eyes.

As soon as she hopped down from her wagon and stepped up onto the boardwalk, Jane hugged her tight. "It's good to see you again, Evie."

"You too, love." When she stepped away from the embrace and eyed Rider, she looked surprised yet pleased, to see him waiting with Jane. Her wise old eyes sparkled with humor. She moseyed over and kissed his cheek. "Why, Rider Magrane, are ye still here in Drover?"

Rider tipped his hat and smiled. "Where else would I be, Mrs. Smith?"

"It's Evie, boyo. I figured you for long gone by now, but mayhap I took ye wrong."

"How's that?" Rider looked offended. "I thought you approved of me."

"Maybe I do and maybe I don't. Can't say fer dead sure. But I kinda figured you for one of those fellers like our Jane's brother, tha' no-good David Warner."

"Is that so." Rider's blue eyes flashed and a muscle twitched angrily in his jaw. "And how would I be like him?"

"All show and no stay, boyo. All show and no stay."

He bristled. "Now, why would you think that?"

"I wonder," she said enigmatically. She turned her back on him and glanced up and down the street. "Now, where are those wee bairns?"

Rider took her by the elbow, leaned down and looked her square in the eye. She spread her legs, folded her arms across her flat bosom and gave him a mocking smile. Completely bewildered by their strange conversation, Jane couldn't help but feel she'd missed something that must have gone on earlier between these two. Perhaps in the barn when Evie thought Rider was stealing from her? Still, she thought Evie liked Rider. She'd even told Jane to marry him.

"I'll have you know," Rider said through gritted teeth. "We were just on our way to speak with the minister about marrying us up."

"And about damn time if I do say so."

Rider gave Jane's package back to her. Throwing up his arms in apparent exasperation, he grumbled. "I give up."

Jane looked at his flushed countenance and decided to keep her own counsel. Rider looked ready to explode. Evie looked like the bird who'd swallowed the canary.

"Jane, I'll meet you later at the church," he said,

pointedly, "after you've conducted your business, and chatted with Miz Smith. I may even stop at the saloon for a few drinks with Jake and Martin."

None too gently, Evie smacked him on the forearm. "Not too many . . . and don't you be late, boyo."

With an expression of pained tolerance, Rider said, "Don't you worry none about me, Evie. I'm never late."

He turned on his heel and headed back the way they'd come. Jane proudly watched him walk away, his back straight, his long legs moving with purpose and grace. He'd stood up to Evie, never letting her get his goat or drive him to say something unkind, even though he'd been sorely tempted.

She turned back to Evie and smiled. "Kind of hard on him, weren't you?"

Evie chuckled. "Nah. Those Magrane boys are made of stern stuff. 'Twill be more than a mere woman to break tha' kind of man.

"Now," she said, tucking Jane's arm in her own. "Where are those wee ones?"

Jane and Evie spent the next hour together. Evie purchased what she called "trousseau" items for Jane, embarrassing Jane with the intimacy of her choices. Jane traded her quilt for a wedding gift for Rider and a few supplies for home. She told Evie about Sukie and Mary Jo's arrival, and how her son, Mack, found Sukie in her bath. They laughed over that, wondering which of the two of them was the more embarrassed.

Deep in conversation, Evie and Jane drew near the mercantile store. The owner, who had been sweeping dirt out onto the street, glanced up at their approach. His brows drew together in a fierce frown. He shook the broom in Jane's direction. His eyes flashed fire and brimstone like a traveling preacher. "Did I see you talking with that good-for-nothing coward, Rider Magrane, Miss Warner?"

Surprised by the vehemence with which he spoke, Jane nodded. She puzzled over his unconcealed hatred of Rider. Recalling that Rider had warned her about people's reactions to seeing him again, she was still taken aback by his thundering rhetoric. Jane turned to Evie to assess her reaction.

Evie stood silent and unmoving, her chin tilted and set in a stubborn line. She brought her fists to her hips and stared at him through narrowed eyes.

"Answer me, young woman!" he bellowed. "That man is evil, pure evil. You would do well to stay away from his kind." Anger blazed in his eyes.

Evil? Jane half expected him to charge her at any moment. She shivered and it had nothing to do with the cold air.

Evie placed her hand on Jane's quaking shoulder and squeezed, then gave her a reassuring smile.

When she turned back to the store owner, her expression had turned to stone. "Gresham Carlisle, have ye never heard the expression about letting sleeping dogs lie." She gave the mercantile proprietor a scornful glare. "He's paid his dues."

"*Hmpff.* An eye for an eye, Evie Smith. In my book, he hasn't paid enough yet. They shoulda stretched his neck for what he did."

"Ach! Ye have the gumption to quote the good book, and in the same breath talk about your own darn book? That's blasphemy, Gresham. The Lord would no' understand."

The man actually flushed, and the fire faded from his

eyes. He turned his back to them and stomped inside. The door slammed shut behind him.

Evie threw her arm around Jane's shoulder. "Jane, love, there's a new general store just around the corner that I hear tell gives a better bargain than Gresham Carlisle could ever give ye. Let's be off."

"Why was he talking about Rider that way, Evie? Surely Rider didn't do anything worth hanging for."

"It makes no nevermind. I believe the poor man is near out of his mind with grief."

"I'm sorry. I didn't know that. His wife?"

"No, love. His child, his only son. But it's been a long time and he shouldn't be carrying around his grief so long. It does no good.

"Jane, love, ye'd best get yourself over to the church. Ye wouldn't want to keep Rider waiting long . . . well, no' too long anyway." She chuckled deviously.

With obvious reluctance Evie said she needed to skedaddle and deliver her freight. They parted after Evie agreed to come for supper with Mack later that evening.

Rider waited for Jane. None too patiently. Like a caged animal, he paced in front of the white clapboard church and parsonage with its white picket fence. Then he reversed direction and began again. With each step his booted feet thudded louder, his heart beat harder. Every ten minutes or so, a hand would part the lacy curtains at the front window of the parsonage and an obscured face would stare outside but no one came out to question him. He wasn't sure how he would answer. "I'm waiting for my darling bride-to-be to make up her mind about marrying me?" How pathetic that sounded.

Between his talk with Evie Smith and his ill-timed

encounter with the Ferlins, it felt as if his unspoken lies were closing in around him, and he'd never accomplish his goal. Panic threatened to crumble the walls he'd so carefully constructed while in the penitentiary. A cold sweat broke out on his brow. He whipped off his hat and wiped away the perspiration from his temple. With each second Jane didn't show, uneasiness skittered along his spine and uncertainty dogged his footsteps.

He was sure that in the time they'd spent together, Evie had talked Jane out of marrying Rider, a good-for-nothing man she didn't love. The old coot probably gave her some cock-and-bull story about waiting for her handsome knight in shining armor to come riding up on his damnable white horse and whisk her away to his damnable castle. A castle in the clouds was all it was. By God, he'd set her straight as soon as she came down the street.

Damnation.

Who did that Evie Smith think she was anyway? Just because she was as old as Methuselah didn't mean she knew everything. She had no business butting into his business.

Jane would marry him, whether she wanted to or not. He could be convincing. He could be persuasive. He could be chivalrous, charming and knight-like. He could be . . .

That's it!

Rider stood dead in his tracks and stared up the street. A woman was coming in his direction. Jane.

With a determined stride, he walked out to meet her. Rider had no intention of waiting for her to deny him.

Her cheeks were chapped and reddened with the cold. Strands of long, brown hair loosened from its braid danced around her eyes and mouth. With her mittened hand she brushed the flyaway curls from her face. She smiled when she glanced up and saw him coming her way.

When Rider reached her, he took her packages and set them on the ground. He removed his Stetson, brushed an unsteady hand through his hair and placed his hat atop her packages. He went down on one knee. He pulled off her mittens and tossed them at their feet. Clasping her hands in his, he slowly brought them up to his lips. He looked into her face as he tenderly kissed her knuckles. Surprised delight softened her features and a slight smile turned up the corners of her mouth.

"Miss Warner, will you do me the honor of becoming my wife?"

Her brows knit together in a bemused frown. "Rider, I thought we already agreed to this."

"I'm trying to be romantic here, Janie. You're not helping."

"Oh," she mumbled. "Sorry."

"The hell with it." He rose, pulled her into his arms and kissed her. Not knight-like either. No chivalrous, heroic, courtly kissing for Rider. He kissed her like he wanted her, which was the way he honestly felt. Hot and wet and urgent. Drawn-out and demanding.

He dug his hands into her hair and pulled it free of its tie. Tangling his hands in her thick silky strands, he tilted her head. He angled his mouth so he could hold her to him, claiming her soft, warm lips. Parrying with his tongue, he drew hers into his mouth and suckled. He slipped his hand down her back and cupped her fanny, pulling her close so she could feel his eager, willing, unchivalrous male body.

"Young man."

Sharp knuckles rapped none too gently on Rider's shoulder. His head snapped up and he stared into a pair of unnerving steel-blue eyes. Bushy white eyebrows rose into a high, rounded forehead demanding his attention. He couldn't mistake the meaning behind the clerical collar or the no-nonsense glare.

The overall effect efficiently cooled Rider's enthusiasm. "We need to be married," he croaked.

"That's quite apparent."

Though her face was a becoming shade of crimson, Jane chuckled. She ducked her head as another giggle escaped her lips. She brought both hands up to her face and gave way to her amusement, bursting out with full-hearted laughter.

Rider hoped like hell she wasn't laughing at his kisses but at the absurdity of the embarrassing situation.

He was not amused. Neither was the minister.

"Do you think you can wait, young man, or should I perform the wedding ceremony now right here on the street?"

Rider choked. "How about tomorrow, say eleven o'clock, at the Warner farm?"

"Will that be soon enough?" He waved his hand toward the church. "We do have a church handy."

Rider's ears burned. He picked up his Stetson and pushed it low on his head. "I think tomorrow will be fine."

"What about you, young lady? Can you keep this young man's ardor cooled until then?"

"I believe so," Jane said with a trace of laughter in her husky voice. She looked up and smiled at Rider, a tender curve of lips rosy and swollen from his kisses. A sensuous spark radiated from her toffee-colored eyes. Her gaze settled on his mouth.

He didn't think a team of oxen could keep his ardor cooled until tomorrow.

"Very well then. Until tomorrow. In the meantime, behave, young people."

Rider picked up her packages and waited until the parson disappeared inside his home. "I can't make any promises to behave."

"I can, and by the way, Rider," she said, laughter brimming in her shining eyes, "I will marry you."

Morning dawned blustery and bitterly cold. Wind rattled the window glass and stirred the curtains. The sky hovered low and gray. A bank of heavy snow-laden clouds loomed on the western horizon. How fitting, Jane thought as she snuggled deeper under the bedcovers. *A perfect day for my wedding.*

She lay in bed, tired and bone-weary. She hadn't slept well the night before, kept awake by a tumble of confused thoughts. All night her mind circled like a lazy hawk, first with thoughts of the boys, then with thoughts of Rider.

Just the idea of facing Rider and her sisters made her want to wriggle beneath the bedcoverings and never come out. Voices echoed down the hall—John Michael's throaty giggle, Rider's deep masculine baritone, all muted by the wind whistling around the house. She smelled bacon frying and coffee brewing. Still she lay abed. Procrastinating.

Was she suffering from pre-wedding jitters or were her concerns real? She wished she knew if she were doing the right thing for the boys. She hated to admit that Sukie might be right. That maybe three women could put the farm to rights.

She snorted in a most unladylike fashion and pulled the covers over her head. Who was she trying to fool? She hadn't even known how to milk a cow before she came to David's farm. Sukie and Mary Jo knew even less than she did about farming. And Jane knew next to nothing.

They would marry—she and Rider, two people who had many things in common except the most important one, love. Jane repeatedly told herself it didn't matter. They had to put the boys' welfare before their own. They did like each other, and that should account for something.

Rider quite obviously desired her. And she desired him. Even now her cheeks heated when she thought of how she felt when his arousal pressed against her while they stood in front of the church yesterday. It seemed a promising beginning for two people to fall in love.

The boys liked him. He had a way about him that could be endearing and charming. He was a hard worker. Yet still an aura of mystery surrounded him. He was a man who kept his private thoughts to himself.

Reluctantly, Jane climbed from bed. The chilled floor seeped right through her woolen socks. Though hesitant about greeting the day and facing her family, she wasted no time washing up and dressing. As she sat on the bed after lacing up her boots, she took a deep, fortifying breath. Straightening her spine, she left her room but not before planting a false smile on her face.

Sukie stood at the stove with a fork in her hand and Jane's apron tied around her waist. She frowned at Jane's late arrival to the breakfast table. Planting her hands on her hips, she said, "You're late. We're already eating. You'll have to fix your own plate."

She's my sister. I love her. Jane counted to ten before replying. "I'm sorry I'm late, but I think I can fix my own plate. I've been doing it for a number of years."

Rider, teasing the boys, looked up and winked. Mary Jo gave her a tentative smile.

Sukie wasn't through. "Lucky for you, Rider got the boys up—"

"You got that wrong, Sukie," he said. "They got me up. These young'uns are early risers."

"Still, Jane should have been up earlier—to get the stove going and wake the boys and—"

"Leave off, Sukie," Jane said, her patience stretched beyond the breaking point. "I'm not in the mood for one of your lectures today."

"Well," Sukie huffed. "Aren't we a ray of sunshine this morning, and on your wedding day, too?"

Like a sore tooth, breakfast went from bad to worse in a hurry. The boys sensed the adults' tumultous emotions and acted out because of them. Teddy burst into tears when Sukie barked at him—for the fourth time—about playing with his biscuit, instead of eating it. Rider scowled at Sukie then snatched both boys out of their seats. He stomped from the room growling to himself about her being as cold as a mother-in-law and equally nasty-natured.

Tears coursed down Mary Jo's cheeks. Jane wanted to weep herself.

And there were still four hours to go until the wedding ceremony.

Sukie, of course, failed to see that she had said anything wrong. "What's he all het up about? Mary Jo, stop that sniveling."

Humming to herself, Sukie went back to clearing up the breakfast dishes as if all were well.

Jane wanted to slap her. The woman had about as much compassion as a fence post. Jane wiped Mary Jo's tears away, and brushing her hair from her face, kissed her forehead. Though she should have been helping Sukie clean up, she walked Mary Jo to the front room and sat her down on the settee. She squatted in front of her and took her sister's chilled hands into her own. "Why are you crying, honey?"

"What's going to happen to us, Jane?" she asked. Her voice squeaked like a frightened mouse. "Are you going to make us leave here when you get married?"

"Of course not." Jane's throat tightened at the dread she heard in Mary Jo's voice. "You'll always have a home with us. You can stay as long as you like. Forever if that's what you want."

"I know we should go back to Kansas City, but I'd rather stay here with you and the boys." She leaned close and whispered, "I like Rider, too, no matter what Sukie says about him. He's always nice to me, just like a real brother."

Tears blinded Jane's eyes and choked her voice. "I'm glad to hear that."

Her voice still quivered as Mary Jo asked, "What about David?"

"What about him?"

"What will happen when he comes home?"

Jane doubted he would ever come home, but she didn't have the heart to tell Mary Jo. "We'll just cross that bridge when we come to it, honey."

"I hope he's happy now."

"Me, too."

Mary Jo brightened. "Maybe he joined the circus."

Jane couldn't hide the surprise in her voice. "The circus? Why would you think that?"

"I always thought it would be fun. I'd like to ride an elephant or one of those fancy white horses. Wouldn't you?"

"That would be nice, I suppose. I never thought about it."

"I have. I used to dream about it sometimes. Maybe he'd be a clown."

"I can't see David as a clown but maybe . . ."

"He used to tell funny jokes and stories before he got married and left home." Mary Jo smiled. "He would be a good clown."

"I'm sure he would, honey." Jane kissed her little sister's cheek then stood and pulled Mary Jo to her feet. Wrapping her arm about her shoulder, she started down the hall. "What say you and me go check out your dresses and see which one you'll be wanting for the wedding. Evie gave me some lovely lace to dress up mine. Maybe we can sew a little on to yours, too. We'll have you looking so pretty, Rider might change his mind and decide to marry you instead."

Mary Jo giggled and hugged Jane, brightening up Jane's spirits more than she thought possible. Now if she could just refrain from strangling Sukie before the day was out, she'd be a happy woman.

Jane stood at her bedroom window dressed only in a fine linen batiste chemise tied with blue satin ribbons and two lace-trimmed, embroidered petticoats, all gifts from

Evie. She stared at the bleak landscape and shivered. With a fingernail, she scratched her new name in the frost. Well, not her new name quite yet, but it would be soon enough. Jane Magrane. It sounded like a child's nursery rhyme. *On the day of her wedding to her beloved swain, Jane Magrane tripped on her train, and her ankle she sprained.*

Jane shook her head, then pulled her best Sunday-go-to-meeting dress, a dark brown wool made when Jane was much younger, over her head. It fit reasonably well, though Jane had been surprised when she discovered it was a bit tight across the bosom. She sewed several rows of Evie's gift of delicate Irish lace across the bosom to disguise the tightness. The fabric also trimmed the collar and cuffs, making the dress seem almost new.

Even after trimming Mary Jo's gown, Jane had enough left over for a short veil. She draped it over her head and held it in place with a silver hair clip.

Buttoning up the dress, Jane stared at herself in the mirror. A face as pale as fresh milk stared back at her. Smudged dark circles beneath her eyes gave proof of her sleeplessness the night before. She pinched her cheeks to give herself a bit of color. She leaned closer to the mirror, placing her hands flat on the dressing table and stared at herself. She bit her lip, shaking her head. This was as good as she was going to look. Plain brown hair, plain brown eyes, plain brown dress. Plain Jane.

"I wish Mama was here today," she told her reflection in the mirror.

"Papa, too," Sukie whispered. Somehow she'd entered the room without Jane's notice. She stood behind Jane, and patted her shoulder. "They would have been proud of you, Jane."

''Do you think so? Do you think they would have liked Rider? I know he doesn't love me but he makes me feel safe. Since he's been here I feel less careworn and not so worried about the boys' future.''

''If that dress is any indication I'd say you're eating better, too. Mama would just be glad you're getting married and not living here alone with that man any longer.''

This was not what Jane needed to hear today. She rolled her eyes. ''Sukie, we're hardly alone.''

Sukie tossed her head and started for the door. ''Still, I wish you happiness.'' She glanced back over her shoulder before she left the room with her last parting rejoinder. ''I doubt you'll get it from him, though.''

Jane groaned and dropped into the rocking chair set against the wall. What did she expect? She turned, just so, to catch the view outside the window and wait for the minister's arrival.

She closed her eyes and tried to let the rhythmic rocking motion soothe her disquieting thoughts.

Jane wondered what Rider, dressing for the wedding in the boys' room, was thinking about. The responsibilities of the farm? His newly acquired family? Or the wedding night?

Could she become pregnant without having her monthlies? Could she even take the chance? She couldn't leave two children plus a newborn in Rider's strong, yet capable, hands.

Yet how could she could keep her attraction hidden when she so wanted Rider to touch her, to kiss her, to hold her. To make love to her.

And she wondered if she could tell him the doctor thought she might be dying. What would he think?

Marry in haste, repent in leisure.
—Nineteenth-century proverb

Chapter Thirteen

Rider thought he must be the most nervous man ever to have taken a bride. His cold hands shook. He yanked on his sleeves, then tried fastening the buttons on the shirt cuffs with stiff fingers. The awkward task took more than a little cussing but he finally completed the deed. Then he attacked the buttons on the white cotton shirt, misaligning them twice before getting it right. Smoothing a trembling hand down the front placket, he heaved a sigh of relief.

For probably the fifth time that morning, he looked at himself in the cracked mirror hanging above the scarred maple bureau in the boys' bedroom. His eyes fell to the new shirt with its neat tiny stitches, the fabric soft and spotless. Jane surprised him with the gift she made herself, calling it a premarriage present. He was oddly touched.

He peered at his face. His dark hair fell across his

perspiring forehead and brushed past his collar. It begged for a trim, but he owned no scissors. He had yet to work up the gumption to ask Jane if he could borrow hers.

Skittish as a green-broke pony, his heart pounded in his chest and sweat broke out on the back of his neck. He tried not to think about the wedding night, but whenever his thoughts turned to Jane it was the first thing that came to mind. Instead he tried to concentrate on what should have been first and foremost in his head—paying off his debt to David Warner.

He hoped the man, wherever he was, would understand what he was about to do. He knew a man might not take kindly to a stranger marrying his sister just to fulfill an obligation and redeem himself. Even to Rider, it seemed a selfish motive, and a feeble reason to marry. He didn't love Jane in the way he thought he should, but he liked her well enough and he sure as hell desired her. Love might come to them with time.

He didn't fancy the idea that he was about to spend the rest of his life as a farmer. But it was the price he was willing to pay.

Jane fretted about the boys and their future, and he hoped this marriage would put her mind to rest. Still, he wondered what she thought of him. She was marrying a stranger, too. At times, she stared at him with eyes that hinted of desire, of longing. The few times he'd kissed her, she participated and seemed to enjoy herself. But maybe that was simple wishful thinking on his part. He didn't know.

He stared hard at his reflection. The man who looked back at Rider from the mirror wasn't the same callow youth who thought rustling cattle was an easy payday.

No, Rider was a changed man. And he hoped to God, he was a better man.

He leaned close to the mirror, running his hand over his clean-shaven jaw. He brushed back his hair with his fingers, and reckoned he was as presentable as he was ever going to be.

He heard the minister's horse and buggy pull up outside. It was time.

There was no music for her wedding, but Jane could hear the wedding march in her head. She'd heard the name of it once at a wedding when she was a young girl—Low and Grim or something like that. A German musical composer, whose name she couldn't recall, wrote it. Played on a real church organ, the music had stirred her fanciful little girl's heart. The lyrical notes gave rise to romantic notions of candy and flowers, and summer evenings sitting with a handsome beau courting her on the porch swing. She'd always been a hopeless romantic as a girl. These days she was more practical and realistic than romantic.

But she didn't need wedding music to know this was her wedding day. Just remembering how handsome her own groom looked sent her heart thumping like a bass drum in a marching band.

When Rider passed by her in the hall on his way to let the minister inside, he grinned. His face, once so gray and lean, had filled out since his arrival. From working outside, a healthy tan graced his rugged features.

Before moving on, he commented in a low voice on how pretty she looked. He smelled clean and woodsy, like the air on a brisk fall day when she walked through the nearby copse of cottonwood trees.

Jane took the opportunity to admire his masculine physique as he walked away with an air of self-confidence. His ebony hair, mussed as usual, gleamed blue-black like a star-filled night sky, and she noted with some amusement, needed trimming. She wondered if he would allow her to cut it for him. She fondly remembered how David hated to sit still so their mother could cut his hair.

Rider filled out his new shirt stretching the seams taut across his broad shoulders. He'd put on weight and now instead of sagging a bit, his black trousers hugged his muscular thighs and the narrow curve of his buttocks. He'd even shined his boots to a high, glossy sheen. Outwardly he seemed calm and quite happy to be getting married.

"Look who's here early, Janie," Rider called out. McCampbell and Evie sauntered in behind the minister. To Rider's and Jane's chagrin, they discovered they didn't even know the minister's name.

"As I recall, the two of you were somewhat occupied when last we met." He held out his hand, smiled blandly and introduced himself. "Reverend Donald Millstone."

Rider clasped his hand and smiled. "Thanks for coming, Reverend."

Evie stuck out her hand. "Howdy-do, Parson. I'm Evie Smith and this is my son, McCampbell."

Reverend Millstone shook Evie's hand somewhat reluctantly and then shook Mack's. Mack, however, had eyes only for Sukie across the room. She blushed at his blatant stare and pretended an interest in the puzzle Teddy and John Michael were putting together. Mary Jo sat on the floor with the children, quietly observing.

Evie and Mack ushered everyone outside to help unload their wagon, filled to overflowing with fat scented candles, gold and silver ribbons, huge dried sunflowers, chairs from home and enough food to feed fifty people. They brought a haunch of cooked beef and two smoked hams, a pot of beans, and three loaves of fresh-baked bread including a pan of corn bread. They also brought half a dozen put-up jars of peaches, a jar of strawberry preserves plus a lovely white-frosted wedding cake. Tears welled in Jane's eyes as she watched the Smiths bring in their gifts of food and decorations, friendship and love.

Evie bussed Jane on the cheek before commanding the household with chores to perform and setting the parlor to her exact specifications for the ceremony. She gave Jane strict instructions to sit down, watch the festivities and enjoy herself. After butting heads with Sukie on where things should go and how they should be done, she instructed Sukie in no uncertain terms to stop fidgeting and help Mack put out the food.

Evie put Teddy to work setting candles on every flat surface in the room, lighting them as he went. Rider pushed the furniture aside and moved every chair in the house to the parlor, lining them up in two rows. Mary Jo tied ribbons and the smaller sunflowers around the chair backs making each one look like a giant Christmas present. Evie placed the rest of the sunflowers, some as high as three feet tall, in the butter churn and in milk pails scattered about the room. With the rest of the ribbon, she tied bows around the flower stalks.

Jane watched Mack and Sukie working in the kitchen setting up the food on the kitchen table. At first, Sukie eyed Mack carefully and moved around the kitchen with caution. She wouldn't get close to Mack. He seemed content, grinning at her like a cat in a creamery. And typical of Sukie, she merely frowned in return. Poor Mr. Smith. It would take more than a smile to thaw out Sukie. More like the sultry late-day heat of an August afternoon. And everyone knew what came after a hot, humid afternoon—wild, wind-tossed, light-up-the-sky thunder-and-lightning storm-filled nights.

When all was done to Evie's satisfaction, she sat down and put Teddy between Mary Jo and Sukie. John Michael, quiet for a change, sat on Evie's lap and McCampbell sat beside Sukie.

It was time to begin. Between yellow heads of sunflowers, a row of candles on the mantle glowed with tiny golden flames. On the windowsills, the parlor tables, even on the kitchen shelves and countertops, what looked like hundreds of candles flickered and shimmered like stars. As if in a fairy tale, Evie changed a dismal gray day into one filled with bright sunlight and transformed the inside of the farmhouse into a magical world fit for a princess's wedding.

Before she went to stand in front of the minister, Jane leaned down and hugged Evie. Tears swam in her eyes as she whispered in Evie's ear, "You've made this house look like a beautiful church. It's wonderful. You're just the best of friends."

" 'Tisn't much, Jane. I figured a gal's weddin' day oughta be special is all." If Jane wasn't mistaken, tears trembled on Evie's eyelids as well.

Reverend Millstone moved to stand with his back to the fireplace hearth. He beckoned Rider and Jane to join him.

On wobbly legs, Jane walked to stand where Rider stood waiting for her. He held out his arm, then clasped

Jane's chilled hand in his as he turned them around to face the minister. For the first time that she could ever recall, his fingers felt as cold as her own. And they trembled ever so slightly, as did hers.

He gently squeezed her fingers and whispered low for her ears only, "We'll do fine, Janie. Don't you worry about a thing."

Reverend Millstone clutched his worn black Bible to his chest. He looked at Rider, then at Jane, his expression serious, his bushy white eyebrows set in a straight line. He cleared his throat and began. "Dearly beloved, we are gathered here to join this man and—"

"Wide," piped up John Michael, "Wide." His voice rose as he repeated the name.

Rider turned around and smiled. He placed his finger to his lips. "Shh, Gopher. We're trying to have a wedding here."

John Michael held out his arms. "Up, up."

Evie tried shushing him but the more she tried, the louder he hollered. He stood on Evie's lap and held his chubby arms out to Rider. He began crying, still calling out Rider's name and repeating, "Up, up!" Before long his voice was loud enough to wake the dead.

Jane moved to get him but Rider shook his head.

He released her hand and leaning over, plucked the child into his capable, strong arms. John Michael slowly quieted. Fat tears clung to his lashes as he sniffled the last of his tears away. He lay his head against Rider's chest, his little fingers clutching Rider's shirtfront. Popping his thumb in his mouth, he closed his eyes and snuggled against Rider.

Cradling the toddler in his left arm, Rider took Jane's hand again. Gone were his chilled and trembling fingers.

His eyes brimmed with tenderness. Oblivious to John Michael wrinkling his new shirt, he winked at Jane then turned to the minister.

A lump formed in her throat as Jane fought tears of joy. Why had she ever doubted this man? How could she have missed it before? Rider loved John Michael as if he were his own son. When he gazed down at the baby's head nestled against the crook of his neck it was there for the entire world to see—the affectionate smile, the gentle, caring eyes. The very look of love. Jane found herself wishing that Rider would, just one time, look at her with that same loving expression on his face.

She turned, half expecting him to read her thoughts. Instead he startled her by saying to the preacher, "Go ahead, sir."

"Would you like to put the child to bed?" the preacher asked in an understanding tone.

Rider shook his head. "No, that's not necessary. I can hold him."

"As you wish."

The preacher continued, but Jane, her mind a haze of wonder and confusion, scarcely heard a word. She couldn't take her eyes off Rider quietly, calmly, holding John Michael in his arm. He looked so natural with his large, work-roughened hand supporting John Michael's little diaper-clad bottom. Rider's intense gaze fixed on the minister, his lips parted, his jaw relaxed. In that moment, a singular crystal-clear reality caught in time, Jane fell in love with Rider Magrane.

The people in the room ceased to exist. The candles stopped flickering, the wind quit blowing. She didn't smell the food waiting on the kitchen table. Time stood still. If she lived to be a hundred years old, she would remember this exact moment for the rest of her life.

Clasping her hand in his, Rider stood next to her with his head erect, his strong face in profile. A sleeping child in his arms.

Suddenly, Jane realized the room was strangely quiet. She glanced around and saw every face in the room, expectant and waiting, some smiling, some frowning. And all centered on her. She looked up at Rider. Amusement flickered in his blue eyes. His lips twitched. He cocked his head and leaned toward her as he mouthed the words *I do.*

Heat rushed to Jane's cheeks. "Oh . . . oh, of course, I will, I do."

Rider's face visibly relaxed. He mouthed the words *thank you,* and leaning down pressed a fluttery, soft-as-a-cloud kiss on her forehead.

Jane heard a hushed heartfelt sigh behind her. Probably Mary Jo, she thought. Another young girl with romantic notions about love and marriage. Jane prayed that Mary Jo could hold on to her precious, childish dreams for a long, long time.

"I now pronounce you man and wife. Mr. Magrane, you may kiss the bride."

Careful not to wake him, Rider handed John Michael to the minister. Although his eyebrows shot up in surprise, he took the babe without comment.

Rider faced Jane and placed his hands on her shoulders. He caught her gaze and disarmed her with a dazzling smile. Lifting the lace veil and laying it back over her head, he bent toward her. He tilted his head and touched his mouth gently to hers. At his tender touch her knees buckled. As his clean, masculine scent assailed her, Jane swayed. Rider's grip on her shoulders tightened. He held her steady. Velvety-soft and sweet tasting, his lips caressed hers, creating a delicious sensation that rushed right down to curl Jane's toes. She opened her mouth and accepted his touch, trying to tell him with her lips how she felt. He seemed to know. Fitting his mouth to hers he deepened the kiss, capturing her heart in the process. She heard Rider groan and then the kiss went on and on until Jane thought she might explode from the unbearable tension building between them.

Scattered applause and shouts of laughter shattered the highly charged, emotional moment.

Rider's head jerked up, his eyes heavy-lidded, his lips parted. His breath rasped in and out of his chest. Like a kid with his hand caught in the cookie jar, he blushed, then grinned. The lobes of his ears and his cheeks turned bright cherry red. If the heat in her own face was any indication, Jane must look much the same.

Evie broke the awkward moment by hooting and hollering and waving a red checkered neckerchief above her head. Mack stomped his feet on the floor and John Michael woke, bellowing like a calf looking for its mama.

Reverend Millstone winced, then handed the bawling child to Rider. When placed in his arms, John Michael quieted but not a minute later began calling for his dinner.

The preacher, quite loudly, cleared his throat. The wedding celebrants hushed, even John Michael stopped caterwauling long enough for the man to speak. With an imperceptible smile on his lined face, he said, "Ladies and gentlemen, may I present to you, Mr. and Mrs. Rider Magrane."

* * *

Rider stood alone, his arms crossed over his chest, and watched the small wedding reception. As he leaned against the wall by one of the broken windows, a draft cooled his neck and kept his mind alert. A week or so ago he'd covered this window and one other with burlap sacking and waxed paper. It was supposed to keep out the cold but it didn't let in any light either. He'd be glad to replace it with the glass he'd traded for in town—one of his wedding presents to his new bride.

Thinking of Jane, he searched the room for her, a diversion he'd found himself doing all afternoon. She stood with her back to him in front of the fireplace speaking with the parson and Evie. The man kept nodding and patting Jane's shoulder with a paternal gesture. He wondered what they were discussing.

Testy and impatient, Rider grumbled to himself. He hadn't spent a minute alone with his bride since their passionate kiss at the altar. Even hours later his blood boiled when he thought of that kiss. When he sought her out to talk to her, she was as nervous as a . . . well, she was as nervous as a new bride. What did he expect? Every time he captured her gaze she'd avert her eyes and blush, then catch her lower lip between her teeth. Which was what he wanted to do. Or play with the top button of her dress. Something else he wanted to do. Or touch her hair. Well, dammit, come to think of it, there wasn't much he didn't want to do with her.

Was three in the afternoon too early to take his new bride to bed? Rider heaved a sigh, half exasperation and half frustration. Even though scandalizing Reverend Millstone was tempting, it wouldn't be too smart. Rider figured the whole town of Drover would know about the wedding soon enough, and then it would only be a matter of time before a lynching party arrived.

Furthermore the parson seemed in no hurry to leave, enjoying himself at this unusual wedding party. He'd filled his plate three times already, all to overflowing. Rider couldn't help but think how badly the boys and Jane needed that food. Only by sheer willpower did he manage to keep from saying something ill-tempered or contemptuous to the self-righteous, gluttonous man.

The afternoon dragged on . . . and on. The assortment of food smelled and looked delicious but it all tasted like sawdust in his mouth. He drank coffee until his nerves sizzled like bacon frying in a skillet, and his hands shook like a palsied old geezer.

Rider could have kissed Evie Smith on the mouth when she offered her home to Jane's sisters for the next two nights. Rider could have even kissed that damnable farmer, Mack Smith who was especially happy to escort Sukie to his home. Rider hoped to remind Smith that he owed him one.

Since Gopher wouldn't go anywhere without Jane or himself, and Teddy refused to leave without Gopher, they would stay home. But right now Rider just wanted the Smiths and the minister to go home, and to take Sukie and Mary Jo with them.

He'd watched Jane closely throughout the day and had yet to see her eat. But if her stomach was tied in knots as his was, he understood the reason why. When she left the minister and Sukie she stopped to speak to Teddy who had his fingers in the wedding cake. She said something to Mary Jo and then looked up, glancing around the room.

Their gazes locked. This time Jane held his stare but her eyes narrowed as she studied him. Rider watched her expression, his longing to bed his wife almost uncontrollable, as she fidgeted with the lace sewn across her bosom. A purely female gesture that sent a clear message to Rider's groin. He uncrossed his arms and linked his thumbs in his belt loops.

At that moment they were the only two people in the room. The air fairly hissed with the sexual tension bouncing between them. Rider didn't care who saw them, he was going to cross the room and kiss his wife . . . again, like he wanted to the first time, and never got the chance to finish.

Rider sauntered toward her with only one thought in his head. Her toffee-colored eyes widened in obvious agitation at his approach. He drank in her every feature slowly, languidly, the same way he wanted to kiss her. In anticipation, he ran his tongue over his lower lip.

"Mr. Magrane, it's time for me to take my leave." Reverend Millstone grabbed Rider's arm, pulled him to an abrupt stop and vigorously pumped his hand.

So intent was Rider on waylaying Jane and kissing her, that without thinking he swung around to knock the man into next week. Out of nowhere, Mack appeared next to Rider. He grabbed his upper arm forcibly holding it down and twisted his other hand behind his back. His eyes warned Rider to control himself. Rider barely managed to mumble, "Huh?"

"Your good friends helped you put on a lovely wedding," the parson continued, unaware of Rider's single-minded preoccupation. "I expect now that you're a married man with a wife and children, I'll be seeing you in church on Sundays from now on. Children need the guiding hand of the Lord."

"Yeah, all right," Rider muttered. He stared at the man in total incomprehension.

"I really must be getting back to town. Mrs. Millstone frets about low ruffians and outlaw types that pass by on these country roads, particularly after dark. Women are such worrisome creatures when it comes to their menfolk. I reckon you know how women are but then, we wouldn't have them any other way, now would we?"

By all that was holy, the man actually winked at Rider. *Winked? What the hell?* Rider found himself blinking in confusion.

He gave Rider a knowing grin. "Well, perhaps you don't know yet but you will from here on out. You're a married man now."

"A what? Oh, yeah, I guess I am . . ."

"Thank you, Reverend Millstone." Jane's calming voice, one of sanity and reason, broke through Rider's distracted thoughts. Mack placed Rider's hand in Jane's. She gripped his fingers, until he relaxed his hold. Then he held on to her hand, grateful for the tender touch.

Good Lord, between Mack and Jane, they'd saved him from spending his wedding night in jail. He almost hit a parson, for God's sake, a servant of the Lord. He remembered wanting to knock the man ass over teakettle, and keep right on going. Rider couldn't believe he'd had such a lapse in judgment, to say nothing about his own sanity.

Thank God for Jane.

She soon walked the parson outside to his waiting buggy and was joined by the Smiths, Mary Jo and Sukie. Rider stood on the steps holding Teddy by the hand. Gopher, after an exciting day, lay sleeping on the settee.

They said their good-byes, and Rider, Jane and Teddy

went inside to put the leftover food away and set the parlor back to rights.

Rider heaved a long sigh. Alone at last. Well, almost alone. Soon the boys would be asleep and Rider would have Jane all to himself for the rest of the night. For the rest of his life.

Jane turned the wick down low on the lantern and set the globe back in place. Bathed in a soft, golden glow, the bedroom shadows wavered ghostlike and eerie. Her heart beating like a tom-tom, she climbed into bed.

Her first time in bed as a married woman, she thought, as she pulled the quilt up to her chin. She lay a moment staring at the ceiling, then folded the quilt down, and placed her arms outside the covers. She tugged at the bodice of her new white satin nightgown. It was a thoughtful gift from Evie, but sinfully provocative. The whisper-soft satin caressed Jane's skin, from her bosom all the way down to her ankles. Two delicate straps held the material together. Three pearl buttons fastened over what little fabric covered her chest. If she moved just the tiniest bit, she thought her breasts would fall completely out of the gown. She jerked the quilt back up to her chin.

She fluffed her goose-down pillow then she fluffed the one on the opposite side of the bed. Where Rider would lay. Beside her. In the bed. In the very narrow bed.

Dear God. She couldn't swallow. A lump of fear and dread stuck in her throat like day-old bread. She couldn't breathe. She couldn't possibly go through with it.

She lay in bed, quaking like a leaf. Lightning flashed in the distance, followed by the faint rumbling of thunder. Maybe God would be merciful. He would strike her with lightning and she wouldn't have to go through with this wedding night.

She was cursed, after all. She gave a hysterical giggle, then covered her mouth.

Would Rider wear his long johns to bed? Or would he wear nothing? Just before the wedding ceremony, Evie explained everything to her. Everything. In detail. In very unladylike detail.

The act of lovemaking sounded messy, and terribly awkward and all too embarrassing but Jane did like Rider's kisses. Very much. She loved Rider even if he didn't love her. Love for her might come to him in time. He was a good man, and she trusted him. Besides, she reminded herself, theirs was a practical marriage, for the sake of the boys.

Maybe she could just refuse to do those other things Evie described, and they could stick to kissing. After all during the wedding ceremony, Rider promised to obey her. In sickness and in health.

Jane was beginning to feel very sick.

His bashful mind hinders his good intent.
—English proverb

Chapter Fourteen

Lightning flared in the night sky, just a brief flicker caught from the corner of Rider's eye. Seconds later thunder rumbled, quiet-like, off in the distance. Then all was still. On his way out of the boys' bedroom, Rider stopped to glance out the window. He hoped it was just rain in the thick cloud cover and not snow. He still needed to replace the glass panes in the windows before it got too damn cold and everyone in the house caught the ague. He tiptoed from the room closing the door behind him.

After much coaxing, and a bribery of peppermint sticks, Rider finally got the boys into bed where they were now sleeping soundly. Jane had escaped to the bedroom thirty minutes ago. Was it too soon to join her? And did he knock on the door of their shared room or just walk in?

It scared him half to death thinking about climbing

into that narrow bed with Jane. In his inadequate, fumbling way, would he make the transition of going from single woman to married woman difficult or embarrassing for her? He knew she didn't love him but he didn't know her expectations.

He swallowed hard. Did most women want or expect an experienced husband? Did Jane? Should they talk for a while first or should he start by kissing her?

Kissing was the easy part. He was experienced at kissing. What red-blooded young buck wasn't? He was also experienced at quite a few other aspects of lovemaking but the simple fact remained he was still physically a virgin. As pure as she was—all right maybe *pure* wasn't the right word but he was pretty green.

After all, he'd been in prison since he was nineteen years old. One of Lansing's steadfast rules was that you couldn't talk with the other inmates, though they found ways around it. Still he didn't get much education about women while locked away either.

Rider stood outside the bedroom door, afraid to enter, afraid not to.

He took a deep breath, released it slowly, screwed up his courage, and pushed open the door. Jane turned her head at the creak of the hinges. She lay in bed, bathed in the inviting glow of a lantern turned down low. She had the covers pulled up to her chin. She stared at him with those lovely chocolate-brown eyes of hers. They were as wide as a doe's, in a face as white as the sheets.

"Hi there."

"Hello," she said in a tremulous whisper.

"You've taken down your hair." God. It sounded like he was accusing her of something terrible. *Good begin-*

ning, Magrane. You really know how to make a woman feel comfortable.

Jane nodded. She visibly swallowed before answering. "Evie told me men like that."

Rider entered the room and shut the door with his heel. He leaned back against the wood watching her. The light played over her features, displaying her fine bones and smooth, satin skin to perfection. He ached just to touch her face. "They do. I do, but if it's all right with you I'd like to do it myself next time."

"If that's what you want."

"I would." He walked across the room and sat on the edge of the bed, his back to Jane. The bed ropes groaned. He felt, rather than saw, Jane flinch. He pulled off his boots, tossing them on the floor where they hit with a resounding thud. He began unbuttoning his shirt and said in as casual a tone as he could muster, "What else did Evie tell you?"

"Quite a lot actually."

"I bed—I mean I bet she did."

"Rider, can I ask you something?"

He looked over his shoulder and caught the agonized expression on her face. He wished he knew what to do to ease her fears. Maybe if he kept her talking, she wouldn't think about later. "Anything."

"Have you ever done this before?"

"What?"

She waved her arm over the bed. "This. With some other woman?"

"Nope," he admitted. "Well, not exactly."

"You haven't?" She sounded flabbergasted. "But you kiss like you . . ."

He chuckled as he tossed his shirt onto the floor. "I

never said I hadn't kissed anyone before.''

He turned to gaze at her. She stared back at him, obviously surprised by his admission.

Rider sat back against the headboard and laced his fingers behind his head. ''When I was seventeen I fell in love. Head over heels, foaming-at-the-mouth, sick in love. With Sara Timmons. She had the prettiest blue eyes and the biggest . . .'' he held out his hands, palms up as he fondly remembered cradling her ripe, young breasts. ''. . . Well, let's just say, she wasn't a small woman.'' He smiled as Jane's lips twitched in amusement. ''And she said she loved me. We snuck away whenever we could—in the loft of the barn, behind the smokehouse, in the apple orchard on her parents' place. We didn't care where; we just wanted to be together.

''And we touched and kissed, sparkin' and spoonin', and generally just getting to know each other. Neither of us knew much about love play but we sure had fun learning. We never did . . . uh, exactly complete the act.'' He glanced at Jane to see if he'd said too much but she gazed back at him with an avid, almost amused, expression on her face. The fear and uncertainty seemed to have dissipated, too.

''We came close, damn close many times, but we were both just scared kids. I was afraid of getting her with a baby and she was afraid of . . .''

Rider's ears burned and his face heated like the inside of a cookstove when he remembered *what* she was afraid of, but he refrained from telling Jane that particular part of his sexual introduction.

Rider shrugged his shoulders. ''Well, anyway, that's all there was to it.''

"What happened to her?"

Rider snorted, shaking his head. "She took what she learned, and up and ran off to marry some rich drummer fella from St. Louis."

Jane looked at him with concern in her eyes. "Did she break your heart?"

"I thought so at the time."

"Now what do you think?"

He grinned. "I think I just enjoyed what we were doing together."

"Did your family ever find out?"

"Chance did. He caught us in the barn once."

"Your brother?"

"Yup."

Jane leaned forward, her eyes questioning. "What did he do?"

"Nothing at the time. Later he took me aside and said that if Sara came up in a family way, I'd better make an honest woman of her or he'd toss me into the outhouse headfirst."

Jane laughed. She pulled her knees up to her chin and wrapped her arms around them. "Thank you for telling me, Rider. I know you were just trying to make me feel more comfortable."

"No, ma'am, that's the God's honest truth." He stared at her sparkling eyes and couldn't keep from touching her hair any longer. He pulled a thick strand of it through his fingers. The silky threads caught on his calloused fingers and curled around his thumb. "By the time she ran off, she was one enlightened lady but still a virgin. I expect that drummer was quite pleasantly surprised, though, by all the things Sara already knew and showed him on their wedding night."

Sara could kiss like nobody's business and even now, all these years later, the thought brought a grin to Rider's face.

He gently tugged on Jane's hair bringing her head around to face him. He kissed the tip of her nose, then released her hair. "So, are you feeling more comfortable with me now?"

"Yes," she whispered.

"Good but there's still something else you should know, Janie."

"What's that?" Her voice sounded low and expectant. Her breath whispered against his heated face.

"I'm cursed."

"What?" She bolted upright. The sheet and quilt fell from her chest to her waist displaying firm, ripe breasts barely covered within the confines of a thin scrap of white satin. Rider's hands itched to hold their weight in his palms.

"Yeah," he said, his voice growing thick with lusty anticipation. He tried to recall the nature of their conversation. For a moment it eluded him, but then he remembered he was trying to make Jane feel at ease, not seduce her. "The doc in town who splinted my arm said I was cursed just like he said you were."

"I don't believe it," Jane said. With an irritated flick of her wrist, she brushed her hair off one shoulder exposing a satin-covered breast. Beneath the thin material, the nipple contrasted darkly against the white of the fabric. It pebbled as cold air caressed her skin. She didn't notice but Rider sure as heck did. His blood, from the top of his head to the soles of his feet, surged through his body with excitement.

Jane's mouth tightened with displeasure. "What else did that fool doctor have to say?"

"He, uh . . ." Rider cleared his throat. "He said there were several cases around Drover."

"Several, huh? I just knew that man was a quack. I shouldn't have believed a word he told me."

Apparently feeling chilled, Jane pulled the covers back up to her shoulders.

Rider released a breath he didn't even realize he'd been holding. Jane gave him a quizzical stare. He tried to smile. It probably looked more like a grimace since his back teeth were clenched as tight as Aunt Tildy's corset strings.

"Are you feeling all right?" she asked.

"Right as rain," he lied.

"He told me I was dying," she said in a matter-of-fact tone.

Rider sat up straighter and stared at Jane. All thoughts disappeared except that one seemingly simple, yet wholly complicated, statement. Acid churned in his stomach, as his heart flip-flopped like a fish out of water. "He what?"

"He said I was dying."

"What a crock. Why would he say something like that?"

"I don't know how to tell you without mortifying myself and you at the same time."

"Janie, you can't believe a thing that man says. He spouts nonsense like a fountain."

"There's more that you don't know."

Rider had no intention of clearing the air with *all* of his past history and surprisingly, he didn't feel the need to know Jane's either. "All I need to know about you I know already. If there's something that's embarrassing, forget about it, and tell me later when you're more comfortable with our situation or don't tell me at all. I don't care. It doesn't matter."

"I know it sounds childish but thank you for saying that."

"Forget it. But now I have a question for you, Janie. It's gonna sound forward and I don't know how to put it polite-like so I'll just ask it straight out. Are you expecting me to make love to you tonight?"

She sucked in a quick breath but said in a steady voice, "Evie told me you would want to."

"Forget Evie. Do you want to?"

She nodded. "Rider, I do, but I'm afraid of something."

Rider eased his arm around her shoulders. "What is it?" he whispered. "Maybe I can help you put those fears to rest."

"If the doctor is right and I'm dying—"

"You're not dying."

"No, let me finish. What if we do this and I get pregnant and have a baby and then I die. What would you do?"

"You're not gonna die."

"But what if I did?"

"Then I'd love that baby, just like I do Gopher and Teddy, and I'd go on without you. Not easily but I'd carry on with the plan we agreed to." He stared at her beloved face etched with worry for *him.* A man she hardly knew. He didn't deserve her concern. He was an outlaw, a jailbird, a liar with little to offer and nothing to recommend him. *A man she didn't love.*

He smoothed away the frown lines on her forehead.

"But it would be real hard without you standing by my side."

"Rider." She threw her arms around his neck and hugged him. "That's so kind of you to say."

"It's the truth." He surprised himself by admitting it aloud. It was the truth. He cared for her far more than he'd realized. He'd be lying if he said he was going through with this charade only to repay his debt to David Warner. It hit him like a slap in the face. He inhaled her musky female scent and snuggled his nose against her throat. God, she felt wonderful in his arms and smelled sweeter than a peppermint stick. He smoothed his palms up the outside of her ribs feeling each bone beneath the satin of her gown.

Surprising him, she struggled out of his embrace. He released his hold and stared at her. She rolled onto her stomach, reached beneath the bed and pulled out a newspaper-wrapped bundle. "I have a wedding present for you."

"You do?"

"Unwrap it," she told him, a pleased look on her face.

He tore the paper and string away to find a finely tooled, leather rifle scabbard. He grinned. It was a thoughtful gift, but a tad too late to be useful.

"I thought once your arm healed you'd be riding out to go hunting and would need a place on your saddle to store your rifle."

Rider couldn't help himself. He stared at her hopeful expression, then burst out laughing. The bed ropes groaned as he shook with the force of his laughter. Tears of mirth streamed down his face. As he wiped them away, he glanced at Jane and saw her trembling chin, the hurt expression on her face. He immediately felt contrite. He tried to take her in his arms but she scooted away from him.

Her voice broke as she asked, "You don't like it, do you?"

He held out his arms, palms up. "I'm sorry, Janie darlin', that's not it at all. It's just that to get you a wedding gift I traded in my saddle. If I go hunting, it will be bare-backed."

"Oh."

"I hope you didn't trade anything too valuable for the scabbard."

"Only a quilt I made."

He chuckled. Taking her chilled hands into his, he stared at her brokenhearted face. Tears glittered on the tips of her lashes and shimmered in the corners of her eyes. "We sure as heck made a hash of this all the way around. I trade my saddle for window glass to keep the house warm. You trade a good, warm quilt for a scabbard for a saddle I no longer own. We're a pair, aren't we?"

She gave him a weak, watery smile. "At least we have the window glass. We can certainly use that."

"I know it's not the most romantic of gifts, but it's practical."

"Yes, it's practical."

He couldn't bear the crestfallen expression on her face another minute. He lifted his butt and wriggled his fingers into the front pocket of his trousers. Pulling out a small package tied with string and wrapped in brown paper, he handed it to Jane. "I think this is a more appropriate present for my new bride."

Her eyes brightened as lightning flashed outside immediately followed by a crash of thunder. She started, and glanced out the window at the darkness. She clasped the package tight in her hands. "The storm's getting closer."

"Sure is," he agreed as he watched her slim fingers play with the lopsided bow.

She turned the gift first one way and then the other as if admiring the plain package. She seemed reluctant to open it. Lifting her head, she beamed at Rider. "Thank you."

He smiled in return. "You don't even know what it is."

"It doesn't matter. It was a thoughtful thing to do."

Heat washed up his neck at the unexpected compliment. He couldn't ever recall a woman smiling at him for such a simple thing. "Come on, just open it."

With hesitant fingers, she untied the string, then tore away the paper wrapping. She stared openmouthed at the small, intricately carved mahogany box lying in the palm of her hand. "Why, it's lovely, Rider," she whispered.

"Open it up."

Her lips parted in surprise. "There's more?" She unhooked the latch, lifted the lid and stared inside at the red velvet lining and the necklace lying within its folds.

Rider held his breath.

She gasped when she lifted the gold chain out of the box. She leaned over on her elbow and held it up near the lantern where she could better inspect it. The links twinkled and danced as it dangled from her fingertips. A small rose of carved ivory swayed from the end of the chain. Perfectly formed petals shimmered in the light as if tiny droplets of morning dew clung to their delicate contours.

"Let me put it on you," Rider said.

Jane turned her back and with shaking hands lifted her hair out of the way. She handed the necklace to Rider. He unclasped the chain and draped it around her neck. With clumsy fingers, he fumbled with the clasp until he finally fastened it. He touched the back of her neck and the underside of her hair with his fingertips sending a shiver up Jane's spine. He gave a light chuckle, then kissed the nape of her neck before saying, "Let me see."

Jane twisted around to face Rider. She looked down at the beautiful pendant lying between her exposed breasts. The delicate rose caressed the fullness that peeked above the satin fabric of her nightgown.

"Sweet Jesus," Rider murmured.

Jane watched Rider's chest heave as if he struggled to breathe. His breath faltered when he slid his hands slowly up Jane's ribs until he cupped their fullness in the palm of each hand. His thumbs met in the middle and lifted the pendant away from her heated skin as he caressed her breast.

Then he looked up at her. "Do you like the necklace?" he asked in a hoarse, unsteady whisper.

"It's lovely," she answered, her own voice thick with emotion. "It's a wonderful present. Thank you, Rider."

He made a satisfied sound deep in his throat. "Thank *you,* Janie. You've given me a gift I will always cherish and even when I'm old and gray, I will never forget."

She had no idea what he was talking about. "What gift? The rifle scabbard?"

"No. This. You, the boys, the farm. All of it is a gift from heaven."

His eyes darkened to sapphire as he lowered his lids. He leaned forward, pressing hot, wet kisses that seared the valley between Jane's breasts. The hair along her arms prickled as her heart tripped inside her heaving chest. Still cupping her breasts Rider brushed his thumbs across the nipples with faint feather strokes. They hardened and ached, sending a shaft of yearning heat low in her abdomen. She lay her head against his temple and thrust her fingers through the thick dark hair on each side of his head. He whispered her name.

Jane's senses sharpened. She became acutely attuned to Rider's touch, tender yet urgent. The feel of his calloused fingers against her breasts. His darting tongue, sleek and wet, lapping at her skin. The sound of his labored breath as it rasped in and out of his parted lips. The squeak of the bed ropes every time one of them stirred. The shimmering lantern light. The lightning flashing, the thunder rumbling and moving ever closer.

"I want to touch you," he mumbled against her throat. "And kiss you everywhere."

"I want that, too," she admitted, surprising herself.

He chuckled deep in his throat. "Good thing." His lips slid up her throat, dropping honeyed kisses, and nibbling along her collarbone and the underside of her chin and jaw. Tasting her an inch at a time. Little humming noises emanated from his throat as he made his way up her face, planting barely-there kisses on her nose, her eyebrows and closed eyelids.

He slipped the straps of her gown off her shoulders, and pushed the fabric aside, baring her breasts to the cool air. Silently, he stared at her a long tension-filled moment. She heard him swallow. Then he folded his arms around her and crushed her against his chest. Her heated skin against his heated skin. An unbearably sweet, delicious sensation that stole the breath from her lungs.

"I think you're bewitching me, Janie," he whispered.

"Should I turn down the lantern?"

"No, no," he murmured, his voice sounding as gritty as sandpaper. "I want to see your sweet face when I enter . . . oh, hell, just leave it be, Janie darlin'. Just leave it be."

He covered her mouth with his, his lips slanting across hers. First teasing with his tenacious tongue, then sucking her lower lip inside his mouth.

He captivated her with his mouth, his lips warm and soft, first demanding, then yielding. Her senses filled with the love she felt for him, the desire to be as close as two people could. She was scared and excited, exhilarated and profoundly touched.

When Rider kissed her before it had been wondrous and magical, but this time with her bare breasts crushed against his naked skin, it was so much more. She felt his heart thumping, or was it hers? They were so close she couldn't tell his pounding heart from her own.

Jane flung her arms around Rider's neck. With trembling fingers, she stroked the taut muscles, the hard sinew and straining tendons. She ran her fingertips slowly down his back, loving the feel of him—hard muscles and soft, warm skin. When her hands reached his long johns she felt two indentations. She ran her fingers just inside the loose waist. His silken skin shivered in response to her tentative touch.

Lifting his lips from hers, he murmured, "Don't stop there, darlin'."

"Wh-what?"

"Do you want me to take off my trousers now?"

"No. Yes."

With a slight smile on his lips, Rider cocked his head to the side waiting for her response.

"I guess so."

He rolled off the bed and stood with his back to her and dropped his trousers. He turned, still dressed in the lower half of his long johns. They drooped low on his hipbones. He towered before her, strong and lean, yet hesitant as though he waited for an invitation to her bed.

Lightning lit up the room, illuminating his powerful presence. In those few seconds she allowed her eyes to rove over him, savoring his masculinity, aching for the return of his touch. She held out her arms to him.

Rider smiled before joining her on the bed. He pulled her into his embrace, his lips moving over her shoulder, down her arm. He pressed a velvety kiss to the inside of her elbow and on the tender pulse point of her wrist. Gooseflesh popped up along her skin and skittered down her back. He chuckled deep in his throat.

He slid his hand down to the small of her back, then cupped her bottom and pulled her close to his heated body. Through the thin cotton of his drawers, she felt the throbbing evidence of his desire thrusting against her quivering stomach. Boldly Jane copied his movement by clasping her hand to his buttocks and squeezing. He groaned and cradled her next to his chest. His cool dark hair slid across her cheek as his lips claimed hers in a searing, demanding kiss.

A bolt of lightning flashed across the sky, lighting up

the room. Thunder boomed, shaking the house like it was made of straw, instead of heavy timbers. The wind whistled up the chimney, and rattled the windows and doors.

"Jane!" Teddy called down the hall in a frightened voice. "Rider!"

Rider lifted his head, panting, his eyes heavy-lidded, his lips parted. "What the hell?"

John Michael wailed, crying out, "Wide!"

He jumped out of bed so quickly Jane nearly bounced out the other side. He hitched up his long johns where the erect evidence of his arousal pushed against the straining fabric. He tripped over his trousers and nearly sprawled headfirst onto the floor. Murmuring a rather descriptive obscenity, he stumbled over one boot, then kicked the other aside. He reached for the doorknob, grumbling beneath his breath.

"I'll be right back," he muttered in a voice Jane hardly recognized—raspy and breathless.

Nervous laughter worked its way up Jane's throat. She bit her lip to keep from giggling aloud. For a man who was generally cheerful and optimistic, Rider sounded downright glum.

Jane was certain that this was a wedding night she would never forget. If she knew the boys and their fear of thunderstorms, she was just as certain this was a wedding night her new husband would never forget either.

Children should be seen, and not heard.
—Nineteenth-century proverb

Chapter Fifteen

As far as Rider was concerned four people to a bed were two too many.

He glanced at Jane, innocent and peaceful, tucked beneath the quilt, sleeping on the far side of the mattress. Her long, brown hair lay loose around her head, tumbled and tangled, as if she'd spent the night in rousing love play.

He wished.

Rider sighed, then gazed down at Teddy lying snuggled up against his belly like a baby possum. Gopher sprawled on Rider's pillow, one arm wrapped around Rider's neck, leaving him no room to put his own thick skull but flat on the bed. A headache the size of a watermelon banged inside his throbbing head. He flung an arm across his eyes to block out the sunlight streaming through the window.

Of course, now that the thunderstorm was gone, all

was silent. It passed through Drover as quick as a flea hopping onto a dog. But not quick enough for Rider. Not before ruining his long-anticipated first night of wedded bliss.

And what a wedding night it was.

By the time he fetched the boys from their room, they were both hollering loud enough to bring down the house. Gopher picked up on Teddy's fear and wailed like a banshee every time it thundered. Teddy quivered like a motherless calf and hid beneath the covers.

Rider knew his night was really over when after returning with the boys, he noticed Jane had changed from her provocative satin nightgown to a practical, prudent flannel one. One that covered her silky skin from neck to ankle.

Rider sighed again.

He lifted Gopher's arm from around his neck, and placed it beside him beneath the quilt. He climbed from the bed, dressed quickly and quietly, and trudged to the kitchen to get the woodstove going and the coffee brewing. This morning he needed strong, hot coffee. Several cups.

He had just tossed kindling in the stove and re-lit the fire when he heard a pounding on the front door. Irritated by the intrusion, he yanked it open.

On the porch stood Jacob and Martin Ferlin, looking somewhat less than hale and hearty, with bloodshot eyes, a two-day-old growth of whiskers on their chins and dressed in stained, foul-smelling clothes. They were obviously hungover and in need of serious bathing.

Despite their appearance, Jake grinned and Martin shot Rider a bleary-eyed smile. Rider wondered if Martin knew who clocked him when he chased that gal from the saloon the day before yesterday. On second thought, he doubted Martin even remembered the day before yesterday.

Rider looked beyond their shoulders to where they had hobbled their horses in a copse of cottonwood trees, quite a distance from the house. That explained why Rider hadn't heard their arrival.

He stepped outside and pulled the door shut behind him.

"Ain't you going to invite us in?" Jacob asked.

"I don't much care how you found me, I just want you out of here," Rider tossed back.

"How was the weddin'?"

Damnation. Small towns.

How long would it be before someone told Jane exactly whom she'd married? He should have confessed the truth about himself before she agreed to marry him. Certainly, before the wedding. He'd tried, but the time never seemed right. Well, it was too late now.

Rider stepped off the porch, hoping to lead the boys away from the house. "What d'you want, Jake? Everyone is asleep and I'd just as soon keep it that way."

Martin stepped in beside Rider.

With obvious reluctance, Jake followed. "You are just plumb ant-i-social these days, Magrane. And here we got a fine proposition for you."

"What?"

"You know that Smith fella down the road?"

"Sure."

"He's got a healthy herd of cattle." Jake's eyebrows lifted suggestively. "A whole piss-load of fine fat cows just waiting to go to market. I figure if we help ourselves, he won't miss a few head."

Rider gestured to the cottonwood where they'd tethered their horses. "You boys asking to get it in the neck?"

Jake planted his fists on his hips. "I reckon we're shrewd fellas nowadays. We won't get caught. This time I got me a first-rate plan."

They all thought they had a first-rate plan the last time. Rider glanced at Martin, who averted his gaze. Then he came back to Jacob, the older, and Rider had thought, the smarter of the two. "Have you forgotten your years up in Lansing?"

Martin removed his flea-bitten hat and scratched his head. He lowered his chin to his chest and shuffled his boots like a schoolboy caught cheating.

Jake cleared his throat. "We ain't forgettin', and we won't be repeating our mistakes, will we, Marty?"

Martin stood mute, staring down at his feet.

"Forget it, Jake," Rider said. "It's not worth it."

"We're gonna do it whether you're in or not."

"When?"

"Tonight."

Rider clapped a hand on Jake's elbow and steered him to the corner of the porch. "Jake, I mean it. Don't do this. You'll get caught."

Jake shook off Rider's grip. "Not this time."

"Come on, Jacob. Smith is savvy and so's his ma. They'll put two and two together and come up with you. You and Martin will be in leg irons before you have a chance to spend a dime."

"Hell, Rider, I figured you for better."

"Sorry, but I got a wife and family to think about now. Besides that I don't have a hankerin' to go back to that hellhole. Haven't got fond memories of the place. Do you?''

''Hell, no! But I'm telling you, this time will be different.''

Rider shook his head, and shot a glance at Martin. He merely shrugged his shoulders. ''Isn't there anything I can say to talk you two out of this foolishness?''

Jacob shook his head. ''Nope. We need us a grubstake so we can start out fresh.''

Rider shook his head again and blew out a long breath. ''You ever heard of working for a living?''

Jacob snorted in derision. ''Why waste time workin' when we can just help ourselves?''

''Damnation.'' Rider ran his hands through his hair. ''Did anyone see you come out this way?''

''Didn't check our back trail,'' Jacob said. He glanced over his shoulder, then looked toward Martin. ''You?''

''Nah, I didn't think to look either.''

''You idiot.'' Rider couldn't believe he'd ever trusted these two.

At one time they'd been the best of friends. Rider seemed to be the only one to have learned his lesson—the hard way—from their stint in the Lansing Penitentiary. ''I don't have a hankering to be tossed back inside. If cattle are rustled, I'll be the first one the new sheriff comes gunnin' for. You two will be second.''

''You sound like an old woman. Marty and I have a plan that won't incriminate you.''

Incriminate? Rider winced, rubbing his aching head. ''Only by association.''

''What the hell does that mean?''

Rider grabbed Jacob by the scruff of his collar and

yanked him forward. "It means that if you're guilty, I'm guilty. Just because I know you."

Jacob shook off Rider's grip. He straightened out his frayed shirt collar and smoothed his hand down the front of his dingy coat. He grinned, not the least bit concerned about Rider's anger.

Jacob knew Rider all too well. Rider was quick to anger but it didn't last and he never resorted to violence. It simply wasn't in him and Jacob knew it.

"Then you might as well join us. Tonight at midnight. We'll be waiting for you where the rail line crosses over the Drover Road out by the old Sawyer place."

"How fitting," Rider said, unable to keep the sarcasm from his voice. "That's where it started going bad five years ago."

"Yeah. I'm just a sentimental old fool, ain't I?"

"You got part of that right, Jake. You're a fool. A damned fool who'll never live to be old."

"Now, Rider, no need to be calling me names." Jacob vaulted onto his horse. He grinned as he looked down at Rider. "We'll be seeing you soon, I reckon. You could start a nice little nest egg for your new sweetheart with your take."

"She could watch me hang from the nearest tree, too."

Rider took Martin by the arm and swung him around to face him. "You don't have to go along with this, Marty. You don't owe Jake a thing."

"Yeah, I do," Martin insisted. "He's my brother." He trudged over to his horse. He looked back once, a forlorn expression on his tired, dirty face. He waved to Rider, then mounted and rode off after Jacob.

Disheartened, Rider watched them as they disappeared from sight. He had to try and stop them.

Something poked Teddy in the middle of his back. He yawned, then rubbed the sleep from his eyes. When he opened them he saw Jane asleep beside him. He rolled over to see whether it was Rider or Gopher who was pushing against him. Rider wasn't in bed anymore but Gopher was curled up like a kitten on top of Rider's pillow with his feet pressed up against Teddy's back. Teddy hoped Rider was out milking Emmett; though it was his chore, he disliked going out to the barn once it got chilly outside. His fingers stung from the cold and poor ole Emmett balked when he tried to place those cold fingers on her udder. He guessed he couldn't blame her.

He was glad the storm was gone, though. He hated being a scaredy-cat, but when the thunder was so loud it shook the house and the lightning so bright it lit the room up like a hundred lanterns, he just couldn't help feeling afraid. He missed his mama and papa during thunderstorms.

He heard several voices, men's deep voices, coming from the front of the house. Rider must be one of them, but he couldn't figure out who would be calling at the farm. Except for Evie and Mr. Smith, they seldom had visitors and never this early in the morning.

He crawled out of bed carefully so as not to wake Jane or Gopher. He tiptoed down the hall to the kitchen. There he dragged a chair from the kitchen table up to a window to see if he could see anything. He climbed onto the chair and sat up on his knees. Finding a small crack between the sheets of yellowing newspaper, he leaned his arms on the sill and squinted through the opening.

Rider stood in the yard with two men Teddy had never seen before. Plumes of white billowed from their mouths as they spoke, but Teddy couldn't make out the words. The men wore dirty clothes and were kind of scary-looking. One of them talked loud and had a cross look on his face. The other just stood there stiff as a scare-crow like he wasn't even listening. He thought Jane would say they looked like ruffians or maybe even out-laws. Men that Teddy was supposed to steer clear of because they were bad influences. Teddy didn't know what influences were but these two looked like men he wouldn't want to have any truck with anyhow.

As Teddy watched, straining to hear their conversation, Rider's voice rose. He grabbed one of the men's arms. His other hand fisted at his side as if he might hit him. Alarmed, Teddy jumped up to stand on the seat of the chair. He stuck his eye right up next to the crack. He had never seen Rider that way—so angry his face turned red. It frightened Teddy a little bit. Maybe Rider needed his help. Teddy stared out, trying to decide if he should fetch the shotgun for him. Before he could make up his mind, the two men mounted their horses and rode off toward town.

"What's so interesting this morning, Teddy?" Jane hitched John Michael to her other hip and stared over Teddy's shoulder at the newsprint. "You reading the paper?"

Teddy jumped, and a guilty look crossed his features. "Nah."

Jane knew that expression. Caught in the act. She just couldn't figure out what he'd been doing that he shouldn't have. He didn't read well, and didn't like it much when she tried to teach him his ABC's. He certainly wouldn't be reading on his own.

Jane leaned forward. There was a small space between the pages of newsprint where they didn't quite meet. She glimpsed Rider standing outside, his hands on his hips, his back to the window. He seemed to be staring up Drover Road at something, but maybe he was simply lost in thought.

"You haven't been spying on Rider now, have you?"

"No."

"Ted-dy."

"Well, maybe a little bit but, honest, I didn't see nothing."

"Anything," Jane corrected. She knew he was lying because he refused to meet her gaze. Oh, well. If she knew Teddy at all, he'd give himself away sooner or later. Thank goodness, the boy wasn't a good liar.

John Michael reached out and grabbed a hank of Teddy's hair, and gave it a good, hard shake. Giggling, he refused to relinquish his hold. "Teddy hair."

"Ow," hollered Teddy. Tears formed in the corners of his eyes as he batted at John Michael's hand.

"Yes, that's Teddy's hair." Jane pried John Michael's pudgy fingers off. "Let go and we'll have breakfast. How does that sound?"

He immediately released his hold. "Eat bi'cuit."

"Yes, darling, we'll have biscuits."

"Bacon."

The child was single-minded in his quest for food. "Yes, dear, we'll have bacon, too. Teddy, have you milked Emmett yet?"

"No," he grumbled. He climbed down off the chair and scooted it back to its place at the kitchen table.

"I hope you don't expect Rider to take over your chores for you now that we're married."

Jane had her answer when he didn't reply. "Go get dressed. By the time you get back from the barn, breakfast will be ready."

In a blast of cold air, Rider stepped into the kitchen, his face red, his features pinched. He kicked the door shut with such ferocity that both boys jumped. He started when he saw them, then relaxed. As they stared at him without speaking, he mumbled, "Sorry." He plopped down at the kitchen table and turned to look at Jane.

Still holding John Michael, she stared at her new husband. Teddy, standing by her side, gaped, wide-eyed, in silence.

Jane couldn't believe the sour expression on Rider's face. Teddy took one look at the dark eyebrows slanted in a frown, the narrowed eyes and clamped jaw, and tore off down the hall. Jane felt like following him.

Before she'd seen him this morning, she half expected Rider to tease her about last night but he didn't say a word. In fact, he looked mad enough to chew nails and spit out tacks.

"What's wrong?"

"Nothing," he barked. He seemed to realize how harsh his tone sounded. He glanced at Jane with a sheepish, apologetic look on his face. "Nothing," he repeated in a softer voice. "I just have a few things on my mind."

"About last night?"

"No, Janie, not about last night."

"I'm sorry about what happened."

"You mean what didn't happen." He gazed at her with a wry smile. "So am I."

"We'll have other nights," she said.

"You bet. And mornings and afternoons, too."

Jane turned her back, smiling, although she felt a blush steal into her cheeks. She deposited John Michael into his high chair and went about making breakfast. As if allowing for her embarrassment and his sharp tone earlier, Rider turned his attention to entertaining John Michael.

"Janie," Rider said, his voice low, her name a mere whisper on his lips as the door creaked open and he stepped into the bedroom. Jane turned, just as she was about to take down her hair. He closed the door and came around the bed. Tossing his hat on the bedpost, he sat down beside her. Rider clasped her jaw, tipped up her chin and stared into her face. "It's been a helluva long day and what seems a lifetime since I've properly kissed you. Will you let me do that now?"

"Yes," she whispered. Anticipation stirred inside of her like a tiny flame building toward a fiery blaze.

Smiling, Rider lifted Jane's arms and wrapped them around his shoulders. Her fingers automatically curled into the silken hair at the nape of his neck.

He placed his mouth on her cool lips and her eyes drifted shut. The moment their lips met Jane dissolved in a riot of dizzying scent and sound and feel; the puzzling texture of Rider's skin, the crisp black hair on his chest, the subtle warmth of his body pressed close to her own. She was acutely conscious of the steady rise and fall of his chest. The wind whispered through the eaves, and in the front room a log fell and crumbled in the fireplace. The kiss went on a long while, and Jane found nothing proper about this kiss.

She relished Rider's every touch and kiss, always

tender but never tentative, a promise, a challenge, but never demanding. His mouth melted against hers, softly sweet and agonizingly sensitive. His tongue probed, beckoning her to follow his lead. She willingly followed.

Jane felt his large, calloused hand on her leg, her knee, wandering, exploring. He pushed her nightgown up and ran his hand along the inside of her bare thigh. A tingling sensation thrummed through her blood. When his palm caressed the curls that covered her womanly part, she started. He paused, as if waiting for her to deny him. When she didn't his hand moved upward over her tummy and navel. She was surprised to feel his hand tremble where it touched her. She shivered with expectation, trusting in the light brush of his fingers, waiting, wanting for more.

His breath gave a slight hitch as he raised his head and asked in a husky voice. "Can I take your hair down now, Janie?"

Jane nodded, unable to find her own voice.

He pulled the pins out and plied both his hands through the braid. Pulling the strands loose, he tangled his fingers in its length. "You've got the prettiest hair, Janie." She could hear the smile in his voice.

"What? Why, it's just plain old brown." She turned to see his face, to see if he was making fun of her.

The taut lines bracketing his mouth relaxed into a grin. "It's true, Janie. Smooth and shiny as molasses, and it smells like. . . " He trailed off as he pushed his nose into his palms where he loosely held her tresses. As he inhaled, he murmured, "like taffy."

Jane choked, then managed a bark of laughter. "Taffy?"

"I really do like taffy," he admitted. In the lamplight,

all she could see above his cupped hands were his blue eyes. They sparkled like dew on the petal of a pansy as he watched her.

"And soft, your hair is soft and silky and cool to the touch. Ah, Janie, you've made me a very happy man."

Without thinking, she said, "But we haven't done anything yet."

Rider chuckled, and his eyes danced with merriment.

Jane realized how forward she must have sounded. She bit her lip as he captured her gaze. "That didn't come out quite the way I meant it."

"I know," he said as if to reassure her.

With gentle hands he finger-combed her hair back over one shoulder. "By marrying me, Janie, you've given me a future. Something to look forward to every single day for the rest of my life. I will always be beholden to you for that, and I promise to never take it for granted."

Sometimes this man purely mystified her.

"And by the way, thanks for wearing this here night thing again." He winked at Jane, then his lips curved in a devilish smile. "You look good enough to eat. Kind of like taffy."

He removed her nightgown and tossed it on the floor. His own shirt and boots followed. He pulled her down on the bed where they lay side by side, face to face, their breath mingling, their hands and lips exploring. She licked his chest; he tasted her flesh. His mouth played over hers lightly, and then their lips became as one. He picked up her hand and held it to the warm skin of his bare chest. Lifting his head, he captured her gaze, and her heart turned over in response.

"Darlin', we're going to start now. I admit this is

about as new for me as it is for you but look at it this way. We'll be learnin' together.'' He kissed the tip of her nose.

She smiled at his delightful expression of eager affection.

''I'm going to be blunt here, Janie because I don't know any other way. If, when we're making love, I get too rough or you don't like something I'm doing, you've got to tell me. But once I'm inside of you, I don't reckon I can stop. Do you understand what I'm saying?''

''Yes, I think so.'' She'd give him everything she had to give. She hoped it would be enough to make him stay when things got rough as she knew they eventually would. She hoped by then he would love her as much as she loved him at this moment. Overcome by his genuine concern, she kissed him on the tip of his nose. He grinned in return. ''I trust you, Rider.''

''Thank you, Janie.''

He guided her hand to his trouser button where with shaking fingers she undid each one. He tugged them off, along with his long johns and tossed them on the floor. Pulling the bedcoverings up to his hips, he tugged Jane's waist until she was pressed so close to him, their hearts beat as one. His hands guided her hips toward him so she could feel his arousal, hot and pulsing, against her womanhood. He pushed against her, grinding in slow circles. Jane mimicked his movement, clinging to him, needing to be as close as possible. Against her neck, a moan escaped his throat. Janie delighted in the wickedly provocative sound.

''Dear God, Janie,'' he muttered as his fingers caressed her buttocks.

Rider squeezed his eyes shut and concentrated on the

agony. He didn't think he could hold back much longer. He couldn't think, he couldn't breathe. He wasn't even inside her yet but the urge to release himself was driving him mad. The need burned within him.

Her neck arched and her hair swung back, giving him access to her breasts. He took a pebbled nipple inside his mouth, first one, then the other. He nibbled and sucked, searching for the one thing that would set her to wanting him as much as he wanted her. When she moaned and writhed beside him, he almost lost control.

He gritted his teeth and parted her legs. Swinging his body over hers he kept his weight on his elbows. He held her hips still, kissed her and eased his way inside. She was wet and slick, tight and welcoming.

"Rider?"

"Hmm?" was all he could manage.

"I love you," she whispered in a soft voice so sweet and tender, it very nearly pushed him over the edge.

Dear God.

He thrust once, hard, and heard her gasp. Against all reason, he swelled with pride knowing she'd allowed him to be the one to take her virginity. His own body shook with tension but he waited until her body relaxed, and became accustomed to him inside her. Then he began again, slowly building momentum one hard thrust at a time, but he knew he wouldn't last. Drowning in the depths of her love, he sought completion.

He shouted Jane's name as he came in an onrush of heat and love.

When he was able to catch his breath, Rider eased down beside Jane and took her hand in his. She was still trembling slightly. He kissed her knuckles and heard her gentle laughter. He opened his eyes to find her watching him, her face and throat pink and glowing.

He tugged at the bedcoverings until they covered their damp cooling bodies. He wiped his brow with the corner of the sheet.

"Are you all right?" Jane asked.

Still breathing hard, he replied, "Better than all right, Janie. Why?"

"The way you were groaning I thought maybe you were in pain."

He couldn't help but laugh. "I *was* in pain, sweetheart, but I'm much improved now. I promise it will be better next time."

"Next time?" she questioned.

"Absolutely, darlin'." He grinned at the quizzical expression on her face. "You and me are going to do this all night until I get it right."

Her right brow rose in obvious consternation. "We didn't do it right?"

Janie sounded so troubled, Rider chuckled. He took her in his arms and sought her gaze. "You were wonderful but I came too soon."

"Came where too soon?"

Rider snorted with laughter, then spent the next several hours explaining and showing his curious wife how the male anatomy worked. She proved to be an apt student. By midnight he was an exhausted shell of his former self, and Jane was sound asleep. Sleeping like a babe at his side, replete and, he sincerely hoped, well satisfied. Rider had taken great pains in making sure. After all, she loved him.

Rider knew it was time to find the Ferlin brothers to try and talk them out of rustling the Smiths' beeves but he found himself procrastinating.

He glanced at Jane beside him, warm and soft, her head sharing his pillow, one arm across his chest, her body cuddling against his belly. Her hair lay tangled about her head. He lifted a strand in his fingers and wound it around his fist.

Looking at her beloved face, he felt like he'd come home to the place where he was meant to be. For the first time in five years, he felt fulfilled, content and happy.

He would do anything in his power to keep it that way but he owed it to Jake and Marty to stop them from ruining their lives.

Wide awake, Teddy lay in bed staring up at the stars. He didn't know what time it was exactly, but the moon shining in his window told him it was very late. In his own bed, Gopher was asleep and snoring.

Heavy booted feet moved around in the front room. It must be Rider but he should be in bed, too. Except for Rider and the snapping of the dying fire in the fireplace, the house was quiet.

Teddy climbed out of bed and pressed his ear to the door to listen. What was Rider doing? He snuck out of his room in time to hear the front door close quietly. Rider sure was being careful not to wake up anybody. Maybe he was just going to use the outhouse but why was he going out the front? Teddy pulled on his boots and buttoned his coat on over his nightshirt.

After a quick glance at Jane's bedroom door, Teddy stepped outside to follow him. Beneath the glow of the moon, he saw Rider walking fast down the road toward Drover. Rider wouldn't leave in the middle of the night unless it was important. He might need Teddy's help.

Jane awoke alone. She reached her hand out to where Rider had lain last night showing her the many ways of lovemaking. The space next to her felt cool to the touch. Apparently, Rider had been out of bed for quite some time. The thoughtful man was probably out milking the cow for Teddy.

She rolled over and found she was sore in places she didn't even know existed before last night. She smiled to herself, even after discovering something else. Her woman's cycle had begun again. That stupid doctor and his foolish curse. Shaking her head, she found the cloths she hadn't used in months shoved to the back of a dresser drawer.

Still smiling, she threw on her wrapper and padded down the hall. The kitchen was quiet and cold. She was surprised that the stove hadn't been lit yet and the coffee wasn't on. Nor had any logs been thrown on the fireplace.

A terrible premonition replaced her feelings of love and tenderness from the night before. She hoped Rider was merely in the barn, but it wasn't like him to leave without lighting the stove so the house would be warm by the time the rest of the family rose.

With one hand gripping the back of a chair, Jane glanced uneasily about the kitchen and sitting room. Rider's coat was gone but nothing else looked amiss.

Why, she couldn't say, but at that moment she thought of the doctor's curse. Was Rider going to be a part of her curse? Had he taken her virginity so lightly and then left her and the boys to fend for themselves?

During the night he'd been forthcoming about himself and their future; a future he looked forward to spending with Jane. He had been a giving, thoughtful lover. Was it possible to misjudge a person's character this much? Jane didn't want to think so, but a nagging uneasiness filled her with dread.

A heavy fist pounded on the front door. Jane stared at the entrance but apprehension kept her feet glued to the floor.

He that has no children knows not what love is.
—Seventeenth-century proverb

Chapter Sixteen

Her empty stomach churned as Jane regarded the closed door, reluctant to find out who stood on the other side. Maybe it was the curse. Maybe it was women's intuition. Or maybe it was just common sense, but she knew that whoever stood on her front porch this early in the morning came bearing bad news.

The wooden bar that secured the door overnight wasn't in its frame. The length of wood looked horribly out of place leaning against the wall where she kept it during the day. She took an unsteady breath and with reluctant, trembling fingers pulled open the door.

A tall man, whose head nearly reached the rafters stood on the porch, a brown Stetson clutched in his fingers. His right hand rested on a holstered gun and held back the side of a heavy brown canvas jacket. An unmistakable silver star gleamed on his black leather vest. With a gentlemanly gesture, he inclined his head and gave Jane a grim smile. "Do you happen to know where your husband is, ma'am?"

Jane stared at the star pinned on his chest, her mind unwilling to register its significance. She couldn't seem to find her voice. Her eyes darted between the serious expression on the man's rugged face and the foreboding badge. "Sheriff?"

He nodded. "Sorry, ma'am. I reckon we haven't met. I'm Drover's sheriff, Caleb Asher."

Scared like she'd never been in her life Jane asked, "Is something wrong?"

"Could be. Right now I'm just trying to locate Rider Magrane and get a few facts straight. He is your husband, isn't he?"

"Y-yes."

"Do you know where he is."

Please be in the barn, Rider. Fear tugged at her composure. "D-did you try the barn?"

"Yes, ma'am. Before I knocked on your door, I walked all around your place and didn't see a soul. I take it he's not in the house then?"

"No, he isn't."

"And you don't know where he is?"

"He's in trouble, isn't he?"

"What makes you think so?"

Jane felt herself quaking, but she pushed the door wider and beckoned the sheriff inside. "Come on in, have a cup of coffee and let me know what *you* think." Jane heaved an unsteady sigh.

He ducked his head as he entered the house, looking obviously uncomfortable in the confined space. Jane thought his towering, formidable presence had cowed more than one man in his time, but his deep-set gray eyes held a kind, understanding expression. He had a very honest, trustworthy look about him. She motioned him to sit at the oilcloth-covered table.

He set his hat down, lowered himself to a chair and crossed one leg over the other. He rested his steepled fingers on his knee. Looking up at her with an expectant gaze, he asked, "Do you want to start or should I?"

Forgetting the coffee and the chill in the room, Jane pulled out a chair and sat down across the table from the imposing sheriff. To keep him from seeing how her hands shook, she laced her fingers together.

"I don't know where Rider is," she stated. What else could she say? Just hours ago they'd shared a glorious night of tender lovemaking and lighthearted laughter that she would remember forever and always cherish close to her heart. She told him she loved him, but apparently he took his leave before the bed had even cooled. Surely she couldn't have misjudged him so badly. The fact still remained that she didn't know where he was or if he was coming back. It felt like a fist clenched her heart. Hot tears clogged her throat.

"Now, ma'am." He reached across the table and patted her cold, clasped hands. "Expect the worst and that's generally what you'll be gettin'."

"I suppose you're right."

"Last night your neighbors, the Smiths, had about eighty head of cattle taken from their place."

Dear God. "Rustled?"

"Yes. The varmints took the beeves to the railway stock pens in town. Why, I couldn't say, except maybe they thought the cattle would be shipped out and they could just collect their money and run off before anyone was the wiser. Fortunately, the stockyard master recognized the Smith brand and figured that something mighty suspicious was up. He fetched me to the station where I arrested two fellas right there on the spot. They're in jail now and claimin' they're innocent of any wrong-doing."

"Do you know them?"

"Yes ma'am, the Ferlins. Jacob and Martin. Are you acquainted with 'em?"

Jane stared at the sheriff, her mind whirling with confusion. "No, not really. I did meet them in town a few days ago. They are friends of Rider's."

He frowned, his eyes level. "Yes, ma'am. I believe that's true."

"But surely you don't suspect Rider?"

"Do you know if they've been out here to visit Rider since he's been back?"

Jane shook her head. "No, I don't think so, but it's possible they could have been here without my knowledge."

"Ma'am, can I ask you a personal question?"

She wanted him to leave. She wanted him to reassure her that her husband wasn't a criminal, yet she needed to hear the truth. "Y-yes."

"Do you know where Rider was before he showed up here at your farm?"

"Not really. He mentioned some trouble in Drover and that he'd been gone awhile but he wasn't specific."

"Can't blame him." Sheriff Asher blew out a long breath and paused, looking at Jane speculatively. "I hate to be the one to tell you this but your new husband spent a long stretch up to the penitentiary at Lansing. He just recently got out."

Jane's pulse jittered, and her heart pounded in her

chest. She recalled the times Rider had wanted to talk about his past and she'd put him off or refused to listen. Why hadn't she listened? Her mind raced in a jumble of thoughts, unable to settle on a single coherent one. "Rider was in the penitentiary?"

"For cattle rustling."

"Oh, dear God, no."

He paused before speaking, and then said in a low tone, "Five years ago, he, another fella and the Ferlin boys rustled your brother's cattle, Miss Warner, er, Mrs. Magrane. The other man, Chauncey Carlisle, got killed in the fray by Rider's brother, Chance, who was the Drover sheriff at the time.

"Jake Ferlin is not saying much of anything but he did say I had the wrong men, that I should be looking for Rider Magrane."

Jane's sight narrowed, and the room spun in a kaleidoscope of galloping color. The light dimmed in her peripheral vision so that all she beheld was a pinpoint of pale yellow. Through a veiled mist, she saw the sheriff jump to his feet and rush around the table where he knelt by her side. With a gentle nudge he pushed her head between her knees, then took one of her hands and began kneading the fingers. "Take a couple of deep breaths, then breathe in and out real slow, ma'am. That's the way, just breathe regular-like."

She stayed bent over until the dizziness passed. Then she lifted her head, her vision blurry, her head aching.

Sheriff Asher looked at her with a questioning, concerned face. "Are you all right now, ma'am? You 'bout scared me out of a year's growth, you were looking so peaked there for a minute."

Jane gave a perfunctory nod. She would never be all

right. Rider had lied to her. He promised he would never leave her willingly, although he hinted that there might come a time when he would have to. She ignored him, thinking he was talking about something else, something that had nothing to do with the two of them.

With cold disregard for her feelings and the boys' welfare, he then met with those terrible Ferlin brothers and stole the Smiths' cattle.

How could he not tell her the truth about his past? How could she think she loved him? Because she still did.

"I'm sorry I gave you such a shock. I guess I figured you already knew about his past or you wouldn't have married the fella."

Despair tugged at her heart. "I might not have, Sheriff, had I known."

"Now, ma'am, we don't have all the facts just yet. We still have to find Rider and get his side of the story. If I know outlaws at all and I reckon I do, they will tell a whopper of a story to save their own skins. I got no proof that your husband was involved this time. Only Jake Ferlin's say-so."

"This time," she repeated in a dull voice that didn't sound like her own. She looked up to catch the sheriff's sympathetic gaze. "But Rider didn't think it necessary to tell me what he did before to my own family, now, did he?"

"Ma'am, I got no way of knowing what was in his heart, but I'll tell you one thing. That Evie Smith, she's a rare one, she is. She spoke up for him herself. Even with her beeves missing. She said he loved you and those nephews of yours like he invented the notion, and furthermore, she said he was as loyal as an old hound dog. Said he could no more be involved in this bad bit of business than I could.''

Jane gazed at him in surprise.

He held up his hand. ''Swear to God. That was her exact phraseology. That woman is a pure wonder.''

''What did Mack say?''

His brows rose halfway to his forehead. ''Are you joshing with me, ma'am? When Evie Smith is around, no one else gets half a chance to open his mouth, much less speak. I'm seriously thinkin' about letting her talk to those Ferlin boys. I reckon she could get them to fork over the truth. She even scares me a little bit.''

''Rider once said the same thing.''

''See?''

''Yes, but where could he be?''

''That's the question, isn't it?'' Sheriff Asher picked up his hat and started toward the door. ''You sure you're going to be all right?''

''Yes, I'll be fine.''

''Miz Smith said to tell you she'd be by this morning. If your husband does show up, be sure to tell him I'd like to have a little chat with him.''

''Yes, I'll do that. Thank you, Sheriff.''

With one hand on the handle, he turned back to her. ''Don't you be fretting, ma'am. I have a feeling this will turn out just fine.''

Jane didn't see how. She followed him to the door and watched him as he rode off. She turned away, knowing she had chores to do and the boys to attend to. But her body felt so heavy she didn't know if she could lift her feet. And her weary heart felt like it was breaking in two.

She walked down the hall and quietly opened the

boys' bedroom door. John Michael lay on his back, wide awake, talking to himself and playing with his toes. Teddy was nowhere to be seen.

Rider's first coherent thought when he regained consciousness was that he had to find Teddy. Flat on his belly in a bed of muck and mud, Rider lifted his head and blinked several times, his eyes tearing. The sun, breaking the night from day, hung just above the eastern horizon. The orange globe slanted across his face, piercing the back of his eyelids.

His second coherent thought was that he was going to be sick. He shivered as heat worked its way into his chilled body. He fought down waves of nausea as he levered himself to his elbows and glanced around at what he thought was most likely one of the Smiths' fenced corrals. Jake Ferlin's well-placed knee left Rider light-headed and his groin aching like the devil. He was not happy as he wiped a sleeve across his mud-encrusted face.

Still groggy and disoriented, Rider realized he'd been unconscious several hours. Had the Ferlins gone ahead with their cattle rustling and, more importantly, what did they do with Teddy?

Rider cussed himself for a fool. He never should have trusted Jake. By barging ahead in a hopeless attempt to stop Jake and Martin, he'd inadvertently put Teddy in jeopardy. In trying to dissuade Jake from doing something he'd later regret, Rider walked right into Jake's well-thought-out scheme to trap Rider.

Jake knew all along that Rider would try to stop them. And if Rider refused to go along with the brothers,

Jake's plan was to make it look like Rider was the culprit.

When Rider tried to physically persuade him, Jake kneed him, hard. As Rider fell to the ground, gasping in pain, he heard Teddy call out his name. He looked up just as Martin grabbed Teddy as he was running to Rider's aid. Jake then hit Rider over the head with, judging by the way his head throbbed, an anvil at the very least. He fingered the lump on the back of his head. It was the size of a chicken egg.

Rider sat up then dragged himself to his feet. He looked around. The corral gate stood ajar, and clearly visible in the mud were the hoof prints of cattle as they were lead from the pen. Rider had no idea how many were missing. But it only took one to get a noose around a rustler's throat. His throat. He swallowed hard feeling the rope tighten around his neck.

He strode to the Smiths' cabin, a short distance from where he stood. He pounded on the door. No answer. He walked around the barn calling Mack's name, and then went inside. All was quiet. Too quiet.

He turned to go when he saw a ramshackle toolshed and lean-to at the edge of the property. Thinking that Mack might be inside, he trotted across the yard. He pulled the door toward him. Although shadowy inside, he was shocked to see Teddy sitting in one dark corner, bound and gagged, his eyes red-rimmed and fearful. Rider took a step inside, then heard something behind him. His last thought before he crumpled to the floor was that he'd been hit with that damnable anvil again.

Smith kicked Magrane's scrawny butt into the machine shed and locked the door. His ma could claim the man's innocence until hell froze over but this proved her wrong. He discovered the outlaw prowling his property. Of course, that didn't explain where his cattle were right now, or why Magrane was still here. But he knew that Magrane had accomplices the last time he'd rustled cattle. It made sense that he would run with them again. He was certain he had his man.

Pleased with himself, he moseyed on up to the cabin to wait for his ma to return from speaking with the sheriff. And to spoon with that prickly cactus of a woman, Sukie Warner.

Evie Smith rode home tired as a worn-out banjo string, and mad enough to strangle the next person sorry enough to enter her line of sight.

She didn't like having her beauty sleep disturbed by no-account, hornswogglin' thieves—men of low character like those Ferlin boys. She didn't like having her beeves stolen in the dead of night. And she didn't like having a friend accused of the dastardly deed. She knew deep down in her heart of hearts where it really mattered, that Rider Magrane wasn't involved in this bad business.

Convincing the sheriff and her thick-skulled son was another matter altogether.

She tied up her mare, Irish Lassie, to the hitching post, knowing she'd be leaving again soon, bone tired or not. She heaved a heavy sigh. Before she could ride over to console Jane who was undoubtedly fretting something fierce about her missing husband, she needed to check in with Mack.

She found him all right. The horny son of a gun had Sukie Warner wedged against a kitchen cabinet, his head buried in her neck. The woman was squeaking like a mouse but, Evie noted with a grin, her hands cupped

Mack's backside like she was holding on for dear life.

Evie purposely slammed the front door shut behind her. The couple jumped apart like two kernels of popped corn. They both wore embarrassed expressions, but Mack looked sheepish and Sukie looked humiliated. Served 'em right, thought Evie. They hardly knew each other.

"Hi, Ma."

"Hello, yourself, son. Hello, Sukie. How are you this morning?" Evie plopped herself down at the table and crossed her arms over her chest. "Where's Mary Jo?"

"She's in the barn," Mack said, grinning. "She's quite taken with that orphan lamb we found last spring."

"I expect she'll want us to take it home like some forlorn lost puppy," grumbled Sukie.

Evie shot her an evil eye.

Sukie shut up.

Motioning to the enamel pot sitting on the back of the stove, Evie asked, "Any coffee left?"

Sukie darted across the room, grabbed a tin cup off the shelf above the stove and then dropped it. It bounced on the floor, clanked a few times, and rolled to a stop against a table leg. Sukie threw Evie a look of apology as she picked it up. She wiped it off with a dishcloth, then poured a cup and handed it to Evie without saying a word.

Evie liked company. She even liked a good long conversation now and again, but this woman was a long-winded chatterbox who knew everything about everything, or thought she did. She wore Evie out, and that was no easy feat.

Evie could tell that Mack was fair chompin' at the bit as he asked, "What did the sheriff say, Ma?"

"He found our beeves."

"He what?"

"Aye, they were at the train station, getting ready to be loaded into a car and shipped back east. Luckily, the man at the cattle yard recognized our brand and notified the sheriff."

"How did they get there?"

Evie gave her son a disgruntled look. "How do ye think they got there? They were herded to town by those no-good Ferlin brothers who are now residing in our fair jail."

Mack's eyes bulged like a toad. "What? But I caught him red-handed right here on the farm."

"You caught who?"

"The thief, that's who. Rider Magrane."

Evie jumped to her feet. "Where is he?"

"I hit him over the head, then dragged his sorry ass into the machine shed and locked him in."

Sukie stared at Mack like he'd lost his mind. "You wretched villain, you. You stood right here in this kitchen taking liberties with my person—"

"I took no liberties. You were willin' and likin' it."

"I was not. And my poor brother-in-law was undoubtedly bleeding to death in your machine shed?"

"Aww, I didn't hit him that hard. I didn't think you liked him anyway."

"He's family."

"Bridle yer tongues, both of you." Evie headed for the door. "And come with me."

Rider woke up with the same damned headache. No, worse. Only he wasn't breathing mud. This time the dirt in his face smelled like a combination of axle grease and turpentine. He coughed, trying to clear his lungs as well as his head. Both felt clogged with the muck and mud of a cattle pen. A dull ache throbbed in his groin. As he sat up and tried adjusting to the dimness, he remembered seeing Teddy in the wooden shed. His heart hitched as he frantically searched the small, shadowy room for signs of the child.

Teddy sat next to Rider, shivering with cold, tears flowing freely down his ruddy cheeks. His hands were bound with a short length of rope. Rider untied the simple knots from Teddy's chilled and raw chafed wrists. Rider swore under his breath. He pulled the loop from around his head and yanked a filthy, foul-smelling neckerchief from his mouth. He cussed Jake Ferlin, loud and descriptively, before settling his gaze on Teddy's tear-streaked face.

"I-I thought you were d-dead," Teddy sputtered, his voice ragged with unspent tears and fatigue. He threw his thin arms around Rider's neck and sobbed against his chest. "I was s-so sc-scared."

"Shh," Rider whispered. "Everything's going to be all right now." He opened his jacket, enfolding Teddy close to his heart. Rider squeezed his eyes shut against hot tears and stroked Teddy's bedraggled hair with shaking hands. "You were really, really brave trying to help me out like you did."

"But I didn't do anything," Teddy insisted. His body shook as he took a hiccuping gulp.

Tears rose again and speaking was beyond Rider for a moment. "Yes, but you wanted to. That's what counts."

As he warmed up, Teddy's shivering diminished and his crying slowed. "I knew those men were outlaws. They smelled bad."

A smile tugged at Rider's mouth. After lying for several hours in cattle manure, surely he smelled worse than they did right now, but Teddy didn't seem to notice or care.

Rider rose to his feet and tried the door. Why, he didn't know. He knew it was locked. He sat down with his back against the wall. Over the top of Teddy's head, Rider glanced around the dimly lit room looking for a means of escape. There were no windows, just the one locked door. The only light that permeated the space came from the badly mortared walls, sparse and shadowy. Anxiety filtered in between the cracks and filled Rider with outright fear. He choked on a lump that filled his throat and threatened his breathing.

Rider's heart sped up, and a cold sweat broke out on his brow. His skin twitched as sweat ran down his back. Rider tried to slow his intake of air by closing his eyes and taking even breaths, but with his eyes shut he felt the walls suffocating his equilibrium. He clung to Teddy, taking comfort in the weight of his slight body; the same way Teddy's little arms clung to Rider seeking shelter.

"Rider?"

"Hmm?"

"Are we going to get out of here?"

"Absolutely," he said in a voice he hoped sounded reassuring. In actuality he needed reassurances of his own. Panic settled in his bones. He wanted to jump up and pound on the walls, screaming like a madman and tearing at them with his bare hands. The boundary between remembrance and reality wavered. This wasn't prison; he would get out of this shed. He had to be strong for Teddy. He had to remain calm. Still he couldn't allow Teddy to witness the panic building inside him like a blazing inferno.

Keep talking, Magrane, just keep talking.

With tears streaming down her cheeks and John Michael clinging to her coat lapels, Jane ran all the way to Evie's house. She arrived sobbing, struggling to balance the baby and gasping for oxygen. She stopped near the edge of the yard beside a tumble-down shed and plopped John Michael on the ground. Placing her hands on her knees, she bent over and tried to catch her breath. She wiped her face with the back of a hand and inhaled slowly, then released it unevenly.

She refused to let Evie see her cry. Evie disliked tears. According to her, weeping was a sign of weakness. An attribute men assigned to the so-called weaker sex. Evie figured that men had enough ammunition against women. They didn't need anymore.

Jane turned toward the shed when she heard whispering coming from inside. She scooped John Michael into her arms and rushed toward the building. She tried the door but it was latched with a removable lock that required a key. Still she definitely heard voices. "Is someone there?"

"Aunt Jane! Is that you?"

My God. Teddy. "Yes, honey, it's me. Are you all right? Why aren't you home? What are you doing in there?"

"Some bad men tied me up and locked me in here."

"What bad men?"

"Those bad men that hit Rider with a log and tried to kill him."

Jane stared at the closed door, feeling herself crumbling. Her heart breaking. Her knees wobbled so badly that she almost dropped John Michael.

It was all true. He was involved. But where was he?

She tried to put him out of her mind. She needed to concentrate on Teddy now. He was her first concern. She set John Michael down on the ground and seeing a loose board at the corner of the shed, she pulled at it with both hands. The dry rotted wood broke away easily in her fingers. She pried several more lengths away until she made a hole big enough that she was able to crawl inside on her hands and knees. She pushed John Michael ahead of her. Inside, the interior was dim and poorly lit.

Before her eyes could adjust, Teddy jumped into her arms, crying with elation. They toppled to the dirt floor, where John Michael joined in the melee adding to the overall confusion.

Jane clasped Teddy's dirty, tear-stained, but oh so beloved, face in her hands. "Are you all right, you little thorn, you?"

"Yeah."

"Why did you sneak out of the house like that?" She swept a hand over his hair brushing it off his forehead. "And in your nightshirt, too?"

"I only wanted to help."

"Help who?"

Teddy looked over his shoulder. "Rider," he whispered. "I think there's something bad wrong with him."

Jane didn't recognize this man as Rider. He sat huddled in the corner of the shed, his head bent to his knees, his shoulders heaving. Dried mud blanketed his clothing. In the dim light she couldn't even make out the color of his matted, dirt-encrusted hair, though it looked dark. Something was dreadfully wrong with him. With his body shivering and his breathing erratic, he looked like he was having a seizure of some kind. Hesitantly, she touched his hand where it lay fisted on the floor.

His head jerked up, swinging around to gape at her. "Teddy," he said in a choked voice, raw with tension. A wild-eyed, startlingly blue gaze stared at her from a face covered with dried mud. His eyes, frantic with unknown demons, didn't so much stare *at* her, as through her. She realized, with a start, that he didn't really see or recognize her.

Jane pushed the boys away, both of them whimpering with fright. She put her hands on Rider's shoulders and shook him. He wriggled out of her grasp, his gaze on the hole she'd made in the wall and began to crawl toward it, repeating Teddy's name. Dragging his body on the floor he slowly, painstakingly made his way across the room. The hole wasn't big enough for his large frame but he lunged forward, regardless. Jane stared in shock as he barged through the narrow opening, first ripping his jacket, then his shirt on the jagged wooden edges of the broken boards. Still he plowed forward until he squeezed through the narrow opening into the fresh air outside. She watched him collapse in the yard, gasping for air and calling Teddy's name.

Jane gathered the boys, pushed them forward and climbed out after them.

Rider lay on his belly. Dried blood matted the back of his hair, and fresh blood oozed from several wicked gashes on his back. Mud and manure caked his clothing and boots. Like a prayer, he repeated Teddy's name one last time.

Jane glanced up as Evie trotted out of her cabin, with Mack and Sukie right behind her.

"Oh, you poor sweet things," Evie cried.

Mack swept right by Evie and lifted a trembling Teddy into his arms. "I swear, Ma, I didn't know he was in here."

"Teddy, how on earth . . . ?" Sukie exclaimed.

After a quick reassuring glance at Jane and Teddy, Evie sank to her knees beside Rider. Careful of his injured back, she rolled him over onto his side. She placed a reassuring hand on his forehead and he groaned. Blinking against the bright sunshine, he batted at Evie's hand as if to push it away.

"Rider, can ye hear me?"

"Ma, there's nothing wrong with him that a tall tree and a stout rope can't fix."

"Mind what ye say, son. I've a notion ye do no' know what ye're blathering on about." She turned back to Rider. "Rider?"

He blinked once then opened his eyes and seemed to focus on Evie's face. "Teddy?" he asked in a hoarse whisper.

"Yes, he's fine."

Rider's eyes fluttered shut and his hands relaxed and lay loose at his side. His breathing slowed.

Jane struggled to understand what had happened to Rider and Teddy during the night. She did her best to force her bewildered emotions into order, but she simply couldn't concentrate with all the confusion going on all about her.

Jane was startled when she heard a horse trot into the yard. She looked up to see Sheriff Asher. He stopped and dismounted, taking in the scene before him. It must have looked strange in the extreme but he smiled in a friendly fashion and doffed his hat. ''Ladies, Mr. Smith.''

''Sheriff Asher,'' Evie responded, her tone as chilly as the crisp morning air.

The sheriff nodded toward Rider lying prone on the ground, then said to Jane, ''Looks like you may have found your husband, Mrs. Magrane.''

She nodded agreement, unable to find her voice.

''I have to take him in for questioning.''

By this time, Rider sat up, his eyes glazed and pain-filled but focused. He gazed at Jane, his expression one of concern and sorrow. ''I'm sorry, Janie,'' he said in a low voice, ''about what happened to Teddy.''

She wanted to rant and rave, and rail at him, but not in front of half the county. And she knew once she started, anger would get the better of her. She glanced away and said nothing.

Still she watched with wretched dismay as Sheriff Asher stepped into the stirrup to mount his horse. Patiently he waited for Rider to climb to his feet. Rider's neck was stiff, the line of his back tense and hard as he moved forward. Blood trickled down his spine and soaked into the waist of his trousers. He seemed not to notice. He glanced over his shoulder and caught Jane's gaze. His face took on an expression of silent defeat before he mounted behind the sheriff.

Her husband of less than forty-eight hours rode off to be locked up inside the Drover jail.

The course of true love never did run smooth.
—William Shakespeare, A Midsummer Night's Dream

Chapter Seventeen

Rider had never met Sheriff Caleb Asher. As the lawman recited his recent history in Drover, Rider took the opportunity to study him. Near his own height and weight, he looked to be about ten years older. He carried himself with an air of authority and calm efficiency but not arrogantly so. The sheriff appeared relaxed in Rider's presence. However, he sensed that if he reached for the sheriff's gun he'd find himself on the wrong end of the barrel in no time flat.

Asher surprised Rider by saying, "I knew your brother, Chance, when he was sheriff here."

"That so?"

"We met when I came to Drover. He's a good man. Held no hard feelings against me when I took over the job. How's he doing these days?"

"He's fine, just got married himself."

"Good for him." The sheriff glanced at Rider, before

turning his attention forward. "Just in case you're wondering, I know about your circumstances here. Chance filled me in about the cattle-rustling scheme, how he had to shoot Chauncey Carlisle, and how you and those Ferlin boys came to go to prison."

"I figured as much," Rider said.

With a mischievous glint in his eye, Asher said, "And because of Evie Smith I know what's been happening since: your run-in with Gresham Carlisle, your broken arm and your visit to Doc Hendricks."

They agreed the quack was several bales short of a wagonload.

"Is there anything you can do about him?" Rider asked, thinking of the pain the doctor had caused Jane.

"Last time I checked, being an ignorant fool isn't against the law, but I'll think on it."

"Thanks."

"I heard on the street how you disarmed Martin Ferlin after he'd had a mite too much to drink," Asher said. "I appreciate the help."

"He's harmless when he's sober, but get a few drinks in him and he becomes crazy."

"Thanks all the same. By the way, Magrane, Evie Smith stood up for you when she told me you were back in town. Said you were a good man, as good as your brother. That's high praise coming from that ole woman, so let's just say I'll be fair and listen to your side of the story once we get to town."

Rider inclined his head in acknowledgement.

As they talked on the ride to town Rider found himself liking Asher. Asher was confident and honest. All he wanted from Rider was the truth. Rider was more than happy to oblige, but considering his criminal background, he doubted the wily sheriff believed him. The cautious fella didn't comment however. He listened with an intent ear and nodded on occasion.

When they reached Drover, the sheriff escorted Rider into one of the two cells in the way-too-familiar Drover jail, then slammed the door behind him. The brass key clattered in the lock sending chills rocketing up Rider's spine. He swore beneath his breath as he recalled the vow he'd made when he walked out of the Lansing Penitentiary a free man. He would never in this or any other lifetime spend time behind bars. Now he'd broken the pledge he'd made to himself. Quick as a prairie fire, anger swept through him. Soon the anger would be followed by mind-numbing boredom and deeply profound loneliness if he stayed in jail long enough.

Thank God, Rider had a window that brought in plenty of light, and bars on two sides of him. The enclosed feeling shouldn't hit him again. The sheriff glanced at Rider and gave him a reassuring smile. Why? Rider didn't know why or think he half-understood the man. Asher then left by the door that separated the cells from his storefront office. Despite knowing it was coming, Rider stiffened and then winced as the door banged shut with an inevitable final thud.

In the cell next to Rider's, Jake and Martin sat apart, Jake on the cot and Martin sprawled on the straw-covered floor. Jake gave Rider a mocking thin-lipped smile but Martin, head bowed over bent knees, refused to meet his gaze.

Lucky for Jake iron bars separated Rider from the two of them. Simmering with fury, Rider could easily, without even the thinnest thread of remorse, strangle Jake with his bare hands.

"How could you tie up a little boy like that?" Rider asked through gritted teeth as he stood with his hands clenched around the bars. "Have you got no conscience whatsoever?"

Jake chuckled, a deeply cynical laugh that clanged like a fire-engine bell in Rider's head. "Where it concerns money, I reckon I don't now nor ever did. But, hell, Magrane, I didn't hurt the brat none, and I figured sooner or later someone would hear him hollerin' and let him out."

His indifferent tone infuriated Rider. "Hear him?" he repeated. "How could anyone hear him with a damned cloth stuffed in his mouth? He's just a kid, for God's sake."

Jake shrugged his shoulders and glanced away.

"Martin?" Rider asked.

He didn't reply, just gave his head a slight shake.

Damning both men to hell, Rider turned his back. He paced the length of his cell, trying to think how he could have done things differently. Other than letting the Ferlins run off and commit a crime they'd never get away with, he didn't know how he could have changed the outcome for himself or for them. At the time he felt he owed them his loyalty. He realized, belatedly, that his loyalty lay with his new family—Jane and the boys.

Now Jane would never understand why he hadn't told her about his reasons for coming to the farm, much less his reasons for staying. He should have sat her down, whether she wanted to listen or not, and told her about his past and his connection to her brother.

She would never believe he'd fallen in love with the farm, with the boys, and against all common sense, with her. He had to try to convince her. They were married and, come hell or high water, that vow he intended to keep. When he got out of this jail, whether it was within hours, or if it took years, he would go back to the farm and make it up to her even if it took a load of buckshot in his backside to make her listen to reason. He paced until the sun rose noon-high in the sky and the connecting door swung open.

The sheriff, accompanied by that tough cuss on wheels, Evie Smith, stepped inside. Rider stared at the old woman whose countenance still had the power to scare the living daylights out of him. How she had that ability Rider didn't know, but he didn't discount it. She was one woman whom he didn't want to cross, or match wits with either. He felt he'd come out looking foolish either way. By the way she was glaring at the Ferlin brothers, Rider figured they were about to be in a heap of trouble. If he didn't have enough damn problems himself, he might have smiled.

Sheriff Asher, his Stetson tilted to the back of his head, surprised Rider by unlocking the Ferlins' cell to allow Evie in. When she clomped inside, the sheriff left the door open. He stood outside, his arms crossed, his face unreadable. The boys looked at first shocked, then dismayed.

Evie greeted Rider by patting him on the shoulder through the bars. She motioned for him to turn around so she could look at his back. She made a maternal tsking sound. ''Ye're a pitiful sight, boyo, and dirty as a pig in slop. Saints alive, ye smell like the back end of a mule.''

''Good to see you, too, Miz Smith, though I'd prefer to have your shotgun aimed at my backside than be inside here.''

She beckoned him with the crook of a gnarled, arthritic finger. "Don't ye worry."

He inclined his head to listen.

"Magrane," she whispered in a calm voice, "me and tha' handsome sheriff're gonna have ye out of here quicker than ye can holler 'howdy'."

Her face looked as mean as a startled rattler's as she stared at Jake and Martin. When she lassoed their attention, it turned meaner. Rider felt the rope tighten around their scrawny necks. She began to interrogate the Ferlin brothers while a blushing Sheriff Asher, who had obviously overheard Evie's compliment, stood by. Evie's technique of getting to the truth of the matter was direct and blunt, and soon she had everyone's undivided attention.

After five minutes the sheriff's eyes widened. After ten minutes his jaw dropped. And if Rider wasn't mistaken, after fifteen minutes, he whispered a vulgar profanity beneath his breath not intended for mixed company. The sheriff collapsed into a chair and leaned forward with his palm on his chin.

By now Martin looked as scared as a turkey in November, and Jake was blubbering like a drunkard. Their stories were so disorganized and full of lies that even Rider was having difficulty following.

"Jacob," Evie shouted, pointing her finger at Jake. She glared at him; he stared back through bleary, bloodshot eyes. "Ye are small and yellow and few to the pod. I wouldn't claim ye even if'n I were yore very own ma."

He winced. "Ma's dead."

"And no' surprisin'," Evie stated. "Ye probably put her in an early grave yer own damn self."

Like an axed tree, Jake dropped to the floor and burst into tears.

Martin took one look at his fallen brother and commenced talking as fast as a cotton gin at picking time. He confessed everything, right down to the last ill-planned, ill-considered, ill-timed detail.

When Martin finished, red-faced and out of breath, Sheriff Asher stood up and unlocked Rider's cell. He shook Evie's hand as she came out of the Ferlins' cell. He locked it up behind her.

"Sorry about the misunderstanding, Magrane."

"It's understandable, sheriff. I appreciate the way you handled things. What'll happen to the Ferlin boys now?"

Sheriff Asher turned to look at Evie. She grinned in return. "Kind of depends if Miz Smith wants to press charges. After all, they didn't get away with anything."

"One more thing before I go. About that Doc Hendricks," Rider said. "He's made Jane's life miserable."

"Yes, sir, Sheriff, what are ye going to do about that quack? Do ye want me to take a whack at 'im?" Evie frowned as if in anticipation of being let loose on the unsuspecting doctor.

The sheriff grinned. "Not quite yet, Evie. Magrane and I discussed the man before but after listening to your technique here, I think I can talk him into leaving town. You're one mighty persuasive lady."

"I can be when it's called fer," Evie agreed.

Rider kissed Evie on her wrinkled cheek, and walked out of the Drover jail a free man.

He went down to the Carlisle mercantile to see about getting a change of clothes. Gresham Carlisle told Rider he'd heard about the Ferlins' latest escapades and even went so far as to apologize to Rider for hitting him. He offered his clothes for free. Rider washed up at the bath house, changed and started down the Drover Road toward the Warner, no, make that the Magrane, farmstead. He was more determined than ever to make his new bride understand.

Taking his afternoon nap in the bedroom just down the hall, John Michael snored like a hibernating bear cub. Bathed and ready for a nap himself, but exhausted and loath to admit it, Teddy sat beside Jane on the settee. Although waning a bit, the adrenaline from his night of excitement seemed to be keeping him wide awake.

They sat cuddled together beneath a quilt in front of a hot, blazing fire. Waiting for Evie to return with Sukie and Mary Jo, Jane lost herself in her own thoughts. As if the burning logs could give her the answers she sought, she stared at the blazing, crackling flames.

Little did the warmth cast by the fire penetrate the bone-deep chill in Jane's soul. She couldn't stop shivering or warm her weary body. Images of Teddy and Rider in that cold, dank shed slid in and out of her mind like photographs—Teddy, frightened, but trying his best to be brave; Rider, bloody and beaten, in that horrible trance-like state, repeating Teddy's name over and over. Remembering Rider, panic-stricken, crawling on his hands and knees so intent on escape, caused Jane's heart to break all over again. Yet somewhere deep in the rational part of Rider's brain his concern for Teddy kept surfacing. The look of relief on his face when he realized Teddy was all right brought tears to Jane's eyes. Despite everything else, he loved the boys. The realization hit her like a knock upside the head. Rider truly felt he deserved the blame for putting Teddy in danger. Jane knew he would never willingly have done such a thing.

She remembered when they huddled in the storage room during that bad thunderstorm a few weeks ago. At the time she hadn't recognized it but Rider had been the same way—panicky and anxious. She thought he was selfishly, thoughtlessly leaving them alone. She reconsidered her opinion. He had an uncontrollable aversion to small, dark, closed-in spaces.

Jane squeezed her eyes shut as tears brimmed, ready to overflow. Overwhelmed by feelings of loneliness and foolishness, and yes, even of love, she felt bruised and sore as if she'd gone through Rider's ordeal herself. The crumbling logs as they shifted on the grate seemed to whisper his name, mocking her. She couldn't bear to think about Rider because she loved him still, and always would . . . but she hated him for putting Teddy in jeopardy, willingly or not. And for making promises he had no intention of keeping. And most of all, for leaving her.

She gazed at her nephew, scrubbed clean and pink, his little face ruddy and his eyes bright. Her heart swelled with love. No matter what, she would always have the boys. "I'm waiting."

"For what?"

"I want you to tell me everything about your adventure," Jane said.

"What d'you want to know?"

"Why you left the house in the middle of the night without telling anyone, that's what."

"I couldn't sleep."

"Ha. You couldn't sleep because your tummy was full of wedding cake."

He ducked his head, but not before Jane noted the

guilt written all over his expressive face. "Maybe . . . I don't know. I was laying in bed staring up at the stars through the window. There's a lot of 'em up there."

Jane tousled his fresh-smelling, shiny hair and smiled down at the top of his head. "Yes, quite a few."

"Then I heard Rider moving around and thought he couldn't sleep either, so I went to see what he was doing."

"And eat more cake?"

Teddy tipped back his head and smiled up at Jane. "Maybe."

She returned his mischievous grin. "How did you know it was Rider?"

"I heard his boots thumpin' on the floor. He sounds louder than you do. I jumped out of bed and when I came into the kitchen, he was leavin' the house."

"You followed him?"

"Yep."

"But why?"

"I thought he might need my help."

"To do what?"

Teddy turned to look at Jane, his face filled with dread.

Jane lifted his slight frame onto her lap and held him close, pulling the quilt tight around them. "Honey, you know you can tell me anything. I promise you won't get into trouble."

"I was spyin' on Rider yesterday. You've told me it's not nice to spy."

Jane studied his solemn expression before replying. "I'll forgive you this time and I'm sure Rider would, too. What did you see Rider do?"

"I saw him talking to those two bad men."

Jane's heart plummeted. She had been praying there was a good explanation for Rider being on the Smith property in the dead of night, but this confirmed her worst fears. He was involved. "You did? Where? When?"

"In the yard before breakfast."

That explained the look Jane saw on Teddy's face when she came into the kitchen yesterday, and why Rider had been so distracted when he came in from outside. "What scared you?"

"Rider was so mad his face got red. He was even hollerin'."

"What did he say?"

"I don't know, I couldn't hear good. Rider grabbed one of the men's arms." Teddy showed her by demonstrating on her arm. "Then shook it like this. Rider looked fit to bust."

Teddy gave Jane a beseeching look. "I know I shouldn't have been eaves . . . eaves . . . what's that word?"

"Eavesdropping?"

"It's not nice either, it's like spyin' with your ears instead of your eyes, isn't it?"

"Well, yes it is, but you were worried about Rider so that's kind of different."

"That's why I followed him." His voice rose, then cracked a bit as he continued. "I ran and ran but I couldn't keep up with him. When I did catch him, he was with those two men and they were all hollerin', even Rider, and this time, one of 'em kicked Rider in the . . ." He stopped and glanced up at Jane with a sheepish expression on his face.

"Where?"

"He kicked Rider," Teddy lowered his voice and whispered, "between his legs."

"Oh," Jane said, keeping her expression somber, since Teddy seemed to think this was a most serious business. "That must have hurt."

Teddy nodded. "Rider didn't cry or nothing but he fell down on the ground. Then the really mean man hit him on the head with a stick."

"A stick?"

"No, not a stick." His forehead wrinkled as he fought for the appropriate word. Then he spread his hands wide. "It was bigger than a stick, it was like wood that you put in the fireplace."

Oh, dear God. They might have killed Rider. Could he have been trying to talk them out of taking the Smiths' cattle? Was that why they argued? A glimmer of hope sparked to life in Jane's heart. "What happened next, Teddy?"

His face paled. "Then they tied me up and put me in the shed."

"Oh, honey." She hugged him to her. "You must have been terribly frightened."

He shrugged his thin shoulders matter-of-factly. "A little bit, but I knew Rider would get me out."

How Jane envied Teddy's unwavering confidence in his hero. "What did they do with him?"

Teddy shrugged his shoulders. "I don't know. They just left him on the ground, I reckon. It was cold and dark in the shed, but Rider found me just like I knew he would." Like a little bantam rooster, Teddy puffed out his chest. " 'Cause he's smart and he likes me. But before he could untie me, Mr. Smith hit him on the head, too. Why did Mr. Smith do that? Isn't he your friend?"

"Yes, he is, but he must have thought Rider was doing something wrong."

Tears formed in Teddy's eyes, clung to his lashes and threatened to spill over. "That's when I thought Rider was d-dead. He just laid there and didn't move. I tried to wake up him but he didn't open his eyes or nothing."

Jane hugged him tight. "That must have been scary."

Teddy nodded, his eyes round with remembered fear, but doing his best to sound brave. "It was."

"You were very courageous trying to help Rider, and thoughtful, too, when you were worried he might be hurt." She hugged him tight. "I'm proud of you. You're not a little boy anymore."

Teddy snuggled his head against Jane's chest, denying Jane's definition of him. "Will Rider have to stay in jail? He didn't do nothing wrong."

"I don't know."

"Will he be all right?"

"I hope so, honey."

An hour later Teddy lay sleeping by her side when Jane heard Evie's wagon turn into the yard.

Though weary and obviously dying to stay and listen, Sukie and Mary Jo, with Evie's rather blatant suggestion that they needed a nap, retired to the boys' bedroom.

Once the girls were gone, Evie settled herself in the rocking chair. "Are you all right, love? You're looking a wee bit peaked."

"You remember when I went to the doctor because my monthlies stopped."

"I told ye then, ye were just workin' too hard and worryin' yerself into a frazzle. It happens sometimes. Why de ye ask now, have ye started flowin'?"

Jane nodded. "Since Rider came I've been feeling better, less worried about the boys. I guess you were right because everything is back to normal again."

"That's good, love." With a grim expression on her usually grinning face, Evie stated, "Now ye'd best be visitin' tha' bridegroom and get this wee set-to of yours put to rights."

"A set-to is it?" Jane asked trying without success to disguise her irritation. "I think it's bigger than that."

Evie shook her head, smiling like a politician. "Nah, just a misunderstandin'."

"I suppose you think I should go to town."

"Tha's where he is, love," Evie replied. A gentle softness, unlike Evie's usual no-nonsense tone, lingered in her voice.

Jane sighed. "It's just that I feel stupid and humiliated."

"Humiliated?" Evie barked. So much for gentle softness. Now she sounded more like the real Evie, a mule skinner with little patience for what she considered foolishness. "Get off yer high horse, Jane. How do ye think Rider's feeling right about now? There's nothing honorable about gettin' yerself jailed."

Evie was right, as always, but she was still as vexing as the single-minded rabbit that got into Jane's vegetable garden last spring and ate all her green beans. "Still he could have told me the truth about David's cattle and all this might never have happened."

"Ye'd ha' chased him off wi' a pitchfork if he told ye right off."

"That's probably true." Jane eyed Evie, then gave her a skeptical glance. Evie grinned in reply, confirming

Jane's suspicion. "You knew all along about him, didn't you?"

"Aye."

"Why didn't you tell me?"

"'Twasn't my place."

Jane thought a moment. "I suppose not."

"Let me tell you a little story about me mornin', love. Betwixt me and tha' handsome ole Sheriff Asher, we had a right long talk with those Ferlin boys. They soon found the wrongness of their ways. They 'fessed up, all right. Rider wasn't involved in any of their foolishness. He was just trying to save their sorry hides by trying to stop them.

"Rider's going to be released from jail if he hasn't already. Then what will ye do wi' him?"

"I don't know if I can ever forgive him."

"Why don't ye let him explain his reasons fer not tellin' ye about his past first, then decide if ye can forgive him."

Jane didn't know what to say.

"He loves ye."

Jane shook her head. "No, I don't believe he does."

"Don't be daft. I reckon the reason ye think he doesn't love ye is because he hasn't said as much?"

"Yes."

Evie snorted in derision. "Ye don't know much 'bout men, do ye?"

"No," Jane admitted. "I don't know anything."

"Men, stubborn as any mule, don't come right out and say so but they show ye their love in their actions. Hasn't Rider?"

Remembering the last nights spent with Rider, Jane felt her cheeks flame.

"Not in the marriage bed, dearie."

Jane cleared her throat. "Then I don't know what you mean."

"Open yer eyes, Jane, and yer heart. He's a good man who's trying hard t' do the right thing. He deserves the best."

"But he stole David's cows and didn't even think he had to tell me."

"Let me tell ye one sure thing. Rider didn't get away with stealing those beeves of yer brother's."

"What are you saying?"

"Ye best be asking yer husband that question."

Without another moment's hesitation, Jane made up her mind. She would confront Rider. She deserved answers and whatever it took she would get them, even if it meant talking to Rider through the bars of his jail cell. She stood up and stared down at Evie. "Will you stay with the boys until I return?"

Evie smiled in approval. "Of course."

Jane bent down and hugged the dear little woman to her breast. "You're so smart."

Evie backed out of Jane's embrace and held her at arm's length. "Phooey. Ye live as long as I have, ye learn a few things along the way. Ye just make up wi' yer man and I'll die a happy woman."

Jane leaned forward, catching a whiff of horse and leather. She kissed Evie's weather-roughened cheek. "You'll never die. You're too cantankerous."

Evie tossed back her head and cackled like a rain-soaked hen. "I reckon ye're right."

Much to her surprise, Jane found herself joining in Evie's laughter. "I expect you've got a lot more matchmaking to do."

Evie's chuckle died away as her expression grew serious. She folded her arms across her chest and said in a voice thick with wonder, "Yer sister has my poor son bamboozled."

Jane nodded her agreement. "Sukie does that to folks."

Evie shook her head. "I'm no' that sure I even like her."

"Don't fret, Evie, you're not alone. Neither does her own family."

"Ye expect she might grow on me?"

"I doubt it."

Evie drew a deep breath. "Well, what are ye gonna do? Nature will take its own wee course. I know ye're not looking forward to it but ye best get on wi' it, Jane. Time's awastin' and it'll be dark afore long. Take the wagon, it'll get you to town sooner."

Jane walked back into the warm comfort of her friend's arms. "Thank you," she whispered. "I'm a little bit afraid, Evie."

"I know ye are, but Rider Magrane is worth it. Ye'll see."

"Wish me luck?"

"Ye don't need it, love."

Yes, I do. After all, I'm cursed. And I fear I've married a man who is cursed, too.

Love is the true price of love.
—*G. Herbert,* Outlandish Proverbs

Chapter Eighteen

With the sun beginning its descent but still warm on his right shoulder, determination and out-and-out bullheaded tenacity lengthened Rider's stride toward home. Good intentions aside, he was as nervous as he'd been on his wedding night.

As he rounded a bend in the road that led to the farm, he heard Jane's strident voice before he actually saw her.

"No, no, not that way! Dammit, slow down, you lousy excuse for a horse! I knew I should have walked to town. That's absolutely, positively the last time I listen to Evie."

Smiling, Rider stopped by the side of the road, his hands on his hips. He watched Jane fight her way down the road battling two feisty mules. She held on to a precarious perch atop the mule-drawn wagon. The four-legged animals seemed intent on taking the wagon through a fallow cornfield, rather than down the road parallel to it. Since no mules resided on the Magrane farm, these surly beasts had to belong to the only surly human beast Rider knew—Evie Smith.

Heaving with every breath she took, Jane hauled back on the reins with both hands. Her hair flew around her head like dirt in a dust storm, and her big chocolate-colored eyes snapped with irritation.

She was so intent on handling the mules, she didn't see Rider until she was upon him.

"Now you know why mule skinners swear like . . . well, like mule skinners," he said, in hopes of diffusing her anger.

Jane glanced at him as if seeing him standing by the road was no surprise at all. She stood up, braced her feet and yanked hard on the reins, nearly falling on her precious fanny in the process. Then she glared at him. It didn't bode well for pleading his case. Determination to make her listen, even if he had to hog-tie her to the nearest tree, burned in his belly.

Rider hurried toward her. "Careful," he warned.

"Thanks," she said in such a sour tone that Rider almost turned tail.

Coward, he chided himself. He refused to buck under. He looped his thumbs inside the waist of his trousers and waited.

The cantankerous mules halted and as one, twisted their necks around to stare at Jane, then hung their heads, apparently as worn out as she looked. The one nearest Rider regarded him with a jaundiced eye. Rider kept his distance from its lethal teeth and dangerous hind legs.

With one hand Jane pushed her tangled hair out of her face, and sank down on the wagon seat. She blew out an exasperated breath. "Don't come one step closer.

I have a gun.'' She proceeded to lift a rifle from beneath the wagon seat and point it at Rider's vulnerable belly.

Was she mad at him or the mules or both? Not knowing for certain the state of her agitation, or if she'd ever handled a gun before, Rider lifted his hands to the sky. ''I'm not armed.''

''I know,'' she snapped. ''As I recall, you're not too good with guns, except to blow away barn doors.'' She gave him a look that left little doubt as to the meaning of her next statement. ''And even then you didn't seem to know what you were doing.''

The tips of Rider's ears burned. ''Any more than you do?''

Jane snorted in a most unladylike fashion, then pursed her lips and glared at him . . . again. Rider had the insane impulse to scramble up on that wagon and kiss that vinegary pucker right off her mouth. He quelled the urge.

Instead he beckoned toward the weapon in her unsteady hands. ''Put that gun away. You're not going to shoot me—on purpose anyway.''

''Ha.''

He pretended not to hear her and ignored her frown as he stepped up onto the wagon wheel. The wagon pitched sideways with the addition of his weight jostling Jane's precarious position. With a feminine squeak she reached her arm out and grabbed his shoulder to balance herself. He smiled at the appalled expression that crossed her face as she yanked it away. He waited until the gun was stowed beneath the seat then took the reins out of Jane's hands. He turned the mules around and started back toward the farm.

''Where are we going?''

''Home.''

Jane glared at him. How long could one woman keep glaring?

Rider ignored her perturbed expression, but couldn't forget how close she sat to him; close enough to hear her every breath, close enough to touch her. He inhaled the rose scent that always surrounded her and, as usual, made him light-headed. He wanted to take her into his arms but figured she wanted nothing like that. He stared forward even though his heart thudded with uneasy excitement. He was about to play his hand, gambling his future on each card dealt. He was hoping for a lot of luck, and a woman willing to share it with him.

He turned toward her, smiled and extended his arm in greeting. "Rider Magrane, ma'am."

Automatically Jane took his hand and shook it, then realizing what she'd done, dropped it like a hot rock. Her brows rose in a frown. She stared at him uncertainly. "What game are you playing?"

"I'm here about the advertisement."

She took a moment before speaking. Her eyes met his, then an almost imperceptible smile softened her features. "What have you done before that qualifies you for the position?"

"I've been in prison for the last five years."

"You call that a qualification?"

"No, ma'am. It just means that for five years I've hardly spoken to another human being, haven't been able to spend much time outside, and haven't had an opportunity to take care of the one thing I always promised myself I'd do. By answering your ad I can do all of that."

"What promise did you make to yourself?"

"That I'd make it up to the man I wronged."

"Well, you're too late. The position's been filled."

"Darn, I do like kids. I've always wanted a big family myself."

Jane chewed on her lower lip and tilted her head to the side. "He might not work out."

He glanced her way. Her expression gave nothing away. A glimmer of hope shot through Rider like a beam of bright sunshine. He struggled to maintain a matter-of-fact tone in his voice. "You have girls or boys?"

"Boys."

"How old?"

"Eighteen months and six years."

"That right? This man that you hired, does he like kids?"

"I thought so."

"But you're not sure?"

"No."

Rider gulped hard. "Why?"

"He put one of the boys in harm's way."

"I'm sure he didn't do it on purpose."

"Maybe not, but if he did it once, might he not do it again?"

Rider stopped the mules. The way his heart catapulted inside his chest, he was certain Jane could hear it. He looked at her beloved face, capturing her eyes with his. "He would never do it again."

"How can I be sure?" she asked in a choked voice.

He caught her chin in his hand. "You can never be sure of anything, Janie darlin', but I learned an important lesson in prison. Life is not to be taken for granted. Seeing Teddy in danger scared me more than spending five years in prison ever did. I will work hard to see that nothing happens to those boys."

She stared back at him, her heart in her eyes, her love for him so obvious it stole his breath away. Tears clogged the back of his throat. "There is one thing you can be sure of," he said in a strangled whisper. "I love those boys like they were my own."

Jane threw herself into his arms, sobbing. "I hate you."

Smiling, he held her tight. He smoothed her hair away from her face and held the back of her head against his chest. "I know, honey."

"I m-mean it. You l-lied to me, you cheated my brother and you put Teddy in danger. I really do hate you."

"If you say so."

She lifted her head. Tears clung to her lashes. "You don't believe me?"

He smiled. "No."

Jane struggled against Rider's arms, but he refused to let her go. Surprise tinged her voice when she asked, "Why don't you believe me?"

"Not twenty-four hours ago, you told me you loved me."

"Things have changed."

"No they haven't."

"Rider, how can you be so blind? Okay, Evie told me you didn't have anything to do with the Ferlin brothers stealing the Smiths' cows, but you did rustle David's cows and conveniently forgot to tell me about it."

"Jane, you'd have chased me off with a shotgun if I told you the truth from the start."

"Maybe."

He glanced at the gun beneath their seat. "No maybe about it. Truth is, David got his cows back and we went to prison. This time the only thing I did wrong was try to stop a couple of old friends from making the same mistake twice. And it landed me in jail right alongside 'em."

She stared at him in complete stupefaction. "If they are your friends, why didn't they say anything now?"

"Too scared, I guess. Who'd have believed 'em anyway? Five years ago we were all just snot-nosed kids. Jake and Martin haven't grown up much since. They're just lucky that Sheriff Asher didn't string 'em up right then and there."

"But what happened to David's cows, to the money?"

"I don't know. We had a buyer for 'em, that's all I know, but we never delivered."

"B-but you spent five years in jail."

"For stealing cattle, not because I made any money at it."

"But where did all of David's money go?"

"I don't know. You said he was brokenhearted over his wife dying and all. Maybe he just wasn't much of a farmer to begin with or maybe he sold off the cattle and when he left took it with him. No offense, Janie, but any man who would leave his family like that would take the profits, too."

"I suppose you're right, I should ask Evie. She would know."

"That ole coot doesn't miss much, that's for certain."

"You know, Rider, I didn't understand the time you left us alone in the thunderstorm, but when you were in the Smiths' shed, you weren't yourself and yet your only concern was Teddy. You kept calling his name even when he was right there beside you. I didn't understand it until later. You weren't thinking of yourself, you were only thinking of Teddy. I knew then how much you loved him. How much you would do for him.

"When I had time to think about it, I realized what it meant."

Rider wiped the remaining tears off Jane's cheeks with his thumbs. He smiled at the grim expression on her face, so filled with concern for him. "Does it mean I'm cursed?"

Jane looked stunned, then she choked on her laughter. "No more than I am."

Rider grinned. "You still haven't told me why the doctor said you were cursed to begin with."

Jane blushed. "I had a female problem," she said in a low, awkward voice, "but this morning it took care of itself."

"I can't say I understand, but as long as you're all right, that's all that matters." He pulled Jane into his arms and pressed his mouth to hers, trying to tell her with his lips how happy, how alive, how thankful he was to have her in his life. She returned his kiss with a hunger that took him by surprise. He wrapped his arms around her and kissed her until his tired soul soared. Jane was where his life was.

He lifted his head and stared into her shining eyes, bright with a faint glint of happiness. "If you want to know everything about me," he said, striving for a grave tone, "then there's something else I should tell you, and this is really serious business."

"My goodness, Rider. There's more?" Her brow wrinkled as though she was in deep thought, but her well-kissed lips twitched in amusement. "Let me guess. You've got a wife and five kids back East somewhere?"

He grinned shaking his head.

"No? You're a spy for the government?"

He shook his head again. "No, this is much more serious than that."

"What could be more serious than that?"

"I'm in love . . ."

"You are?"

". . . with my wife."

"But I'm your—"

Rider kissed her forehead. "That's right, darlin', I love you."

"But—"

"Do you still hate me?" he interrupted.

Amusement flickered in her big brown eyes. "Yes, but I think I can learn to overlook your flaws, and in time, like you. You seem like a worthwhile person and you do have good intentions."

"Worthwhile? Good intentions?" Rider rolled his eyes. "Why, thank you kindly."

"Besides you're good with the boys and they like you a lot. You can change diapers and get Teddy to eat his oatmeal. Someday, you might even learn to shoot a gun with a bit of accuracy."

"Do you think you'll ever grow to love me just a little bit?"

"Maybe."

"What would it take, d'you think?"

Jane cocked her head to the side. "Well, we'll see how you take to farming. You don't know a farmer's true competence until harvest time when the crop comes in."

"Hmm, not for another year then? That's good to

know.'' Rider held Jane in his arms and kissed her with all the love, and all the joy that swelled to overflowing in his heart. ''Janie, darlin', that gives me lots of time to convince you.''